ICE COLD
IN ALEX

ICE COLD IN ALEX

CHRISTOPHER LANDON

CASSELL

Cassell Military Paperbacks

Cassell
Wellington House
125 Strand
London WC2R 0BB

First published in Great Britain by William Heinemann Ltd 1957
This paperback edition 2003

A CIP catalogue record for this book is available from the
British Library

ISBN 0-304-36625-0

Printed and bound in Great Britain by
Cox & Wyman Ltd, Reading, Berks.

FOR
TOM PUGH

★

Remembering many years friendship and,
through him, to mark my admiration of all
the R.A.M.C. and R.A.S.C. personnel who
served with ambulance cars in the Western
Desert.

The author wishes to stress the fact that any
derogatory remarks on the conduct of the
U.D.F. made in this novel must be taken in
the context in which they are said. Having
served with the 1st S.A. Division, the author
knows that the truth is entirely contrary.

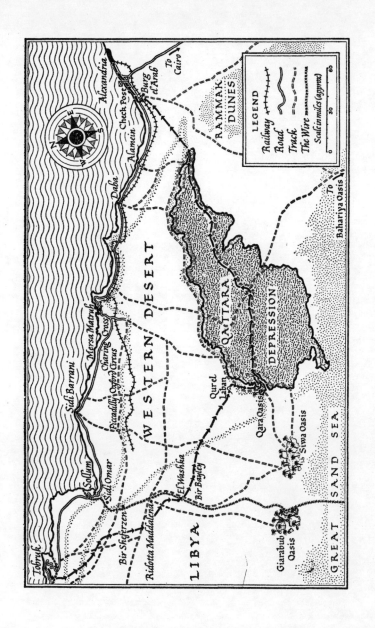

I

THEY served it ice-cold in Alex. . . .

For the moment that he shut his eyes, he could see every detail of that little bar in the lane off Mahomet Ali Square; the high stools, the marble-topped counter, the Greek behind it. Then the sound of the place came back . . . the purr of the overhead fan, a fly, buzzing drowsily, the muffled noise of the traffic seeping in through the closed door.

"If I think of that long enough, there might be a chance of forgetting this bloody noise," but it didn't help.

Then he thought about the beer itself, in tall thin glasses, so cold that there was a dew glistening on the outside of them, even before they were put down on the counter; the pale amber clearness of it; the taste, last of all.

It did not help much either. It did not shut out the sound of the endless shells that screamed over his head —only delayed the inevitable visit to the back of the truck for another whisky. Perhaps, more than anything, it made him realise that for the first time he was entirely afraid.

Jerry had got a ring of their 88-millimetres right up now and were banging the shells on to the edge of the escarpment. The ricochets—perhaps they were doing it for that effect—were screaming out over the harbour in flat trajectory like a curtain of wailing rain. It was doing no damage, except to minds. But that was far the worst.

There had always been noise in Tobruk; in the first

siege, the regular, expected pattern of dive-bombing and shelling, to be sworn at and endured, then the lull of a year, with only daylight stuff coming over high from the west and their growing confidence in the numbers of Allied aircraft ready there to meet it. But now everything was back to where they came in—all the soft-skinned stuff coming back inside the perimeter, the noise of the guns getting closer and closer—and then this last thing, this steady stream of hail that wailed just over their heads.

He knew that the fear had come to stay now—not coming and then draining away, as it had for the last two days. His mind reached back to the first time, when it had come and flapped its dark wings in his face for those few seconds in the moonlight on the Gazala road. The night when those two ambulances had not come back and the C.O. had gone to look for them; when the C.O. had not come back either, and he had gone to look for them both. It had gone away afterwards—but now it was back, all the time, sitting on his shoulder like a vulture, waiting. . . .

He had been scared before—but so had everyone. Perhaps, in a way, it had been a relief from the drab routine of the unending flog up and down the desert between Mersa Matruh and Benghazi. But it had gone on for so long—two years in the wearing-down process of so many days of heat and half-meals, so many nights of no sleep—or, worse, half-sleep, when every little noise is translated by the watching brain into the clatter of tank tracks—that it was not adventure any more. And when it stopped being adventure, he had started drinking.

He shifted his position in the shade of the truck and looked at the nearness of his slit-trench, wincing at a burst of the screaming overhead; that empty aching feeling was welling up from his stomach to the back of his throat now, it was a question of how long he could hang on before he made that move . . . think of something . . . anything. . . .

Two years ago. His mind reached back wistfully to what it had been like then: the rising tide of preparation under clean desert skies before the dash forward to lock in battle with an equal enemy, the few days of excitement before the withdrawal from an honourable stalemate, the break of leave in Cairo or Alexandria before the cycle started all over again. It had gone—all that, and now he was so bloody tired the whole of the time. No one had noticed, no one had said a word; but he had started to drink all the time—just to keep going. He never got drunk; perhaps that was the worst part, that he could not get drunk.

It was snapping point now. He got out, almost levering himself upright against the weight of screaming horror overhead. He went round to the back and groped inside the hanging sheet. Just inside on the floor was an old ammunition box, padlocked, with his name and PRIVATE stencilled on it. Inside, piled on top of his personal stuff, were four bottles of Haig. He lifted one and held it up in the dim light so that he could see the level of the liquid—half-full—against the label. Then he made a mark on it with his thumb-nail, a quarter-inch below.

"There—and no farther." He tilted it back, feeling the raw spirit in his throat and the beginnings of its warmth reaching down to the pit of his stomach. He knew that it would not make the tiredness any better— only allow it to be borne. The cork went back into the neck with a soft sound; he stood for a moment, holding the bottle, thinking back to how it had all begun.

There had been no thought of a general retirement

3

when the Germans started their attack on the Gazala line. Even when they got through in places, the scraps of information that got back to Tobruk were smoothed over with the comforting thought that their armour was now boxed on the wrong side of the line, cut off from their own supplies, with no hope of repair, a sitting duck for our tanks to come in and squash, the moment they chose. The withdrawal of the ambulances from a forward position had followed as a routine movement: a little farther back from the battle would make them easier to control. It had been so casual that he had not even bothered to radio the orders; he had taken them up himself in the car. It had been an excuse to escape from the monotony of Tobruk and he had found the shelling and bombing no worse than he had expected. But as he was on his way back, something started to happen . . . out there, to the south of him, as he motored back to the fortress . . . over the lip of the escarpment, in the flinty plain between Knightsbridge and Bir Hakeim. . . .

He heard the distant thunder of the guns as he drove, heard, in the hours that followed, the breath of rumour that swept through the fortress. That something had gone a bit adrift in the smashing up of those Jerry tanks . . . that 150 Brigade 'box' had gone in the middle of the line, and that the German transports were streaming through the breach to replenish their armour.

Like most of the rest that heard it, he didn't quite believe. And no one seemed to care very much.

The first real personal impact came later: when the last report of the new disposition of the ambulances came in, there were three blanks—three, that had been ordered to leave their old location far south on the line, had not arrived at the new. He spent an hour hanging round the wireless truck with the C.O.—dapper, friendly Major Brooker, the only doctor in that odd formation, a

4

motor ambulance convoy. The operator had twiddled his dials, three times they got a firm, laconic 'No' from the new sites, but there was only silence and the crackle of static from where they had been.

At last, the major had straightened and smiled: then he said, "I'm going out to pull them in, George. Shan't be long—keep an eye on things." He had got into his car and given that half-wave, half-salute of his, and driven off towards the eastern perimeter, into the darkness in a stream of dust. And never came back.

After four dragging hours, Anson knew he would have to do something.

It was one of those things that happened so often: someone like the C.O.—whom you had eaten with, argued with, slept beside, and seen frightened—would get into his truck and say, "I'm going to swan over and see old Joe," or, "—look at that well," or, "—get some beer from the N.A.A.F.I." There would be a grin and a wave, the truck would be swallowed up in the night to the fading beat of the motor, or dwindle to a speck on the rim of the desert.

And that was that: they didn't come back.

Sometimes you found them afterwards. A riddled, burnt-out, twisted wreck, with an untidy bundle slumped in the seat or lying on the sand beside. And the face, always, caught in that last moment of all, was never the face of your friend. Something had gone from it.

But you did all you could: marked the position on your map and sent the identity-disc back to the Graves people, there was the trench to be dug, as deep as the rock would let you go, with the stones piled on top to keep the dogs out. Perhaps later, months afterwards, in a moment of relaxation by the mess truck, someone would say suddenly, "Do you remember Charles—the cunning old basket—the time he——?" But you didn't

5

want to hear it—to remember anything. You shut your mind tight to it; wondered only if the sand was blowing the right way to cover it deeper, made the firm resolve to take a trip out there the next time it was in range and make sure. Then someone else would say, in a tight voice, "For Christ's sake, shut up—and turn on the radio." And the B.B.C. crooner would always be in the middle of singing, 'Sand in my shoes' in that don't-cry-in-my-gin voice. Which didn't help a lot.

Well, it had happened again. The C.O. this time. And Anson knew that he had to go and look for him, and those poor bastards in the missing cars. He was the senior officer now, the only captain in the unit. He had got up from his truck and gone over to where the duty officer was nodding in a chair beside the wireless truck.

"Paul," he said, "I'm going out to look for the old man."

Paul Crosbie was the senior subaltern; he uncoiled his rugger-forward bulk from the chair and stood up towering over Anson.

"Corps H.Q. won't let you, George."

"Corps won't know."

Paul had shrugged. "You're the boss. What shall I tell them if they come on the blower?"

He had hesitated for a moment. "I don't want them told anything—I want you to wake Smith, to take over here—and I'd like you to come with me."

It was quite dark now, with only the faintest glimmer of reflection from the stars, he could only see the faint shadow of Paul's face. He looked away, down to the ground, and added quickly, "That's not an order, Paul. I'd—just like you to come—if you will."

As if in answer, the edge of the moon began to creep up over the line of the escarpment. As the round of it grew, the red-orange flicker that painted the southern

6

horizons like unending summer lightning began to pale; the gunfire—unending muffled roll of a deep drum—thinned and died to a pattern of separate sounds. He had looked over to it—the direction of the flinty plain of Knightsbridge where they would soon have to go—then down at the sand he was turning over with his desert boot. "That driver of mine—he's beginning to get bomb-happy. And I don't want to go alone."

"Of course I'll come." The moonlight was bright enough then to show the glint of teeth as the craggy face broke into a grin; as the big man turned his head, Anson saw the eyes for the first time. And knew that Paul knew.

They had been on their way over to the Humber when he said, "I had better take a map, I suppose." He had come back with a map-board under one arm and a bottle of Haig in the other hand.

"Might get cold, Paul."

"Yes."

"Will you drive?—then I can stand up later—and get a better look-see." He held out the bottle. "One for the road?"

"Might as well."

When he had taken the bottle back and had a swallow, he remembered it was the ninth he had had since the C.O. had gone.

The Humber was an old, open four-seater: battered, sand-stained, but with an engine that had the heart of a lion. They had bumped out of the camp area and then moved quickly to the bridge that spanned the tank-trap on the western edge of the perimeter. There had not seemed to be much traffic moving on the roads inside the fortress that night—and when they had been checked and were through on the open road outside, none at all. None at all, moving their way. But Anson's heart had sunk lower and lower as he saw the endless line of vehicles, head to tail, sometimes two-deep, facing towards them as they waited to get into Tobruk.

The gunfire over on the back of the escarpment had died to nothing, there was almost a complete silence. Only the hiss . . . hiss . . . hiss . . . of reflected sound as they passed each vehicle in the jumbled string of lorries, guns, even some tanks, that waited. Their side of the road was clear. They were the only thing that was moving west.

Hiss . . . hiss . . . hiss. Nothing but that and the occasional deeper snarl from their engine and the rushing sound of sand spewed from racing wheels as Paul had had to swing off the hard going to avoid the wider jams. Each vehicle rushed towards them and was then swept into the dust behind; each one, white and ghostly in the moonlight that was bright now; each one, silent and unmoving. It was like a horrid travesty of a Bank Holiday traffic jam.

There was no contact between them as they passed. Only for an instant had Anson seen the driver or passenger in the cab as they flashed by. They were still too, staring as if they did not really see the Humber, without interest. Things had gone wrong again.

Paul broke their silence. "Another bloody balls-up— or should I go all official and say, strategic withdrawal?" He had sounded remarkably cheerful. "Please God, Jerry doesn't come over and drop a load on this lot—it would be murder." He spun the wheel with an expert flick and the engine roared and the tail bucked sideways before they were round a tank and back on the road again. The solid line was thinning now to groups of two or three, moving slowly: there were long gaps between them. As with the long blocks, Anson had looked at each one in turn, searching for the smaller, square,

8

biscuit-coloured shape of an ambulance car. But there was no sign.

Paul had braked suddenly, peering ahead, and said, "Tanks." A pause. "All right—they're ours—Valentines."

"Keep going," said Anson. As they had passed the low, humped shapes strung out on each side of the road, their turrets pointing backwards, someone had shouted at them. Then there had been nothing but the empty road, a black ribbon stretching straight ahead on the whiteness of the desert in the moonlight.

They were doing a steady fifty then; Anson standing, gripping the top of the windscreen with both hands, the chin-strap of his cap cutting hard into his jaw, the wind of their passing roaring in his ears. The edge of the front seat pressed against the back of his legs and he pushed hard against it—to stop the shaking. It must be the cold . . . he bent for a moment below the shelter of the screen to wrap his white Syrian sheepskin coat closer round him. Something of the feel of it . . . the sight of Paul's big hands splayed out on the wheel, brought back a moment's vivid memory of those leaves in Beirut they had spent together, shared everything together. Until they had met her.

He sat down for a moment and reached for the whisky bottle from the dashboard compartment, pulled the cork and held it out, the other hand poised ready to take the wheel. "I wonder what Ariadne's doing now," he shouted.

If Paul heard, or saw the bottle, he did not react. The hands stayed steady on the wheel and it had seemed a long time before there was the faintest shake of the head as if to dismiss both offer and question. Then he said, "I'd stand up, if I were you, old man. You might miss something."

9

"Sorry."

He had taken a quick hard swig at the bottle and then put it back. When he had hoisted himself to his feet, there was nothing ahead; nothing except the black strip that stretched on, unending, and the white plain on either side. It was then that he had started to search desperately, to find anything there, even the wrong kind of things; the shaking of his legs had nothing to do with cold then and the words that were torn from his lips, to be whirled away into the fog of dust behind, almost a prayer. "They must open up—now. They can't let us go on getting farther and farther in—with nothing happening." For the first time, he was horribly afraid. But they did not oblige.

Another mile and no relief—it would be relief—of those orange buds of tracer bursting into flower as they streaked towards them. Nothing; only the moonlight and the black and white. Then he made his last try.

"Paul——" he had bent, shouting down to the unmoving head, "you know the old track we used to use up the escarpment—by that black stone—about three kilometres on——? They might try and get down there if they were in a jam. We'll try up that way."

Paul had nodded—and another answer had come back to him moments later. Far, far away to the south, beyond the escarpment, three green star shells had climbed up into the sky; he knew that one—the panzer signal for advance. He was just bending to pass this on when he had seen something else: the black rock . . . nearer than he had expected . . . farther from the road than he remembered . . . much larger. Before he could speak they were on it and past it, in the instant of passing there was no mistaking the tight-packed night-laager of tanks . . . no doubt about the square, chopped-off turrets of German Mark IV's. But they were by without the sound or sign of a living soul.

That finished him. His legs were uncontrollable now and for the next kilometre he managed to hold himself up by the strength of his arms alone. Then he sat down suddenly. "Stop her, Paul."

Paul had thrown out the gear and cut the engine and let the Humber coast to a halt. "That track's about another kilometre," he said.

Anson tried so hard to gain control; he knew, the moment he spoke, that he had not succeeded. "Did you —see that lot?"

Paul let his hands drop from the wheel. "The square-heads? Yes. Having a nice kip before the pounce."

Anson had looked at his watch. "It will be two hours —if we turn back now. If they move—and straddle the road—we'll never get back at all. We've done all——"

"Of course we have, George." His voice had sounded a little too casual. "It's entirely up to you. If you say, 'Go on'—we go; if you say, 'Go back', we do. It was your idea of a party. I'd rather be in bed."

Both had listened for a moment: except for the cracking from the cooling engine, there was not a sound, only the soft moonlight flowing over the black road and the white desert.

"We go back. And, for God's sake, get past that like a bat out of hell."

Paul had turned to stare at him. "That's fine. What happens if they have stretched a wire across the road. Would you like to drive?"

"No."

"O.K." He had stabbed at the starter button and in two quick reverse turns was facing back the other way. The moon was behind them then, the way ahead clearer, empty, everything still. They could not see the thing that lay in front of them.

Paul had said, "Well, here we go—first stop, Victoria," and then the Humber had leapt forward in the full power of first gear.

He had crouched, watching the speedometer needle tremble and surge forward as the car accelerated up through the gears . . . sixty-five . . . seventy. Now the ribs on the sand-treads of the tyres were roaring so loud that he could not hear the noise of the engine. They must be very close now. He had looked up at Paul, straight and stiff behind that wheel . . . he could not duck. With all he had left, he heaved himself upright, gripping the top of the screen, and the wind struck him like a blow. The black mass—on their right—was rushing towards them . . . was it his watering eyes, or tortured imagination—but was that a gleam of something stretched across the road in front? HE MUST NOT DUCK. Fifty yards . . . he could see the damned wire now . . . he was certain. . . . Then everything snapped, and with a scream of, "Stop—stop!" he had collapsed back on the seat with his face buried on his knees. Paul had made a noise that was half-way between a grunt and a laugh and put his foot right down to the floorboards. They were by—they must be by; but nothing had happened. He waited, hunched, for the roar of exploding mines or the tear of the wire that would overturn the car and decapitate Paul; but it had not come, not a shout, not a shot, nothing.

Slowly their speed had dropped, the tyres now giving a faint hum instead of that roar. Anson sat huddled in the passenger seat, stared down the empty black ribbon of road that unfolded in front of them, as he waited for Paul to speak.

He had waited, while the minutes dragged by in

12

silence, staring into the moonlight as they closed nearer to Tobruk, thinking. . . . Of all the fun they had had together, he and Paul, of all those leaves—the times in Alex and Cairo and Beirut.

Beirut most of all—because it connected them both in the web of Ariadne. Cretan Ariadne, with the slim grace and look of a deer; Ariadne they had met together, taken out together in perfect accord the girl they had both loved in their different ways. Or were they different——? That was something he would never know now, that was why he was thinking of it all for the last time, for it would never be the same again. There would be no more leaves together. He had seen the look in Paul's eyes just before he had turned the car back down the road.

He had taken another pull at the bottle before Paul spoke.

"Don't you think you had better lay off that, Skipper?"

He threw the whisky back in the locker and they did not speak again until they had been challenged at the tank screen—so thin, so pitifully few. As they had walked back to the car after reporting their find to the squadron commander, Paul said suddenly, "Has it struck you we could have stopped the car in front of them—got out and done a fan dance—sung the 'Horst Wessel'—and there would not have been a cheep out of the lot?"

"Why, Paul?"

"They were just as scared as we were. It must have looked very like the setting of a trap."

He had said, "I'm sorry, Paul. I——"

"Forget it." Paul's voice had been brusque but kind. But he knew that really it never would be forgotten.

The day had been almost normal.

There had been no word of the C.O. or the ambulances —and deep down inside him now he had known that

13

there never would be. He had gone about his routine work in a dead, numb sort of way. He had not spoken to Paul.

The fear of the night had gone, but the hurt of it was still there: so was the whisky, and it did not remove anything of it. Only, it seemed to move the whole thing to one side, so that he could stand and watch it, disinterested.

All through that day the sound of gunfire had increased, had come closer, as the ring tightened. He hardly noticed it—or the raids: just went on with the job, hoping that no one would notice him. His brain had been quite clear; only there was a jerkiness in the way his legs moved as he walked and a numb tight feeling in the muscles of his face.

There had been a counter-attack at dawn and the ambulances were out again, feeling their way through the twisting paths in the minefields beyond the perimeter, running back with their load down the snaking road that led to the harbour and the cluster of tents and the one standing building that made up the General Hospital. It had taken all the morning to get them into the swing of their new routine, and it was not until after the midday meal that he had had a chance to go round the resting sections and talk to the men.

Stiffly, in that jerking stride, he had trudged round the camp, from vehicle to vehicle, squatting down at the bivouacs that were beside them, exchanging a few sentences with the occupants before moving on. Always with one eye cocked at the burnished bowl of the sky for the sign of a glitter of wings, one ear attuned to the mutter of gunfire.

The men . . . he knew them all. Most were hardened old sweats, stripped to the waist and capless in the high sun, burnt native brown, scarred on hands and knees with two years of desert sores. If they got their rations, their fags, and their beer—if they could be contemptuously affectionate to all in authority, that was enough. They had learned to accept the desert, to take the changing fortunes of its war with philosophy: after two years, England had almost vanished, Cairo and Alex were home. They ignored the nuisance of noise of any bombardment that was not personally dangerous to them: jumped unerringly for a slit-trench on the instant of anything that was. Through either, they would curse —foully, but again with a certain affection—at the giver.

They were just the same, as he had talked to them . . . almost. He did not get the change until he had been to three or four vehicles. It was something in their look, questioning, not quite holding his eyes, when they asked for news of what was doing. It gave him the first return of the feeling of the night before.

"When are we going in for another bash, sir?"

"Soon, I think. There was a counter-attack at first light and I hear it's going well."

"Good, sir."

But it wasn't good, because, for the first time, they were not believing him. They knew it was just words— that he hadn't got a clue.

The signal to report to the medical brigadier at Corps H.Q. came through at four. He changed into a clean bush-shirt, had a quick pull at the bottle, and got into his car alone to drive down the hill. Everything was normal as he drove off the camp site and on to the road; the shelling had died in one of those uneasy lulls, and he was glad to see that the men had flattened a patch of desert and had unrolled their strip of coconut matting for a cricket match. He stopped to watch for a minute. Paul was there, bowling at that moment—crafty leg-breaks. He remembered that, apart from routine, they had not spoken since the night before. He let in the clutch and started down the road to headquarters.

The brigadier was a typical desert oddity. Medical officers, even on the staff, do not as a rule attract much attention, but 'Dangle-toes' was a name, apart from this reference to his stature. Always, as long as there were troops in the desert, he would be remembered for the fabulous tale of the day that his headquarters had been overrun at dawn by German tanks. He had got out of a delicate situation by the simple expedient of speaking a little German—and understanding Germans.

He had been asleep when the bother started, and before anyone had come to winkle him out of his dugout had dressed quickly in his best tunic, with tabs, his best hat, with the maroon band. He had stalked out to storm at the bewildered commander of the panzer group, screaming, in his atrocious German, the facts of his own importance, insisting that they loaded his entire kit on his own truck and that he was driven by his own driver into captivity. They reacted, as he had hoped, to noise and brass: they did it. When he had moved off in state, and under escort, towards Tripoli, he had waited till dark and then slipped out sideways past the escort and regained Allied territory. He had arrived triumphant, but speechless with rage. Those —— Jerries had forgotten, worse, deliberately omitted, to load his portable wash-stand!

He was small, very thin and, through some whim of hygiene, always kept his head shaved close to the scalp. He looked like a Hun—and was a bloody good bloke. At the moment Anson made entry to his dugout at Corps Headquarters, he had been sitting cross-legged in a tin bath, with nothing more on than a pair of rimless glasses. Anson had thought of Gandhi.

16

"Ah—Anson. 'Afternoon." He reached forward, fishing for something in the three inches of grey scummy muck that was a week's water ration.

"Good afternoon, sir."

"Well. Sit down. Let me finish this lot. How's everything?" He always spoke in jerks.

Anson sat on the one camp-chair and began the recital of the unit's state. As he listened, the brig still trawled the water in front of him with his hands: at last, with a grunt of satisfaction, he pounced to-pull from the depths a fragment of what had once been a loofah. Without interruption, he began to scratch his back.

When Anson had finished he said, "—and there's no news about Major Brooker, or the ambulances?"

"None, sir. I don't think there is anywhere else to check. I've packed up all the kits—shall I——?"

Outside there was a crump—crump—crump, as a stick of bombs dropped quite close. The water in the bath had shivered in little circles and some sand fell with a soft noise from the sides of the dugout. The brig had not moved, except to lift one arm and explore the mysteries beneath it.

"Now—there's a thing," he said. "Never a moment's peace—for either side. Take a man going to the latrine. Why shouldn't he? Normal natural function. Then that happens. No wonder they get constipated."

Anson's fingers had been slowly relaxing from the grip he had on the under-side of the chair. The brig had shot a quick glance at him and gone on scratching.

"I think I'd like a drink, Anson—and I expect you could do with one, too. The Scotch is on the table. There's the water bottle. No, not that one—the next. That's real Charing Cross." In the desert, the merit of various wells was judged as fine as a vintage.

When he had handed down a mug to the bath, his

17

hand had stopped shaking. The brig went on talking as if there had been no interruption.

"Poor Brooker. I'm afraid he's had it. We shan't hear anything now. You are to be temporary O.C. by the way. I can't find a doctor that's suitable to take over—and your R.A.S.C. don't object, so you can carry on." He stood up in a rush of scum and reached for a towel. "After all, there's no medical work in an M.A.C.—just an ordinary Service Corps carrying job, even if it is a rather special load."

"Very good, sir."

The brig was finding his shirt and shorts. "Now, immediate details. 'A' and 'C' sections to carry on just as they are—with the other two resting at an hour's readiness. Less six cars from 'D'—that I have a special job for."

"A special job——?"

The brig finished his drink. "The nurses at the hospital," he said, "they're to go back to Alex—tonight."

Anson had stared for a moment, trying to gauge what was going on behind the glint of those glasses. "Is it—as bad as that, sir?"

The little man made an impatient movement. "Good God, no, man. But it isn't very pleasant here——" He cocked his head and listened. The dull tattoo was beating up again from the south: now, close, something sighed overhead, to finish in a deep crunch, followed by a long rumble. "Things like that," said the brig.

He swung round. "Anyway, I never wanted them here. It was Army that insisted, said it needed a woman's touch to make the poor bastards feel they were on the first stage of the road home. But that hospital isn't fit for that any more, Anson. It's too damned crowded. It isn't fair to the colonel—or the girls."

He stopped suddenly to glare. "And what the hell has it got to do with you?"

"Nothing, sir." He changed the subject hastily. "How many will there be going?"

"Thirty-two and the matron. No kit except essentials."

"That will mean eight cars."

"Eight——? Why eight? Why not send the whole damned unit if you're feeling so generous?"

"I was only thinking of the sleeping, sir. They are bound to be at least one night on the road. There are four bunks in each car—I thought eight cars would make it about right."

"Five cars," said the brig, gently, "that's all they get, Anson. They'll have to double up—or sleep on the floor. They may be glad of one night's discomfort . . . soon."

So it was like that—however much the brig tried to smooth it over. There was going to be another siege. Then the first thing was to think of his own men. He had weighed the situation for a moment and then said, "Those caves, sir. The ones by the shore, east and below the hospital—you know them? There's no one there at the moment. We'd be nearer you—and the hospital, the troops would like the bathing, too. Can we move in?"

The brig had smiled, not unkindly. It was the moment when both were certain of the other's knowledge. "If there's room—and you're first, go to it."

Anson had got up. "Is there anything else, sir?"

"Not at the moment, Anson. Just five cars to be at the hospital for loading at seven. The drivers—I want nice types——" he looked down at his congealing bath for inspiration, "—married men."

For the first time that day he had felt like laughing. It was typical brigadier. There was quite likely to be further embellishment. As he waited for the probable instructions on chastity belts he thought of the work

19

entailed by this proviso in searching the company roll. But the brig did not seem to have anything to add; he realised in the same instant it was not a question of the nurses' virtue—it was only five, but the brig was getting five married men out of Tobruk as well as the girls.

"An officer to go with them, sir?"

"No. A good sergeant—to come under orders of the matron."

Anson saluted. He was half-way up the dugout steps when the sharp voice called him back. "Oh, Anson—in your movement order, give the sergeant explicit orders as to propriety."

"Propriety, sir?"

The brig waved his hands. "Dammit, man. They'll be two days on the road, and there's not a bush worth calling by the name between here and the delta. I imagine they'll want to powder their noses. Instruct the sergeant to take orders from matron; when she gives the word, to pull the cars off the road and form a hollow square—them leave them in peace."

It was almost the last straw. "And when they have delivered them, sir, where do they report back?"

"Here—or as near as they can get."

Quite suddenly, he thought he had never seen the brigadier look so old.

Things had followed the expected pattern after that.

It was a vague unrelated pattern, for Anson was only a grain of the mass: he knew—but could not ask for confirmation, his only source to the higher, over-all picture, the brig, was closed to him now, because he knew that he knew. There would be no answer as to 'why'; only the rate of the 'how' of disintegration could reach down to his awareness in the narrow limits of his job.

It was after the ambulances had left for the hospital

that the signal from the brig had arrived; it said,
ALL CARS RETURNING EX PERIMETER TO
REMAIN YOUR HQ AND NOT REPEAT NOT
RETURN LOCATIONS. It didn't make sense and, as
they were in the middle of the move to the new site at
the caves, made extra work in directing the empty cars
back. "Hasn't Dangle-toes anything better to do——"
Anson had snarled as he tried to sort the tangle out. It
had taken him twenty minutes to find the five most
married and moral for the hospital lift.

Then he had looked up to see Smith, the junior
subaltern, poking his head into the back of the office
truck. "Well, what do you want?"

"Can you let me have some money from the Imprest,
Captain Anson?"

"What do you mean—from the Imprest? It's the field
cashier's job to deal with your advance-of-pay chits. The
unit's not a bloody bank."

Smith had looked uncomfortable. "I know that. I'm
sorry, but I can't find him."

Anson stopped in his writing to stare. "The field
cashier? But he's just down the road, man. Where he's
been for months. I saw his tent this afternoon. He'll be
back later—probably gone out to pay a unit."

Smith stared at his feet. "I've just been down there.
The tent has gone."

"Nonsense!" He had thrown down his pen. "Get in
the car and I'll take you down. I bet I find him."

But Smith had been right. He wasn't there—or anywhere that they had the time to search. The place that
they knew, where they had come to cash their cheques
for months, was just a beaten square of sand with an
untidy rim of sandbags pulled back from the edges where
the tent had been struck. A few tattered shreds of paper
were blowing across the open space. That was all.

Anson had lifted his eyes to the huddle of tents a little farther down the road . . . the N.A.A.F.I. There were some transport there, and a lot of figures milling round it. He was all right now, he had had another drink and the whisky was singing high in his head. He knew what was going to happen. If the paymaster had gone, it was only a question of 'how long' before the N.A.A.F.I. bonfire went up. . . . Then he had looked at Smith's face. There was just the same look there that the men had had that morning. And nothing he could say, nothing he could do about it. If the brig wouldn't tell him . . . then he couldn't speak. . . .

"He's probably swanned off to find himself a cosy little cave—like we have. We'll find him later. Come back to the office now, and I'll cash that pay-slip."

On the way back in the car, he had pulled out his own wallet and counted. Three pounds and fifty-odd ackers . . . but money wouldn't matter any more.

So to this wait by the truck—waiting, turning the whole thing over, wondering, afraid. Then this last bloody thing had started—that had just tipped the scales. And now he was going to drink when he knew he shouldn't. . . .

He was late for the rendezvous at the hospital; two sudden, vicious raids cost him half an hour crouched in the ditch by the side of his car. When at last he arrived, the broad turn-round outside the main building was empty. The convoy must have gone. He had better go and find the C.O. to apologise for not having been there to see them off.

He ran up the steps and turned into the main corridor. The whole place had a quiet, deserted feeling and he did not meet anyone. First turn to the left, then second door on the right, that was the colonel's office. He stood for a moment, looking at the plate with the C.O.'s name on it before he knocked. There was no answer, so he pushed the door open and went in.

The colonel was not there, nor the carpet, nor the big desk, nor any of the things he remembered. The room was stripped of everything. Only bodies covered the floor now; wrapped in blankets, laid reverently side by side . . . but packed like sardines . . . about three deep.

The smell of wounds and guts and death beat about him with its horrible sweetness. He managed to pull the door fast and grope his way back blindly towards the entrance. There, on the corner of the steps, all the defeat and bitterness and whisky of the last days won as he rocked to and fro, vomiting.

When it was over, the colonel's voice came to him suddenly. It seemed to be a long way off and when he turned his head to look he could not see for the tears that were blinding his eyes. The voice said, "Drink this, George. And take the pills—you'll feel better."

He groped for them, took them, and then bent forward, resting his head on his knees until the shaking had stopped. Then he turned to look at the man he had known and worked with for months. He was glad the voice had been the same, for otherwise he would not have recognised him.

There was a long white coat, buttoned to the throat, and it was stiff and stained the whole way down the front . . . all shades of red that merged to the edges in an older brown . . . like a butcher's smock that had been worn a long, long time. The face above it seemed so thin now, so sucked in at the cheeks, that it had taken the cast of a skull; the eyes had dropped back in the sockets and the little of them that showed had an opaque look.

23

"I'm sorry, Colonel. I went straight to your office—I didn't know——" He wiped his mouth on the back of his hand and looked away.

"It's I that should apologise, George. I should have put up a notice. The mortuary is full—there was nowhere else to put them." There was a pause and then he had said, "—and we can't get any help in the burying. . . ."

Anson said, "But I'll send a squad down——"

"No, George. There's going to be plenty for your blokes to do without taking on outside jobs."

For the second time he said, "It's as bad as that, then?" and there was no attempt to brush the question aside as before.

The colonel said, "Yes."

The light had nearly gone then and, as often happened, there was a lull in the firing, a sort of respite before the night came up and the big bombers were over. They sat, in the peace, side by side, on the steps.

"Did they get away all right?"

"The nurses? Yes, just before that raid. It was good of you to be so prompt with the cars, George. It's a great weight off my mind."

He said, "They'll be O.K. I got through to Eastern Control. There's an 'all clear' report from there to the frontier. They should be in Egypt by dawn."

"I know." The colonel got stiffly to his feet. "Stay a minute and I'll get you a drink. By the way—what's the time?"

"Twenty to eight."

"About time I had a break. I've been operating since ten. I'll go and tell them."

He sat quite still waiting for him to come back. The mutter of the guns started up again, the light flickering against the sky to the south. The evening breeze was coming in off the sea, making the few tattered palm fronds that were left whisper and rattle against the stems. Even the moving air felt heavy . . . like the moment before a thunderstorm.

The colonel came back carrying one glass and a small cedar box bound with a bright label. "I won't have a drink, but I'll smoke a cigar. I've been thinking about that all day." He looked affectionately at the box. "My wife's last Christmas present—only it didn't arrive till February. I thought I'd save them for the next one. But——"

Anson took the drink. "I shouldn't have this. I've been on it all day. I made a B.F. of myself last night."

The colonel's thumb made a brittle sound as it broke the seal.

"It won't hurt you now—I've fixed your tummy. I knew there was something wrong. The brig told me."

"But——"

"He just knew, George. But he thinks very highly of you. And, by God, he's going to need you."

"Is it another siege, then?"

The colonel didn't answer for a moment. He pierced a cigar carefully, lit it, and then blew out a perfect smoke ring. He watched it for a moment before cutting it to fragments with a stroke of his hand.

"What has the brig told you?"

"Sweet Fanny Adams."

"Then I can't tell you—can I—officially. But I think you will find out very soon—that we're for it. Beyond that—it's only guessing. Even THEY haven't got that far." He stopped for a moment and stared out towards the pale flicker on the skyline. "But I've made my plans," he said.

"Plans——?"

"Yes, George. To go quietly into the bag with that

lot." He jerked his head at the bulk of the hospital behind him.

"But—you can't mean . . . ?"

The colonel just looked at him. "I do. I think this place will fall like a pack of cards." He looked out once more to the south. "It's different this time—they are resolute, first-class troops, those Germans."

"They couldn't take it before."

"It was only the Ities then—and no treachery."

"Treachery——?"

The colonel said, "Perhaps that is the wrong word. You had better forget it. But I've heard some very funny talk." He drew on the cigar for a moment. "All I'm interested in is starting clear here when the balloon goes up. There's a hundred cases to get away. We've signalled for a hospital ship—but there's no answer yet."

"Couldn't we lift them?"

"Far safer by sea—and they have always played fair with hospital ships. Over the desert—there might be accidents—even if you could get through——" He broke off abruptly and held out the box. "Have one. And let's talk of something else."

From time to time people came in and out of the entrance to the hospital, but none of them seemed to notice the colonel in his butcher's smock and the captain of the R.A.S.C. sitting on the corner of the steps in the dark, smoking their cigars. They talked of many things as they sat there—the pubs of Nottingham; the best way to make steak and kidney pudding; rowing. Once an orderly came out and plucked at the colonel's sleeve, holding out a signal that he said was "Most Secret and Immediate."

"Dear God," the colonel said, "they are all like that now," and put it under the cigar-box.

It was pleasant sitting there—and strangely peaceful.

26

Anson began to forget everything. Then, from east and south, first in little wedges of sound that grew each moment in volume, the 88-millimetres started the second barrage that sent the hideous whine skating out over the circle of the harbour.

He remembered what the colonel had said. This was the first part of the softening-up process. And the fear of the night before came back to him, only this time it did not leave.

It was impossible to go on talking. The colonel bent close to his ear and shouted, "I'll have to get back.' They both got up and walked over to the car, the colonel unfolding the signal he had retrieved from under the cigar-box. "It's too bloody dark," he said.

"There's a masked light on the dash."

The colonel climbed into the passenger seat and smoothed the paper out under the dim, shaded light. "How nice of them. There's no hospital ship available —so they're sending a transport—with doctor—and eight nurses. Due in harbour at eleven. As there's no protection from the red cross, they must be away before moon-up—that's two. Only three hours."

"How many cars will you want?"

"In the dark—better a few, and work fast. Five good ones."

"All right. I'll lay them on to report to you at nine— to be on the safe side."

"Thank you, George." He got out of the car and then leaned back over the door. "Here—take these."

Anson's hand groped out to feel the bundle of cigars, wrapped in a slip of paper. "I won't have time to smoke the lot," the colonel said, "and I thought you wouldn't mind doing something for me—I remembered earlier. My missis's address is on the paper. When you get out of this—please write to her. Say how you sat here with

27

me—and that we smoked her cigars and enjoyed them. That I was well, but very tired. And we had done a good job."

"You'll be able to do that before I can."

"I don't think so. Good luck to you, old man."

He turned away abruptly and soon the Humber was creeping back up the road to the centre of the perimeter. Then, a sharp turn to the right and he was bucking back down the track towards the caves. As he walked towards the office truck after parking the Humber, he was not a bit surprised to see a thin streak of light showing through the black-out, to find, having let himself through the curtain, that the brig was sitting at his table, writing furiously.

"I'm sorry, sir. I'd no idea——"

"That's all right, Anson. Mr. Crosbie told me you had gone to the hospital. I've had a look round the new quarters. Very snug."

He started stuffing the papers back in his brief-case and then his glasses glinted in the light of the pressure lamp as he swung round to stare.

"How are you feeling?"

"All right, sir."

"Well, bring that map-board round here. I want to have a talk to you." He glanced at the orderly, sitting in the shadows by the telephone—"Alone."

"Go and get yourself a cup of tea, Corporal," said Anson. "I'll answer that."

When the corporal slipped out through the black-out curtain, the brig pushed the map-board into the yellow circle of light, while Anson leaned on the table beside him. From outside, over the quiet hiss of the lamp, the sound of the bombardment was rising again; but under the lee of the cliffs there was less menace to it . . . the noise was more like that of distant surf. The brigadier

28

started talking in the quiet impersonal voice of a chairman addressing a shareholders' meeting.

"There is a change in the whole tactical plan. We are going to break off contact with their armour and go back to the 'wire' "—his finger traced the line that was the barbed-wire entanglement separating Libya from Egypt —"re-form there, and then come in again. It's got to the question of speed of recovery on both sides again. But we command the air, so it should be easier.

"While this is happening, the plan is to hold as much of the coast road as possible—but not as far as Tobruk."

So the colonel had been right in fact—but how far would the guessing prove to be . . . That fear surged up in him again, sick and sour.

"And I suppose we stay inside again . . ." he said at last.

"Not all of you—and not for long. The estimate is that the garrison will be contained for a maximum five weeks. And it will be immensely strong this time. And lashings of everything they want in the way of supplies already stocked."

"But some of this unit will be with them," Anson went on doggedly.

"Yes. Twenty-five cars with one officer. To come under the C.O. of the hospital. They will provide all the medical transport for the garrison. How are you going to detail them?"

There was a long silence. He knew what had to be done; what he had to say.

"Unmarried men, sir—and myself."

"The first, excellent. The second—no."

The relief made him feel ashamed, but he had to go on.

"I would like to stay, sir. I should stay. I wouldn't like those that have to—to think anything else. It won't be very funny for those in for the second time."

The brig did not answer for a minute. He had pulled his pipe from his pocket and started filling it: as he bent forward in concentration, his shaven head shone like a billiard ball in the glow of the lamp.

"Look, Anson—though you may forget it, I happen to be a doctor as well as a brigadier on the staff. I suppose you would argue that I should stay inside with the hospital and set an example? Well, I'm not going to. For two reasons. The first is that my doctoring is so far behind that I wouldn't be any bloody good—I doubt if I could even give an enema properly. Second, and far more important, I'm too valuable to be frittered away in a gallant gesture. Corps H.Q. moves out of here at dawn tomorrow, and I'm going with them. The same thing applies to you. I want an O.C. back with me at the wire, running the unit, not mucking about in here doing a subaltern's job."

"I see——"

"Crosbie," said the brig, "he's the one for it. I don't imagine he suffers from nerves——"

"Nor does Smith, sir. Both are unmarried. And Crosbie did go through the last siege."

"So much the better. He should feel quite at home. Crosbie it is, Anson."

He said, slowly, "Would you mind telling him—that—yourself, sir?"

The brig gave him a long searching glance. "No. Get him here now." He picked up his signal pad and started writing.

When Paul was found, they walked back together to the office truck in silence. The brig was still sitting at the table with two folded signal forms in front of him. He started without preamble.

"Crosbie, I've given Captain Anson certain orders

with regard to the disposition of this unit. As a main part concerns you, I thought I would brief you personally." He pushed one of the signal forms across the table. "Here are your orders."

Paul, so big, so broad, seemed to tower over the little man as he bent forward to read the message under the lamp. A long silence, with only the mutter of the guns coming through to them from outside, then the paper crackled as he folded it carefully and put it in his pocket.

"Quite clear?" said the brig.

"Perfectly, sir. I am to take over command of a section of this unit remaining on this site and coming under orders of C.O. hospital, Tobruk." There was no expression in his voice.

"Any questions?"

"The rest of the unit——?"

"That has nothing to do with your orders—but they are going back to Sollum."

"I understand, sir. Will I have my own section?"

"No, Captain Anson will detail the other ranks staying. They will all be unmarried."

"So—we're going to be boxed in again," said Paul.

The brig hesitated for a moment. "I think it is only fair to tell you, Crosbie, that Captain Anson volunteered for this job—but I refused him."

Paul did not answer.

"Well," said the brig, "I'd best be getting back to Corps. We have all got a lot to do. Will you drive me, Anson?"

The three of them walked back to the Humber. When the brig was in the passenger seat, he turned to Crosbie, standing beside the door and leaned out to grip his arm.

"Well, so long, Crosbie—and good luck. I know I can rely on you. It won't be for long. Five weeks at the most—and you'll be quite snug in these caves. I'll look forward to the time you and Anson dine with me in Alex—and we can have a good laugh about it all."

"I can hardly wait for it, sir. Good night."

Anson was just able to see the black shadow of him, outlined against the stars. He knew then that he would always remember that moment. He said, "Will you check the nominal rolls while I'm gone, Paul? Put the names of all the single men in a hat. Then we'll draw sergeants, corporals and drivers as necessary, when I come back."

"What about Mr. Pugh?" Crosbie's voice came back to him out of the darkness.

"Who is Mr. Pugh?" It was the brig.

Crosbie answered before Anson could speak. "Mechanist sergeant-major, sir. He qualifies. A widower—since the blitz on Plymouth." There was an edge in his voice.

"No," said the brig. "He goes with Captain Anson."

They moved off, groping their way down the track and then on to the road; neither spoke until they were nearly back at Corps H.Q. Then the brig said, suddenly, "I'm sorry about all that, Anson." When he had got out of the car, he held out the other message form.

"There are your orders. The rest of the unit to move off at 02.00 hours. To reach the eastern check-point by 02.25. The senior subaltern to be in charge. They will go straight to the old location at Sollum. You will stay and tidy up detail with Crosbie. Then report to me at first light here. I'll come along with you."

Anson thought for a minute. "Can I keep Mr. Pugh to come with us, sir? It will give him a little more time on the vehicles staying behind—and——"

"And what?" said the brig.

A raid had started. It was one of the usual high-level

night pattern—so usual, that neither of them had taken much notice. To them, it was just a lot of extra noise. For a second both looked at the pale slanting fingers of the searchlights, the heavy flicker of the A.A. guns and the orange flare and crump of bombs.

"And what——?" asked the brigadier, again.

"Mr. Pugh—he's sort of the keystone of the unit, sir. I think there may be a few rough edges over this business —and he'd be invaluable in helping me sort them out."

The brig had not answered for a moment. He was looking along the line of the harbour. A fire had started in one of the depots; little pin-points of yellow and orange that licked and jumped out from the first explosion. Then, nearer, another patch of light appeared, starting this time without any explosion, without benefit of the burst of a bomb.

"Good old N.A.A.F.I.," said the brig, "I thought they wouldn't miss the chance. Yes, keep your Mr. Pugh, as long as he doesn't have too much kit. There is to be no question of him staying behind. Good night, Anson." He got out of the car and scuttled off into the darkness that flickered in the lights of the fires.

All that had followed after that was the vague, unpleasant, condensed pattern of a nightmare. The look of the men as they had waited for the names to be called out of the hat; the little sounds that gave expression of the relief of those not staying; the frozen silence of the others when they heard that they were. Paul standing beside him, calling out the chosen in a clear, expressionless voice, withdrawn, seeming already to have taken over control. There had been the rush—too eager, almost indecent—of those going down the road to prepare their vehicles and pack up. The deadly tiredness coming back to him, the furtive drinks. Last, and most clearly of all, his talk with M.S.M. Pugh.

33

He had sent for him as soon as he had got back to camp. It was not the actual words that were said, but the way of saying them, that would always stay in his mind.

Mr. Pugh had come in quietly through the black-out curtain at the back of the truck to stand silent, waiting. Tall and very thin, with a russet pippin of a face and the bluest of blue eyes. They had known each other for so long, and always the older man, the junior in rank, seemed to be cast in the role of parent.

"Hello, Mr. Pugh."

"Good evening, sir."

Even after these years, their relations, in any circumstance, were always of the most formal.

Anson had leaned forward against the desk and knuckled his hands into his eyes, trying to think, trying to bring himself back from that dark sea of tiredness and despair. Then he pushed the bottle and a spare glass across the table. "Sit down and have a drink," he said.

"Thank you, sir."

He had watched the sergeant-major tilt the bottle to pour a small tot, then swallow it neat. His eyes had taken in the dark stain of grease on the side of the jaw; the black worn nails of the hand that was holding the glass. Then the overalls, anonymous but for the gleam of the brass coat-of-arms on the sleeve. As always, Tom Pugh was on the job.

"You've heard?" he said.

"Yes, sir. I've started workshops on the division of spares. I wondered what——"

Anson held on to the edge of the table, fighting to say sparingly what had to be said.

"First—the cars that are staying. There'll be twenty-five. And they're to be the best in the unit—regardless of who has them now. You know which they are—

so tell the platoon sergeants to get them transferred at once."

Tom Pugh wrote in his notebook: he looked up and said, "The present owners won't like that much, sir."

"I couldn't care less. And it will take that cocky look off their faces when they start on that safe road east."

"Very good, sir. And then——?"

"Then——" He stopped to stare. Then——? He couldn't remember. He looked all round the truck and then buried his head on his arms. . . . "I'm sorry, Tom," he whispered, "I'm so bloody tired. . . ."

It was the first time a Christian name had ever passed between them, but the warrant officer took no more notice than to slip one key in his form of address. "You've had enough, Mr. Anson," he said quietly.

Anson moved his head sideways, looking at the whisky bottle. "You mean—of that?"

"No. Of everything."

Four years of respect and understanding and something deeper flowed between them in the narrow space while the pressure lamp hissed and spluttered to break the silence. Then Tom Pugh got to his feet. "I'll look after it, sir. I know what you want. You get some sleep."

"Mr. Crosbie——" said Anson, and stopped.

"I'll explain to Mr. Crosbie. And I'll come back and see you before you go."

"But you're coming with me."

The M.S.M. stood quite still. In an instant he was the warrant officer again. "I'd rather stay, sir."

"No. You can't be spared."

"I'd rather, sir. I've nothing to go back for——"

There was another silence. Anson thought of that day in Matruh when he had had to break the news of a house obliterated by a bomb in far-away Plymouth. "Neither have I, but that's not the point. The brigadier says we both are non-expendable—so we go. His direct orders."

"Very good, sir." Tom Pugh looked down at the air-mattress that was laid out under the table. "You lie down—just for an hour. I'll attend to everything. Call you, if necessary." The soft Devon voice sounded so very persuasive.

"Just an hour then——" He almost folded up as he levered himself out of the chair, rolled on to the mattress without even bothering to loosen his belt. "Only an hour," he said again.

"Yes, sir."

There was the sound of the chair being moved and then the truck went dark as the lamp was turned down. He heard the scraping of boots and then two hands pulled up a blanket to his neck and tucked it in all round him. There was a patch of the night sky showing where the black-out was parted and the thump of someone jumping off the tailboard.

He stared for a moment at that chink of light, flickering, faintly tinged with orange, the reflection of countless fires. Then he went down into the sleep of exhaustion to the sound of the mutter of the guns . . . and something else . . . a new, different noise. Beyond the cliffs, on the road, the steady grind of an unending column of vehicles . . . creeping in low gear . . . without a light . . . winding out towards the east on the last night of Tobruk.

II

MR. PUGH rolled over on his back and wiped the sweat out of his eyes. He said, "I don't want no more of that kind of talk, Corporal Bellamy. Pass me a three-eighth-inch ring spanner."

It was stifling in the narrow space under the engine of the lorry, the four blankets that were draped to the ground on all sides of the engine effectively prevented any air as well as light from escaping outside, while the four inspection lamps that blazed inside gave off the combined heat of an electric fire. As he turned on his back and adjusted the blanket to the contours of his body where it straddled outside, Tom Pugh winced at the sharp edge of a stone that was biting through the tarpaulin and into his left shoulder-blade. He marvelled again at the state of mind in base workshops and civilian garages that insisted on minimum facilities before they would attempt the renewal of big ends.

Above him, the bowels of the engine—gleaming crankshaft and loosened connecting rods, tied to the sides of the crank-case with wire—seemed to be grinning. It was a challenging grin—"what's wrong with me?" He stared back, up at the glint of metal, framed in the black space where the sump had been removed. 'It's easier for doctors,' he thought. 'Patients can talk. But machinery goes on uncomplaining, until it breaks.'

An arm holding a ring spanner came in through a crack in the blankets, groping its way towards him like a blind worm. Tom took the spanner. "Thank you. When I've switched off the lights, you can come in and get cracking. Bring the split-pins and locking washers with you."

He switched off the lights and then, with a grunting and a humping, Corporal Bellamy wriggled through the curtain to join him. Tom Pugh felt to see if the blankets were tight round both their legs and then switched on.

"Start on number four, Corporal. If you'd done that

37

inspection properly, it wouldn't be necessary for a W.O. to have to get under here and show you your job."

The corporal was a natural grumbler. "If the mucking officers knew what they were mucking well doing—and what was mucking well happening—instead of boozing—none of us would be mucking about under this mucking son of a bitch in the middle of the mucking night——"

With immense skill, Tom Pugh flicked a gob of oil off the crank-shaft and into the corporal's left eye. "Sorry, Corporal," he said pleasantly, as the other rolled away, cursing and rubbing. "When you're ready—hand me up some of those pins and tabs—and let's get on with it."

As they worked on their backs, reaching up into the dark shadows of the crank-case, he went on with a monologue.

"You don't like being left here, do you, Corporal? Just nothing to do, except sit on the soft sand on your fat arse—and a nice little cave to run to when the bombs come down? You would rather be coming with the captain and I—probably get shot up and chased all the way—just like it was at Sidi Rezegh, if you remember that?

"You wouldn't? Well, you will—if there's another word of that kind of talk—and under close arrest, on a charge of mutiny. That's a promise. And they aren't very kind to mutineers at these times, Corp, they find nice hard walls to stick them up against."

There was a healthy silence.

"You heard what the captain said, didn't you?" Tom was tightening steadily.

"The captain—he didn't look too good," said Corporal Bellamy reflectively.

"No. He's had too long wet-nursing clots like you." Tom felt in the tin between them for a locking washer.

38

"But you heard him say—three or four weeks—no worse than last time. And I'll tell you something you don't know—and you can tell it to your precious friends—the captain volunteered to stay——"

"Go on, S'major."

"SIR—to you," Tom snapped, "—I happen to hold the King's Warrant. But tell your friends. I was there and I heard it."

"Heard what, sir?"

"You know that little brigadier—the medic they call 'Dangle-toes'? Well, when he was telling the captain what was going to happen, the captain said, 'I must stay, sir,' and when I heard that, I said, 'I'd like to stay too.' And the brig—he didn't half bawl us both out. Said 'No' and that we'd bloody well got to obey orders."

"That's different," said Corporal Bellamy.

"Yes." As he bent over the last split-pin and then ran his square fingers, lovingly, over the work done, he was thinking that it had been the only thing he could do to help—and at least some of it was true.

"This seems ship-shape, Corporal. Get the sump on— fresh oil—and test the pressure. Don't let me ever hear again of you failing to report a low one on inspection— or you'll be on a charge."

He switched out the lights and crawled out of the blanket tent.

Outside the flickering darkness and the noise that had been muffled by the blankets, almost unnoticed in his absorption over the repair, came back with a sense of surprise. He got to his feet and groped his way back to the running-board. Then he sat down and bowed his face on his hands. He was so very tired.

After a minute he stirred and looked at his watch. Better give the captain a little longer. What else was there to do? As duty, nothing, for all the vehicles were sorted out in the order of their going and the best shape he could have them in the limited time. From loyalty, so much—if he had been in a position to do it. He wondered where Mr. Crosbie was, thought of him and Captain Anson and then wished he was not in uniform and could do what was necessary. Knock their two silly heads together. . . .

An eruption of noise down by the harbour made him look up. The searchlights were circling in a cone and the orange reflections tinted the dark sea from the explosions on the point. A raid—and a bad one. "Poor sods," he said out loud. He was thinking of the drivers of the five ambulances, down there, so close to it while they cleared the hospital. Then his mind went back to the problem of his commanding officer.

It was a little thing that had started the essence of their relationship. On that overcrowded troopship, coming out. He, the just-promoted warrant officer, Mr. Anson with one pip up. It had been the time when the first letters home had been due for censorship, and he had held his back for three days because he could not bear the thought that any other eyes should see the things he had written to Ann. Somehow, Mr. Anson must have guessed, and sent for him, to that stuffy little cabin where he sat with piles of letters waiting to be read and stamped.

"Mr. Pugh—I don't want to have to read your letters home. If you promise me that there will never be any-thing military in them that there shouldn't, seal them and give them to me personally, and I'll sign."

In the moment of his promise, something had been born. And he had never forgotten it.

Nor the other time . . . in Matruh, when he had been told about Plymouth. Mr. Anson had been so wise. There had been no fumbling, no awkward sympathy, no

40

offer of leave that would have been an insult, just quiet orders for a reconnaissance of a well far to the south, and at the very last moment, before he set off, the news. Alone, except for the company of a moron driver, between clean sand and clear sky, he had had three days to get to grips with it. He had not forgotten that, either.

Down over the harbour the noise was dying. He could hear Corporal Bellamy swearing under the blankets. It brought him back to the present.

'Officers boozing'. . . . He turned that remark over in his mind. If it had become so obvious, he supposed it was fair. He, watching the long slow change from a different angle, had not realised. And there had always been Mr. Crosbie to help him shield it . . . until today. But something had happened—they were against each other now. It had been sudden, he could pin-point it to last night . . . when they had gone out to look for the C.O. It must have been something serious. They were avoiding each other; once, today, when he had seen them talking, he had not liked the look in Mr. Crosbie's eyes.

Though he had meant what he said in the first place, now he was glad he was going. He would pick the chance of seeing the final crack-up of the captain rather than have to spend the next month cooped up with Mr. Crosbie in that mood. A month? . . . he wondered. It had all sounded very convincing, but he knew that the captain did not believe it . . . and he knew that the men did not believe the captain. That was the trouble of being a W.O.—you were too close to both sides . . . saw too much. He wondered if the brigadier believed it. No, it would be flannel from there too . . . flannel all the way down.

He looked at his watch. Time to wake the captain. Then he would stay close. Six hours before they left to pick up the brig, six hours in which he must keep those two apart or in the restraint of his presence. It must be done, now at the end. They had been such good friends.

He groped his way through the dark patches of the vehicle lines, past the shadowed quick movements of the men packing up, the purr of idling engines, subdued talk. The office truck was black and silent. He climbed up over the tailboard and when he had turned up the lamp, called, "Captain Anson," softly.

There was a sharp crack as the figure on the bed jerked up so suddenly that he hit head head on the under-side of the table, then in one movement he had rolled sideways and was on his feet. Tom saw the eyes open, but not awake; the glisten of the tight skin on the cheek-bones. This half-sleeping was the most dangerous thing of all.

"What's the time?" The voice jerked.

"A minute before 01.30, sir. I thought you would like half an hour before the convoy leaves."

"Yes. Thank you, Mr. Pugh——" The eyes had come back and were focused on the table. Then a hand strayed towards the bottle that was there. Tom said, "Let me——" and grabbed the bottle quickly to pour out two small tots. "Luck, sir." He put the bottle down on the chair behind him.

Anson looked about him vaguely. "You say they're nearly ready to go—is everything all right?"

"Yes, sir."

"I suppose we'd better have a look round them."

They went out into the darkness to the deeper shadows where the convoy was forming up. As they went from vehicle to vehicle down the line, Tom, from the feel of the ambulance or lorry, the faint glimpse of the driver's face, would give all details of load and fitness. The two subalterns who were going with them followed behind.

42

Apart from Tom's quiet voice, there was hardly any sound, the men, standing by to finish the lashing down, were silent, with no spirit of the start of an adventure about them. Once in the darkness a voice passed them, calling, "Timmy . . . Timmy . . ." and someone close said, "Dodger's lost his mucking dog again." Beyond, separated, watching, were the dim shapes of those that were staying behind.

Tom Pugh turned from the last truck. "That's the lot, sir. They're the worst—as you said—but they shouldn't give any trouble."

"Good." Anson turned to the two lieutenants. "We'll get in the rear ambulance—then I'll brief you. You had better come too, M.S.M."

When the rear doors were closed and the ventilators stuffed with rag, they put on the inside light and sat in pairs opposite each other on the bunks. The interior of the car seemed very clean and white, smelling of new paint. Tom Pugh breathed a sigh of relief now that he could see the captain properly. That glassy look had gone from the eyes, the voice when he spoke was natural, firm.

"You, Smith, will command. Prosser take the rear and whip-in. Control are sending a motor-cyclist to guide you up to the eastern check-post, but they're pretty vague about the state of the road beyond there—or the position on the flank. The best thing you can do, is get cracking from there—non-stop—with at least a hundred yards between vehicles. Go to the old location at Sollum and put out a unit sign. Let the men have one bathe and then get them working." While he had been talking, he had scribbled on his message pad. "There's the movement order."

Smith said, "Mr. Pugh—does he come with us?"

"No. With me, later. I've got to report to the brig at

43

first light. Unless he mucks about, we should catch you up fast enough to be at Sollum almost as soon as you are there. But I want Mr. Pugh to do one or two things for Mr. Crosbie before we go——"

He broke off suddenly. "Has anyone seen Mr. Crosbie lately?"

"He was in that far cave, fixing up his new cook-house, about half an hour ago," said Smith.

"Good. I'll see him later."

Tom was still watching. That muscle had stopped twitching at the side of the captain's face. Then he remembered something.

"Those five ambulances, sir. The ones that have gone to the hospital to clear it. What happens to them?"

"Hell, I'd forgotten them."

"I fixed that direct with Crosbie, sir," said Smith. "He's sent five of his—so it doesn't matter."

From outside, through the thin plywood and canvas walls, came the soft 'chug . . . chug . . . chug' of a motor-cycle. "There's your escort," said Anson. He reached up to the light switch. "See you for tea or supper, then, Prosser—I'll come up to the front with you, Smith, and see you off."

They all went out into the dark that was not quite dark now as the tip of the moon was coming up over the escarpment. Tom walked up behind Anson and Smith to the head of the column where the motor-cyclist was waiting beside the lieutenant's truck. He heard the captain say, "Look after them, Smithy." Then the red-cap, who had been looking round, turned to kick his starter; like a soft wave passing down the column, the noise of the running engines was increased one by one. The vehicles started to move past them, lurching, gleam-ing ghostly in the beginnings of the moon. Dim faces looked out of the cabs, little puffs of sand spurted white

44

from between the wheels, there was the soft snarl of power in low gear. Tom stood close behind the captain, counting, forty-six . . . forty-seven . . . forty-eight . . . then Mr. Prosser's truck. That was the lot. The sounds faded into nothing.

The captain gave a deep sigh, but before either of them spoke, another voice came from behind.

"So I just missed the farewell party." It was Crosbie.

Tom moved closer to Anson, instinctively. This was exactly what he had feared.

Anson said, "Hello, Paul. How's it going?"

"All done—and ready for your inspection, sir."

Tom moved a little closer, almost between them. He didn't like that tone. Anson did not answer for a minute, but just stared up into his friend's face. At last, he said quietly, "If you read your chit from the brig, Paul, you would see that you came under orders from the hospital as from midnight. The colonel can inspect, if he wants to—I just wondered if I could help in any way."

"You——" said Crosbie, and stopped, for Tom had cut in with a quick, "Listen." There was the noise of vehicles coming towards them and then four ambulances came round the edge of the hill, swaying ungainly as they bumped towards them down the track.

Anson looked at his watch. "From the hospital—and about time too."

Crosbie said, "Only four—what the hell's happened to the other one?"

They pulled up abreast of them and a sergeant got out of the leading cab and came over. He saluted. "It was pretty bad down there, sir. We got that raid right in the middle of loading. But we got them all on."

"What's happened to the other car—hit?"

"No, sir. The colonel kept it. He gave me this note

45

for you. Said you were to get it at once." He held out a folded signal.

"Thank you, Sergeant."

When the four cars had bumped off down the track to their lines, Anson unfolded the paper and held it up to the moonlight. All Tom could see was that it was very short.

"I thought you said that I was in command here now." There was that edge in Crosbie's voice again.

Anson folded the note carefully. "It happens to be addressed to me personally." He looked at Tom. "Are you very tired, M.S.M.?"

"Not too bad, sir." He had had no sleep and he was dropping on his feet, but he was wanted.

"Will you drive me to the hospital now? I must see the colonel." Then he said, "I'll see you when I come back, Paul."

They were off the track and on the road leading down to the hospital when Tom said, "What's the trouble, sir?"

"I don't know. The note just said, 'Further complications, you must help me, George. Please come down at once.' Could be anything."

Their arrival at the entrance to the hospital coincided with one of those complete lulls that made the silence more frightening than any form of activity. The moon was bright now and, in a way, that only seemed to make it worse. As they drove on to the wide gravel sweep in front of the main entrance, the ambulance, parked up against one wall, scarcely showed but for the darkness of its red cross. When they had stopped and got out, Tom was surprised to see an orderly standing near it. As they walked over, he stiffened, gripping his pick-handle. But he did not challenge, for both of them were well known.

"What's cooking, Corporal?" said Anson.

46

"Guarding the ladies, sir."

"Ladies——?"

The corporal lowered his voice. "There's two in the back. Nurses. They came up on that transport. Got left behind somehow. I'm here to see no one disturbs them."

Anson said, "Well, I don't know what the hell I'm supposed to do about it. Stay here, Mr. Pugh. I'll go and find the colonel." He ran up the steps into the entrance.

Tom moved off a few paces, away from the sentry and towards the back of the car. He pulled out a packet of cigarettes and lit one, carefully cupping his hands over the flame of the match. The moonlight was like soft silver water flowing over everything, smoothing out all the scars and wreckage that lay around. He drew deep on the fag, letting the coils of smoke float up like white snakes from his nostrils. He listened and there was nothing but the faint mutter of the guns starting up again far away, over the escarpment to the south. 'I don't like it,' he thought, 'these lulls—they're too frequent—too long. It's not like them to let up.' Then there was a different, closer sound. He turned quickly to see the back door of the ambulance opening.

At first there was only the widening band of black that showed the darkened interior, then something slim and light slipped between, closed the door and came down the steps.

It was a girl—not a bit like a nurse, he thought—in those slacks and khaki shirt. As she walked over to him, he saw that she was slim and tall and, somehow, serene. The fair hair that was tied back tight behind her head glowed in the soft moonlight and the mouth, big and generous, was smiling. He could not see her eyes. She stopped in front of him and held out her hand.

47

"Good evening. You must be Captain Anson. I'm so sorry we're going to give you all this trouble."

He saluted, but did not take the hand.

"Good evening, Miss. Captain Anson's gone to find the colonel. I'm his sergeant-major, M.S.M. Pugh. We were sorry to hear you had been left behind——" he looked towards the ambulance—"but I thought the corporal there said, 'Ladies'—or are you on your own?"

"No, there's another sister with me—but she's rather shocked and the colonel's put her to sleep for a bit. I had to come out of there. I was dying for some fresh air."

He fumbled with his packet and offered her a cigarette and she lit it from the tip of his own. She blew out a cloud of smoke and turned to look around her while the moonlight pressed down on them gently. "So this is Tobruk," she said. "How different from all that I had imagined."

He said, "It isn't always as peaceful as this." Then, "How did you manage to miss the boat?"

She laughed. "Oh, it was all too silly. Sister Norton —that's the other one—should never have come on this trip. She's too highly strung—and very young. I don't suppose she has ever been in any real bombing before. While we were loading—she and I had come ashore to help—there was a raid. Things started coming down right on the harbour——"

"I saw it," he said.

"Well, Sister Norton just panicked. She ran away. They could only spare two men to help me find her— and it was all so dark and strange. It took hours. She was right over on the other side of that lagoon thing, crouching by the water. Then she wouldn't come back —we had to carry her. And by that time the transport had gone—something to do with the moon. You can't blame them."

She stopped as the sound of voices came from behind them. It was the colonel and Captain Anson coming down the steps.

The colonel smiled at Tom. "Good evening, Mr. Pugh." Then he turned to the girl, "How is she, Sister?"

"Still sleeping, sir."

"Good. Sister Murdoch, this is Captain Anson." As they shook hands, he added, "Your trouble." Tom had not taken his eyes from the colonel's face. They were old friends and now he was shocked to see how he looked. In this light he would hardly have recognised him, like a walking skeleton.

The colonel said, "We seem to have made a mess of this all ways, Sister. Captain Anson's main convoy has gone—and he doesn't think much of the idea of trying to catch up with them."

They were by the car now; Anson leant against the bonnet, rubbing his chin. "It would mean special permission to go through the perimeter, sir. And that would take time. I don't mind taking one of Crosbie's vehicles—but he's got so few spare drivers——" He looked across at Tom. "Of course, Mr. Pugh could start on ahead with them——"

Tom said quickly, "There's a couple of vehicles up there I should look at before we go." It wasn't true—but neither did he want to go dodging about in the night with a couple of girls, nor leave Captain Anson to the mercy of whisky or Mr. Crosbie.

Anson said, "Well—if the sister doesn't mind—the best thing is to leave them here for the moment. It's only a few hours before we meet the brigadier, anyway. We'll come and collect you then, and go on my movement order. A sort of special convoy. And either I or the M.S.M. will drive the ambulance."

The girl said, "That seems simple. We'll do whatever you wish, Captain Anson."

The colonel looked from one to the other. "And you'll deliver them, George?"

"I promise. Either I or the M.S.M. will drive until there's——" he hesitated—"no risk. Then send them on with a sound man to Alex."

"I'm profoundly grateful, George. I know they will be all right now. But I must get some sleep—so I'll say good-bye—and the best of luck—for the second time." Then he turned to Tom and held out his hand again. "And the best of luck to you, Mr. Pugh."

The three of them stood watching him; straight, tall, with the grey hair shining in the soft silver light as he turned and walked towards the entrance of the hospital.

Anson looked at the girl. He said, "Get some sleep. In the morning we won't disturb you. One or other of us will get in the car and just drive it away. But I want you to keep in the back until I give the word."

She smiled and said, "We are under your orders, Captain Anson." Then she turned and walked over to the ambulance. The big square door closed behind her.

The moon was going when they got back to the caves and the first breath of the dawn wind was coming off the sea; already there was that minute shading of colour in the sky between black and grey. They reached to the back of the car for blankets and sat with them huddled round their shoulders. The wind grew and it was colder.

"Time for an hour's kip, if you want it, Mr. Pugh."

"No, sir. I'm fine as I am."

"Don't forget you may be driving those bloody women."

Tom smiled. "And don't forget you may be driving—the brigadier."

There was silence while Tom pulled the blanket closer

round him, taking off his cap and letting the wind ruffle his hair. He closed his eyes with no thought of sleep. He was too tired for that, he just wanted to think. . . .

There was no problem forward—except the extent of the disaster into which they were plunging. That it was to be that, he was now quite certain. He did not have to wait to see the brigadier to be convinced—although he knew that would do the trick. The brig . . . that amusing, gutful, little flanneller . . . he was thinking of him, without disrespect, from the Olympian heights of a W.O. . . . in the morning he would get that stream of bouncing confidence, but he would be able to see the eyes behind those glasses while they told the tale. Which appeared to be more than his officers could. . . .

He had seen all he wanted at the hospital, the colonel, a man he knew and trusted, resigned, calm, saying good-bye, and then going back to his job. And, from him, Tom knew.

He opened his eyes and looked towards the east, no sun yet. Perhaps it was good that a curtain lay between that and what would happen before it set again. There was no point in thinking forward then, only back . . . and there were so many things.

He thought of the garage. The little square white-washed house with its two green pumps on the corner of the village cross-road by the post office. The village, deep in its hollow to the west of the Tamar, with the tall elms round the church, the thatch of the cottages and the smoke hanging straight on summer evenings. They had been so happy there—but now it was like a dream; as if it had never happened.

There was no link, no children—and thank God for that—nothing to draw him back . . . yet he couldn't stop remembering. How she had slaved at those cream teas in the summer, how they had scraped and gone without to put in the second pump, repair jobs, big and small, that had paved the way in the modernising of the business that had been left him by his blacksmith father.

Then the war. The stirrings of conscience that he should do something. The arguments that he was too old and then the tears that night he came home from Plymouth, sheepish, enlisted in the R.A.S.C. The kaleidoscope of north-country billets, postings and promotions. His meeting up with Mr. Anson. . . .

He turned to look at the hunched figure beside him, the head forward, nodding. The first fingers of real light were creeping into the east of the sky. He shook the shoulder gently. "First light, sir."

Anson stirred and stretched. "I'd better find Mr. Crosbie."

"Shall I come?"

"No, stay and start her up. I'll bring him back with me."

He watched the captain, stiff and awkward, get out of the car and walk away. A wave of feeling rose up inside him that almost stifled, it was the focus now—of everything, after a lost wife and the children that might have been. They had been together, up and down that desert, for so long, they had grown up, militarily, side by side— he to the highest rank that held any interest, Anson to captain. 'He should be a major soon,' he thought—then remembered the other things that had happened. His captain was not growing any more. He was withering, and that was, must be, Tom Pugh's only problem.

That day in Plymouth—the one he had heard of in Matruh—it did not hurt any more. Only, it was so terribly hard to understand. The chance that a one-day visit to her sister should coincide with the lone raider, the fighters on his tail, dropping his load on that distant suburb to get more speed for the desperate run home.

52

There had been no hate in the mind that loosed those bombs, he knew, only fear. And in him, now, there was no hate either. It had happened. And there was nothing to go home to.

Voices behind him now, and the soft crunch of desert boots on the sand. He turned to see the captain and Mr. Crosbie walking side by side, yet apart. He got out of the car and stood waiting for them.

"I came to say good-bye, Sergeant-major. I hear you have everything laid on for this trip—even female comfort."

"We'll be seeing you very soon, sir."

"I doubt it." Crosbie was not looking at either of them, but far, far beyond. The light was coming now. Grey.

Anson moved uneasily and said, "Well, I'll say it. So long, Paul, and good luck. We must get cracking—and I know you've got the hell of a lot to do."

"I have." He ignored the outstretched hand and threw up a stiff mocking salute. "Permission to fall out, sir?—and remember me to Ariadne."

"Paul——" The captain looked very old suddenly, standing there, his hand groping.

"Permission to fall out?" As Crosbie repeated it, his voice went brittle. Then he said, "You ripe bastard," very softly and turned away. Tom stared at the ground because he did not want to see the captain's face. He heard the soft crunch of boots fading into the distance.

When he thought it was safe, he said, "We'd best be moving, sir," and Anson had answered, "Yes," in a flat voice, and they had got into the car without looking at each other, and Tom had started her up and driven down the track and on to the road without once looking back. Dawn was with them now; it was easy to see the details of the harbour, the black smudges of smoke still

53

rising from last night's fires, the dark line of the escarpment away to the south. Still that heavy, uneasy silence clung to the whole place.

The ambulance stood like a square box against the run-in to the hospital; there was nothing else there and no movement. He ran the Humber alongside and then turned to look at the captain.

"Will you take the ambulance, sir?"

"No. You hop in and follow me down to Corps H.Q. I'll get ahead and meet the brigadier." He was looking straight in front of him, his voice still had that dead, flat tone.

When the Humber had moved off, Tom got into the cab of the ambulance. It was a wide platform with no doors at the sides, the bucket seats of driver and orderly separated by a gangway that led to the door communicating with the back; the windscreen, top panel hinged open, was smeared with oil and sand to stop the tell-tale glint of sun that might be spotted by hostile aircraft. He sat relaxed in the driver's seat for a moment and then turned round to look at the door beside him. There was no sound from the other side. After he had started the engine and adjusted the choke, he let her idle for a minute. He was just leaning forward to put the gear lever into first when the door opened and the girl put her head out.

"Hello, Sergeant-major." She smiled and he thought it was a very nice smile. He noticed all that he could see of her was as spick and span as he had thought it was last night in the moonlight.

"Are we off?" she said.

"Yes. To Corps Headquarters first. I think the captain has to get permission from the brigadier to move you."

"And then——?"

54

He shrugged. "Back to your hospital at Alex. Two days—if we are lucky."

"Will it——?" she started, but he looked at his watch and then said, "I'd best be moving—that brigadier gets very testy."

She smiled again. "All right. And we'll keep in the back, like Captain Anson said, until you give the word." The door closed and he let in the clutch and went off up the hill after the Humber. He thought, 'I ought to have asked after the other girl—can't waste any more time now—must later.'

It was full light now and all the old scenes of the well-known road slid by one after the other as he turned and twisted up the loops climbing up from the harbour. Well-remembered, but now so different. He stared more and more intently as he swung from one lock to the other on the bends. He used this road so often . . . the last time only two days before . . . one was accustomed to a particular turn by the look of the camps that were close to it. Now it was all changed, for the camps were not there any more, only empty, untidy, turned-over squares of desert where the tents had been. A lot of people had gone in the night.

Farther on, up the higher slopes, there was a new pattern. The transport, pulled just off the road in long straggles. It was the tanks that made him stare hardest, for there were so many, far more than he had ever seen inside the perimeter before. Silent, canted sideways in the ditches, he could see their crews, wrapped in their ground-sheets, lying like grey slugs beside them. But they were not casualties, pulled in for repair . . . he saw no splattered holes drilled through turrets, no damaged tracks. He started to whistle.

In and out . . . in and out, as he pursed his lips. He tilted his cap on the back of his head and then the words came back to him . . . "Where do us be going . . . and what be doing of there. . .?" The old Devon song . . . Tavistock Goosey Fair. It struck him that he did not know where he was going any more than those poor b——s by the side of the road did.

The song died suddenly as he stared down the straight stretch of road ahead. If it had not been for the Humber drawn up on the verge and the three figures standing beside it, he would not have known he had reached Corps H.Q. Like the other camps, it had gone.

"God!" he said. "They don't half get their finger out when they do a swan." He pulled up behind the Humber and got down.

The brigadier was standing talking to Anson, waving his arms, and Tom could see that the captain was angry. Another officer—remembered vaguely as a staff captain, medical—was busy loading a pile of kit from the sand into the back of their car. He saw the brig was wearing his best hat and tunic. A bad sign. He went up to the correct distance and saluted.

The brig looked at him, gave a faint waggle with one hand, and said, "You're late." Then turned back to Anson.

"I'm sorry. I sent my truck on with the Corps transport because I thought your car would be quicker. Now I find you've involved yourself with two sisters and an ambulance. Do you expect me to TRUNDLE back to Egypt in convoy? No, I'll take the car—and Ponsonby can drive it. YOU CAN, CAN'T YOU, PONSONBY?" he roared at the staff captain, who dropped the pack he was carrying and said, "Oh, yes, sir," hurriedly.

"Do you want us to take our kit out?" It was Captain Anson and there was a tremble in his voice. His face was very white.

The brig looked up from where he was leaning on the

56

bonnet, writing furiously in his message pad. "No. Dammit, man—you'll have the lot back this evening. We'll look after it." Then his face changed. "Look— I'm ordering you, Anson. There isn't time for argument." He stabbed his pencil in the direction of the escarpment to the south. "They are making a strong thrust, east of here, towards the road. Corps got out in the hell of a hurry, and I don't like being too far behind the commander—it's uncomfortable. Here are your orders——" he ripped a sheet from the pad—"in case we get separated. These girls are your responsibility. To be delivered to Alexandria by a reliable officer."

Tom was thinking . . . 'A thrust to the east of us . . . on the road . . . when and how did they manage to get that far. . .?"

The brig had jumped into the passenger seat. "Come on, Ponsonby. Don't stand there. I'm in a hurry." He turned to grin at the two of them. "See you for supper," he said. Then their cherished Humber bounded like a wounded animal as the staff captain let in the clutch with a bang and disappeared up the road in a cloud of dust.

They climbed into the ambulance in silence. Then Anson said in a tight voice, "I'm going to catch that little bastard. How long would it take to lift the governor on this crate?"

"All of half an hour, sir. Not worth it—fifteen miles lost. And listen——"

During the argument, neither had realised how the sound of the guns had been growing, how the direction had changed so gradually from south to south-east. It had swung right round now over to the strip that held the coast road, the only access to the frontier of Egypt.

"Yes," said Anson, "perhaps, for once, Dangle-toes is right. Get cracking, then."

Tom let in the clutch and soon the engine was snarling

under its full thirty horses as they swayed round the last twist on the road before the long straight run to the eastern perimeter. They were high now, the escarpment clear to them, a long brown cliff that flanked the south about ten miles away. Ahead, the black ribbon of tarmac and the telegraph-poles stretched out in perspective, empty but for a faint dot that might have been the Humber. Tom had his foot down on the floor now, tense over the wheel while the air roared in through the open screen. Once or twice he managed to flick his eyes over towards the escarpment. Was it imagination?—or was there a haze hanging over it?—vehicles moving? The second time, a little farther east, he saw something quite definite. A ripple of pale flashes that came from the crest. The noise of their passage was too great to hear anything—he did not see the bursts. He swung his eyes back on the road, keeping them there, not speaking. There was no point in telling the captain that they were outflanked already—and that Jerry was shelling the road.

Now the tank-trap on the perimeter and the huddle of tents near it were rushing towards them. He threw the gear into neutral and started coasting to a halt. There were only two vehicles there, a lorry and the Humber jammed up tight behind it. Remembering the advantages of dispersion, he pulled up a clear fifty yards behind.

There seemed to be some form of argument going on up there, for the brigadier was standing up in the front seat of the car, waving his arms as usual, clearly haranguing the M.P. who was standing in the road. Anson said, "I'll go and see what's happening," jumped down and started running up the road towards the check post. There was still no sound from the back of the car. Tom unhooked the captain's binoculars that were hanging

58

from a peg behind the driver's seat and then knocked softly on the communicating door.

"Yes——?" It had just opened a crack, only enough to see her face.

He spoke very softly, "We're at the check post. There seems to be a delay, and the captain's gone up to sort it out. How is she?"

"Awake—and terribly scared."

He said, "Look—Jerry's started shelling the road and it seems as if we shall have to run the gauntlet. There isn't much protection in these things—just wedge all the cushions and blankets beside you to the right, and when we move off, lie on the floor. I'm afraid it may be a bit bumpy."

She took it quite calmly. "I'll do that."

"Are you sure—you can manage?"

"I'll have to."

He said, "I'm just going over to that mound there for a moment—to see if I can see anything."

"We'll stay put." The door shut with a click.

He got down and went over to the little mound that was a few yards off the road. He slung the glasses round his neck, then focused them down towards the check post.

The lorry and the Humber looked misshapen and fore-shortened. The figure of Anson, covering the last few yards, moving in that curious slow-motion gait of magnified distance. The brig had sat down now and then he saw dust puff from under the wheels of the lorry in front; a second later, the noise of the revving exhaust came back. He swung his lenses out to the south, on the escarpment.

The sun was right up now, a blood-red disc that rested on the edge of the desert, beyond the point where the straight line of road and telegraph-poles vanished to

59

nothing. The colours to the side of it had changed to a pattern of dun and grey and sage, it stretched to the south as far as the ridge of the cliff. There, clear now, like ants on an earth bank, was a host of transport. He thumbed the fine adjustment to get them clearer. . . . Yes, they were moving . . . down the cliff towards them. There was no fear, only an aching responsibility for their load.

He swung the glasses back on the way ahead. The lorry had moved a distance now, across the tank-trap and on to the road. He could see every detail of the barbed wire and the minefield as it passed them, dwindling down the line of telegraph-poles. Suddenly, short and then in two groups over, slender columns like black and yellow poplar trees spouted from the desert to grow up in the sky. The 'crump' of them came afterwards, the lorry was invisible beyond in the cloud of dust. Perhaps it had got through; but Jerry had the range of the road.

The roar of an exhaust came back to him again, and he lowered the glasses quickly to the bridge of the tank-trap. It was the Humber being given the gun. He kept his eyes trained on it, hardly aware of the pound of Anson's boots coming back down the road, the shout of, "Come on, Pugh, there's talk of closing the bridge."

It was strange to see the foreshortened, open body of the car he had maintained and nursed so long dwindle like that down the black line of the road. The brig was standing up, arms waving, for a second the light caught the maroon band of his cap. Tom smiled, he thought of the stream of bad German that was being hurled at the enemy. He wondered if it would be effective at a range of four thousand yards.

He saw what happened—exactly, in slow motion—because he was looking straight at the car for that split-second of time. One moment it was there, the next, an orange flower seemed to burst into bloom on the right-hand side of the body; the long bonnet whipped round backwards as a running dog might turn to snap at a fly and then everything was lost in a blot of smoke and dust, with one dot that might have been a body turning slowly in an arc high in the air. When the dust cleared, there was just a spiral of black smoke climbing straight in the sky.

He lowered the glasses, feeling rather sick; the first thought was not for the men . . . or the car. His own tool-kit, the special set of ring spanners, that he loved and would not lend, they had been stowed in the back.

He looked down at Anson. "They've had it . . . a direct hit."

"Christ! Dangle-toes . . ." Anson was very white. Tom understood that thought so well. It was a blasphemy that a pillar of the desert could be obliterated for ever, just like that. Then the captain's hand was dragging at his sleeve, pulling him down the slope. "Come on. Quick—while there's still time."

As they ran back towards the car, Anson jerked, "Are they—all right—inside?"

"Yes—I told them—what to do. The other—she's just come round."

They scrambled in and started her up and Tom crashed into gear and accelerated towards the empty strip of concrete that was the bridge. But there were two figures running away from it now, down the road, in their direction. They were shouting—Tom could see the open mouths—waving their arms; no words came to them through the roar of aero engines that were coming in from the east.

"Get a move on, Tom." Anson's voice rose and cracked through it. But the two figures had halted now, spread across the road, barring it, their tommy-guns at the ready. They were M.P.s.

When Tom had halted in front of them he leaned out of the cab and looked upwards, watching the glint of silver wings against the sun as the fighter-bombers circled in the dive of their attack towards the escarpment, then the shooting stars of tracer weaving their patterns to and fro, the fountains of sand spouting among the distant enemy transport. In seconds it was over and the planes were turning and climbing back to the height for their return to base. The noise of the engines died away. The voices of the M.P.—a captain—and Anson came clear to him from the other side of the cab.

"Sorry, old boy. I've just got the orders. Close the road and blow the bridge. You'll have to turn back."

Tom turned to see him standing with one foot on the step, the tommy-gun crooked under his arm. There was a sheen of sweat on his face.

Anson said, "Don't be a bloody fool. I've told you twice—I've got two nursing sisters in the back. And orders, direct from Corps, to get them back to the Delta. Look——" He fumbled for the brig's signal in his pocket.

The policeman stiffened. "I don't care if you've got the Archangel Gabriel. That bridge is going up in a minute. So get back."

"Drive on, Sergeant-major." Anson's voice was tight.

As Tom hesitated, the tommy-gun came up from under the arm until it pointed straight at Anson's stomach. He saw the finger curling round the trigger.

"I shouldn't, Sergeant-major. You'll have a dead duck beside you if you do."

He put the gear lever into reverse. "Best keep clear of any flying bits," he said. Then he let in the clutch and the ambulance started backwards. The M.P. jumped on the step, holding the windscreen pillar with one hand, gun still pointing. Neither he nor Anson exchanged another word.

Straining round to look past the bulge of the spare wheel cover, he was surprised at the empty road behind them. Surely there should have been others, they could not be the last out. No, there was something else . . . a good way behind . . . heavy stuff, by the haze of dust it was making.

He heard the M.P. say, "Thirty seconds . . . best turn sideways, or the blast may get your windscreen." He locked the wheel hard down to back off sideways on the soft sand, then cut the engine. As he relaxed in the seat, Anson was knocking at the communicating door. He heard him say, "Lie down, Sister—there's going to be a big bang——" over that, the voice of the M.P. chanting, "Ten . . . seven . . . five . . . four . . ." He turned to look down the road to the bridge and then it heaved up slowly with bursts of orange and black between the cracks and the blast of it slapped him in the face. With the noise that followed, the whole thing dissolved into a cloud of dust and smoke; a block of concrete whistled through the air to bounce on the road in front of them, burst, and roll in smaller fragments to the side.

And that was that. They were inside. As Tom sat and watched the dust clear, he thought, without anger, without even bitterness, of the trail of incident that had led up to this moment; the different streams of thought that had caught him for a moment to pull this way and that; the brigadier, warm and comforting, the captain, fighting his own battle, patently not believing, but backing up manfully what he had been told to say; the chill of rumour, his own personal doubts. It was bloody hard for a W.O.—sitting in the middle.

Well, they had said Tobruk would be invested . . . but surely there could be no planned investment, if it happened at such a speed. He wondered how accurate they would be over the second part . . . its strength . . . the time before it was relieved.

The M.P. was talking to Anson. "Sorry, old man. But I wouldn't have fancied your chances out there. Safer inside."

Anson said, "Sorry I created," and they shook hands. The policeman slung the tommy-gun. "Well, I'd better go back along the road and organise the stuff that's coming up." For the first time, Tom noticed the clatter of tracked vehicles that was growing to a roar behind them.

They swung back on the road and started back towards Tobruk and dropped the M.P. at the first screen of tanks that were coming up from behind. As they went on, the sight of the 25-pounders and the Bofors that crowded the road while they moved up in support gave Tom a little hope. They drove on, not speaking, without slowing, without a halt. As always, the red crosses of the ambulance gave them absolute right of way. Only when they had got to a road-fork that branched right to the harbour had Anson said, "Left, Sergeant-major," and soon after that, as they ran along a higher ridge, parallel to the sea, were those earlier thoughts chilled.

There was a lot of transport there, a lot of troops in camps or resting at the side of the road. He saw some British armour and some of the Second South African Division. Trucks passed them or came in convoy from the opposite direction. It all looked very busy and impressive . . . until you looked very close.

Then the pattern of movement became aimless; the second's glance at the faces at the side of the road a little disquieting. There was a groping, bewildered look creeping over all.

Anson's voice cut across these thoughts. "Did you check this crate for everything?"

64

"Only the petrol, sir. She's full—twenty-four gallons —but I couldn't very well get in the back to look at the water and rations. I know there are the usual small spares issued, and a front and rear spring."

"Mechanically?"

"One of the best maintained in the company. Driver Grimes has always had her. He didn't half kick up when he had to leave her behind."

Anson looked down to where a name was painted in white on the drab dashboard. "Good old KATY," he said absently, "I suppose that's his wife?"

"I think so."

There was a silence and then Anson said, "Well, the first thing is to stop and check everything. I came this way to be nearer the supply depot. If the girls agree, I've got a kind of plan."

He did not enlarge on it, but Tom had guessed. He said, "One thing—tools. We only have the issue kit. Not too good, sir. Mine is—was—in the back of the Humber."

Only the snarl of the sand tyres on the tarmac came up to them as both thought of the blackened scrap-heap on the Bardia road, then Tom said, "And we've only got one jack."

There was a lull in the transport passing them now, a high bank on the left of the road that hid anything above; then round the next bend was a semi-circular indent cut into the side that looked like a road-mender's quarry.

"Pull in there," said Anson. "We'll talk to the girls— and work it out."

When they had pulled off the road and cut the engine, the captain got up stiffly from the passenger seat and went to the door between them and knocked. "Will you come out, Sister?"

In a moment her head appeared and she said, "Where are we——? and what was all that noise——?"

Tom smiled at her. "Still on the inside—looking out, I'm afraid."

Anson said, "Can you both come out here—we've got to have a talk."

"I'll try and make her—but she's being awfully difficult." The door was left ajar and while they lit up their cigarettes, they heard her voice coming from the back, low and insistent, then the incoherent sobbing answer of her companion. The voice rose, there was the unmistakable sound of a slap. The two men's eyes met and held. Another complication. Then the fair girl came out into the cab, followed by her friend.

". . . The wrath of God . . ." that was Tom's first reaction to her appearance, and he was not far wrong. He could see that at other times she would be beautiful at the moment, the red, puffy eyes, the white, tear-stained face with the red mark of an open hand still showing on one cheek, were not appetising. 'More trouble,' he thought.

She did not answer their quiet "Good morning", and slumped down in the gangway with her back against the door. Not quite crying, not quite silent, she looked like a crumpled khaki sack in those creased slacks and shirt.

Anson had got down to the road and was leaning on the windscreen pillar, facing back towards them; the fair girl had slipped into his seat. He said, "I'm terribly sorry. We did our best—but we just didn't make it. They were shelling the coast road outside the perimeter when we got there. The brigadier had the first run—in my car. It got a direct hit. Then our people blew up the bridge over the tank-trap. That was the noise you heard. They wouldn't let us have a try at it—they turned us back at the point of a gun. Perhaps it was for the best. But I'm sorry."

The fair girl said, very calmly, "What happens now?"

66

"First the sergeant-major is going to check all the stuff we have with us: petrol, water, food—everything like that. On that, if I decide that it is possible, and—you agree, of course, there is one other way to get you out."

"And if you can't——?"

He smiled. "Let's see if it's possible first—before we give in. Tom, have a quick shufty, will you?" He was pulling out his cigarettes and offering them round as Tom went round to the back of the car.

It did not take him long to check the cans and the sealed box that held the emergency rations. He started whistling while he worked; there was more than he had hoped of everything, and the captain hadn't had a drink for hours . . . and didn't seem to want one.

When he went back to the front, they were still in the same positions. The dark sister—Norton, he thought her name was—was sitting straighter now, looking better, though the hand that held the cigarette still trembled.

He said, "The vehicle rations are sealed, sir. That's seven days for four people. Beside the tanks, there's five jerricans of petrol—say, twenty gallons. Sixteen gallons of water in tins, and some, I can't say how much, in the inside patients' water tank."

Anson said, "We could do it——"

The fair girl said, "What——?"

"Break out—go south and turn up back to the road."

"And the alternative——?"

"To take you back to the hospital—to wait for a ship —if there are going to be any——"

"I think I would prefer——"

They had all been so intent on their problem that the build-up of noise above them had passed unnoticed. The drone of engines, the crackle of machine-gun fire, had come gradually; the 'bump-bump-bump-bump-bump'

67

of Bofors fire brought them back to reality and then the scream of dive-bombers rammed it home.

It came down suddenly on them, rising in pitch and volume so fast that in seconds it was almost more than ears could stand. Anson was leaning back, staring upwards, shading his eyes. Then his voice came, sharp, "On top of us—quick—scatter."

As Tom turned to pull the dark girl from the floor beside him, he saw Anson dragging the other one down in the ditch on the far side. As he touched her, she came towards him at first unresisting, then reacted with terrifying suddenness. She jumped across him, straight out into the road, head down, running with arms flailing. He cursed and dived after her, making a flying tackle that sent them both sprawling into the far ditch. The noise above them had changed to the thinner whine of bombs. He was lying on top of her then, just before the ground seemed to come up and hit them, hard and quick, six times. It was all noise and debris then, with the warm dry dust filling his eyes and choking; the soft body beneath him had stopped shaking. He rolled over and peered through the fog for the others. They were both there, crawling back along the far ditch to the ambulance. He picked up the limp body and carried it back.

Apart from scratches, they were none of them touched and they decided that the dark girl, Norton, had fainted, pure and simple, from fright. They put her in the back and covered her with a blanket, then beat the dust from their clothes and wiped their faces, the yellow grit coming away in patches to leave the travesty of a stage make-up.

The fair girl scrubbed with the back of her hand. "So this is what it will be like—until it's relieved." There was the faintest tremor in her voice. "I wish I could have a wash."

Tom pulled out a large handkerchief. "It comes off better dry. Take that." She smiled as she reached over for it and then, for the first time, he touched her; something strange and from the past stirred inside him.

Anson said, "I don't want to frighten you—but, I shouldn't count on this place being relieved too quickly —if ever."

She stared at him. "What do you mean?"

"That Jerry will be in here before we know where we are. That he's only so slow about it because he can't believe it."

"We'll go with you—your way," she said.

"What about—her?"

"Norton? She's in no state to decide anything. But she won't be any trouble. I'll see to that."

"All right. But I want you to know what we're in for. It will be difficult—perhaps dangerous." He turned to look at Tom. "Do you remember that track—the one to the south-west through the minefield—towards Knightsbridge? That one we used in the last siege?"

"I only went over it once, sir. It twists like anything and I bet the marking tapes will have gone by now. Probably been re-mined too."

"I knew it well," said Anson. "I did it in the dark once. They won't have re-mined it. No point up to a few days ago—and then no time. It's worth a chance."

"—That's the chance, is it?" said the girl. "Being blown up if you're wrong?"

"Yes. But I'll back my hunch. The next bit will be the tough spot, getting through the ring outside if the place is contained. The only chance is if they haven't enough troops to cover the whole perimeter—that there are gaps. The minefield is wide and looks strong where that track is, so they might leave it alone."

"And if they don't——"

"And we run slap into them? Try bluff. Hope for the luck to cook up a good story. They're pretty punctilious about the red cross. It might work."

"And if it does?"

He laughed. "You're a devil for punishment. Well, then it's just a piece of cake. Run due south for fifty miles—to be sure to keep out of trouble, then turn east to the 'wire', then north back to the coast to find our unit. We'll send you straight on to Alex from there."

"I don't know much about it," she said, "but petrol, water, and things like that?"

"It will be two-fifty miles at the outside. On what Tom says we have, there's three-fifty miles' petrol—even over the worst going. We've got ten days' water and a week's food. We should be there in two days. What more could anyone want?"

Tom spoke for the first time. He said, "We could break down."

Anson stared at him. "Then it would be the hell of a long walk." He turned to the girl again. "Well——?"

"We'll go."

"Let's get cracking then. Every hour will make it more tricky. But stop at the supply depot on the way past, Tom, and we'll sling on a bit more food."

As Tom bent towards the starter button, he turned to look at the girl. "Can either of you drive, Miss?"

She shook her head.

"Oh——" He stared at Anson. "I was afraid of that. It means there will only be one of us to do the man-handling. And there's some awful soft sand south on the 'wire'."

"Wait till it comes, Tom. The girls will have to push, that's all." Then he said, "Sister, this is going to be rather bloody for you—but the best way you can help at the moment is by keeping Norton quiet and being out of sight. So don't come out of there until you get the word."

"I'll do that." She smiled at them both and got up and went in to the back of the car.

They moved off and soon they were in the main South African Laager area. And things were different. There was no doubt of it now, the look in the eyes of the troops they passed—open hostility, shading to something worse. They did not mention it to each other, but they both knew; Tom hunched a little closer to the wheel, holding it tighter, there was a little click as Anson opened the flap of the revolver holster that was hanging from his belt.

Now shouts were accompanying their passage, and then there was a man standing in the road with a raised rifle.

"Run him down—if he won't move." It came through Anson's teeth.

As Tom accelerated and swerved, he saw for a moment the fear and hate in the eyes behind the sights, there was a stab of flame and then the bullet whammed high and wide behind them. His spirits soared as the captain leant back and inched open the door and said, "Some-one shooting sparrows," in a cheerful voice.

'Four hours now,' he thought, 'and he's still right on top. It's going to work out all right.'

But round the next bend they came on the supply depot and the first cracks that led to the abyss were there in front of them. The looting. . . .

They saw it just in time as they were slowing down to turn into the sweep before the tent of the main office. Anson had just said, "I'll nip in and show them the brig's orders—that should be enough," when they saw the crowd erupting from the trampled side-wall of a swaying tent.

71

Four separate figures broke from the mass, running towards them, staggering under the weight of the rum jars they were carrying; one tripped and fell and there was the moment's sight of the bloody mask of his face as he lifted it from the fragments, the brown ooze of the rum as it spilled and soaked into the sand. An officer was running, revolver drawn, and then a pick-handle flashed and the whole dissolved into a dark heaving mess that flashed away into the dust behind them. Tom had not needed Anson's shout of "Keep moving", to put his foot down hard. The Austin's engine had snarled as the tyres spurted the soft sand and they were out through the other end of the turn-in and back on the road.

"My God!" said Anson.

He slowed as they moved on down the boundary of the depot. There were gaps in the barbed wire, but no crowds milling among the low stacks of rations that were covered with tarpaulins. No one wanted to loot hard tack.

"Drive in the next gap, Tom. Go from stack to stack. I'll try and find what we want, and sling a case of each on quickly."

Like a great bee drifting from flower to flower, they drove a zigzag course between the stacks, stopping only long enough for Anson to jump down, lift the sheet to identify and heave a case on to the cabin floor. They had sugar and bully and milk before there was a crackle of sound from the corner of the enclosure behind them. The biggest tent was dissolving in thin tongues of flame under a pall of smoke, ant-like figures spilling out of it, running across the open space.

"Get moving, Tom."

Before he could start, the door opened and the girl's head came out; she was white, and her hair had come down at one side. "I must have a hand for a moment—

she's so strong, I can't control her." For the first time they were aware of the thin screams and the banging behind her.

"You go." Anson was running round to the driving seat. There was nothing to do except slide from under the wheel and follow the girl into the back, slamming the door behind him.

It was dim in there and full of noise and there was a faint sour smell in the air. He had been out there long enough to know exactly what it was—fear. . . .

The girl on the bunk was crouching up on it, her fingers making a scrabbling noise on the plywood wall as she tried to tear it away; as the other jumped over and started to pull her back, one shoulder showed white where the shirt had split away, then the head, arching back towards him, the eyes tight shut, the mouth a round 'O' from which the screams came in one long high sound that seemed to hit the inside of his head.

"I'll hold her—if you've got a shot of something. It's the only way." It was small comfort to feel the car swaying under them and know they were moving.

The girl was panting. "Yes . . . in my haversack. . . . Hold tight . . . she's so strong. . . ."

He took a grip and at his touch she seemed to redouble her struggles, then, suddenly, the noise stopped as she jerked her head sideways and sharp teeth bit deep into his forearm. The strain was too much for the shirt and it ripped down the front with a dry brittle sound, a smooth pink-tipped breast was straining up through the gap towards him. He almost let go, not from the pain of the bite, but a feeling of revulsion. It was the first time he had seen or touched a woman . . . since . . .

Now the other was back, ripping the cover from the orange capsule, leaning over him to slide the needle into the exposed shoulder. The teeth left his arm and slowly the fight went out of her, in spasms, like a dying fish.

"No more trouble—for a bit," said the girl.

They were standing close in the narrow space between the bunks. Now there was only heavy breath beside them and the roar of the tyres on the tarmac beneath that showed that the captain was back on the road. He saw how tired, how desperate she was. He reached forward and gripped both her arms at the elbows.

"Listen, Miss. We're going to be all right. We've taken on extra food. There's plenty of water and petrol. Captain Anson will get us through that minefield—I know he can. We won't meet any Jerries. And you'll both be in Alex in three days."

"Sorry—"

She was steadying herself against him now and he could feel the touch of her forearms on his—both soft and firm—but it did not worry him as the other had done. Slowly, the trembling stopped, she gave him the ghost of a smile and then sat down suddenly on the other bunk.

"I could do with a drink," she said. "There's a flask in my haversack. Would you like one?"

"I think we've earned it."

He sat beside her, sucking the pin-pricks of blood from the purple bruise, watching the fumble for the flask, then the rattle of the neck against her teeth. 'You wanted that badly,' he thought, 'but you wouldn't scream—whatever happened.'

When he had had his turn, he said, "I'd best get back to the cab with the captain."

She held out the flask. "What about him?"

"No, Miss. Please don't give him one—don't even let him see it."

"Why ever not——?"

He stared at the shining brown linoleum on the floor, swaying to the movement of the car, feeling a traitor as he searched desperately for the right words. "He's had a bad time lately—been on the bottle. But he hasn't had a chance to have one since we met this morning. All his own stuff—was on that car. He's over the worst of it now and he'll be all right if he thinks there's nothing. If he knows there is, he'll start all over again. And then——" He spread his hands in a gesture that implied a finish to everything, then he looked at her desperately. "I couldn't take you through that minefield—my navigation isn't good enough to risk lives on—so far south."

She said, very quietly, "I'm sorry. I didn't know." The flask went back, deep down in her haversack. There was silence for a moment, and then the noise of the tyres deepened as they started to brake. "Hell," he said, "what's up now?" He pushed open the door and went out into the cab.

The road was empty, a little ahead was a pull-in with a single tent surrounded with stacks and stacks of white water tins and jerricans. Anson said, without looking round, "All right in there?"

"Yes."

"I'm going to pull in, Tom. That water point seems deserted. It's worth a few moments to sling on extra petrol and water—to be sure."

They were coasting in to the track that led up to the tent. It was then he had his first sight of Captain Zimmerman.

He was standing in front of the tent, a big, square pack slung from each shoulder. The first impression was the size of the man, broad and tall, like an oak. Tom saw the orange bands of the U.D.F. below the badges of rank on the shoulder straps, the short wide shorts, the calf-high desert boots. As they slid by, he gripped the pillar of the windscreen with one hand and swung himself up on the step, then sat down on the floor of the cab, facing them. He looked up at Anson. "Good morning, Captain." It was the clipped guttural English of the Afrikander.

Anson had stopped now. "Good morning. In trouble?"

"Yes. Can you tell me where there's a chance of getting a truck—to get to hell out of here?"

"A truck?"

"Yes—mine's down the road——" he jerked his head in the direction in which they would be going—"big end gone."

"Where do you want to go to?"

"The Delta."

He had got down from the step and stood facing them, the packs still swinging from each shoulder. It was then that Tom decided he didn't like the shape of that square neck that ran in a straight line into the back of the shaven head, or those deep-set, very blue eyes.

The South African went on speaking, rocking back and forwards on his heels. "Yes, the Delta—where I belong—at my own H.Q. Out of this bloody shower. I wouldn't have believed some of the things I've heard today."

Anson said, carefully, "Such as——?"

"That there'll be no fight for it."

"No fight?"

"Just that. They'll surrender. At least, that's my lot —the 2nd Div. I don't know about the English. But I shouldn't imagine there's much difference."

"I don't believe it."

The South African shrugged. "Man, I heard it. They were always a lousy lot. The general's a notorious O.B."

"I'm not interested in your bloody general. I take it you're 1st Div. What are you doing up here, then?"

"R/T specialist—attached. But they don't need me any longer—and I'd be wasted in a prison camp. So I thought it would be a good idea to get back where I'd be more use."

Anson said, "I've got two nursing sisters in the back here. Got to deliver them to Alex. They got left behind. We were just too late to get out to the east—and one of them is bomb-happy already." He looked at Tom. "Is everything really under control in there?"

"Yes, sir. For a bit. The other sister's given her a shot."

The South African said, "What are you going to do now?"

"Try and get through the minefield—I know an old path—and then feel our way round to the coast behind our own lines. We'll have to keep pretty far south."

"I'd like to come with you."

There was no one near the water point, no sound from the back of the car. They were in a little world of their own. From the south came only a dull mutter of guns and there was nothing in the sky. It seemed so peaceful.

Anson broke the silence. "It's the extra weight, the drain on water and rations—I don't know——"

The big man lowered his packs to the step. "There's one point I don't understand. If you get through this minefield, how are you going to get through the German troops outside?"

"How do you know they are there——?"

He shrugged. "It's common talk in the 2nd Div—and why could you not get out from the east this morning? Be your age, man."

Anson's voice was sharp. "We'll bluff it—I don't

know your experience of German troops here—but they usually respect the red cross."

"You speak German—either of you?"

"No." They said it in turn.

"Well—I do. Worked for years in South-West Africa. That might be useful. And—if we dealt with that one— I could push. I know the going down there. You'll need a strong man." He flexed the great shoulders, then patted one of his packs. "And last—just plain bribery— I've got a thousand cigarettes and three bottles of gin in there."

As Tom's head jerked round to Anson, he was in time to see the pitiful reaction, the jerk of his Adam's apple and the flicker of the tongue over the lips. In a second the eyes were glittering in their agony and the sweat was shining through the stubble of his chin. Breaking point had been nearer than he had feared.

'You stupid, clumsy bastard,' he thought. 'You weren't to know—but now you've done for us all.'

Anson said, "All right—you don't mind if I check your papers." He turned to Tom. "While I'm doing that, slip on six cans of each, will you?"

Sick at heart, he trudged off to the stacks, bringing back two tins at a time, humping them on to the cabin floor, then into the back, stacking them against the back doors. He did not speak to the girl until he had to; she was sitting on the bunk opposite the form under the blanket, head tilted back, eyes closed. The desperation of his thoughts scarcely allowed room for pity that surged up in him at the sight of the drained, defeated face. But, at the fifth trip, the gin bottle was out in front and they were holding mugs; after the last cans were stacked, he closed the door and leaned against it, looking down at her.

"Miss—there's a South African captain outside. I

78

think the captain is going to take him with us. He's got some booze—and they have started to drink already. I can't do much. Please help me."

She opened her eyes. "I don't see I can do much, either. But I'll try. And don't call me 'miss' all the time. The name is Murdoch—Diana Murdoch. What's your's besides Pugh. I can't mouth through 'sergeant-major' all the time."

"Tom."

"All right, Tom. I'll come out with you and see what I can do."

She came through behind him and Anson put his mug down quickly. He said, "Sister, this is Captain Zimmerman, of the U.D.F., who is coming with us to push. And this is my sergeant-major, Mr. Pugh."

They both shook hands and then the girl looked down at the bottle and mug on the floor of the cab. "What's this—a party?"

"Sort of 'One for the road'," said Anson.

She looked at him steadily. "I thought the first part of the 'road'—was through a minefield. Is that the usual kind of training?"

There was a faint sound as Zimmerman banged the cork back into the bottle. "The lady's right," he said. Tom watched Anson tilt the mug to drain the last dregs.

The girl said, "Then we go—now?"

"Yes." Anson turned to Zimmerman. "I should warn you. This track, it's old, we don't know if the tapes are still there to mark it—it may have been re-mined——"

"What are the chances?"

"About even money, I should think."

"Fair enough." He looked round at them for a moment. "After that—the chance of being stopped. If I may say so, we won't have a hope, however well I talk, if you wear that——" his hand pointed to Anson's holster—"or those cap badges. They know them all, and they never let any but medical personnel through."

"But we aren't doctors—any of us."

"We all must be—to them."

"It would be—like going through as a spy. They would shoot us if they found out." Anson's voice was a mixture of fear and revulsion.

"They'll put you in the bag if you don't. If it does happen—that we're stopped, the only chance is to let me do all the talking. But I won't be able to do anything if you have those."

Anson took off his cap and looked at it for a moment, then unstrapped the holster. With a quick jerk, he sent them both spinning to the side of the road. "We'll have to, Tom." Then he turned to the girl. "We'll have to rely on you to look after the back. Keep on the bunks—as far forward as you can—in case a back wheel hits something the front one's miss. And don't come out at all until I tell you."

She said, "All right, Captain Anson," and went into the back.

"You drive, Tom." Then Anson gave a last hard look at the South African. "It's understood, of course, that I command this party?"

"Of course."

Tom let in the clutch and they moved off from the water point, making for the winding road that led up the ridge that guarded the inside of the minefield.

He drove fast and the noise of their movement and the fact they were on the lee of the hill seemed to blank out all other sound. The three of them sat in a row, Anson in the passenger seat, Zimmerman on the floor against the door, listening to the snarl of the tyres on the black road, eyes flicking at the scattered transport that was all they were passing now. Tom thought of the silence in a concert hall after the conductor had raised his baton and before the orchestra crashed into sound. It was just like that.

Anson said, "About two hundred yards ahead, Tom. You can see the marker cans on the track going up the hill."

He slowed down and swung the car off the road, taking a line on the row of empty four-gallon cans that were strung out up the hill. It could hardly be called a track, for the going was far different from the soft sand at the other end of the perimeter; slab rock, with the space between covered in loose grey shale and flat stones, the lurking place of countless scorpions. The heavy box of the ambulance car lurched and swayed as they went up the slope, while the stones clattered from under the wheels. When they had reached the crest, a small shallow valley unfolded before them and then another, higher ridge that cut across the sky. Beyond that, Tom knew, was the descent into the minefield.

But there was something there that he had not counted on, the first pattern of any form of defence. Scattered there, hulled-down below the further ridge, were seven or eight tanks . . . Grants, he saw, by the big gun sticking from the side of each like a towel-rail. 'Poor sods,' he thought, 'there's only fifteen degrees traverse on those—and if they fight in retreat, they got to move in reverse, at five m.p.h. maximum to get them to bear at all.' His eyes were still searching as he followed the line of cans, then his spirits rose a little when he saw troops digging and the blunt muzzles of 25-pounders sticking out from the scars in the sand. If Jerry came over the top he'd catch a packet from that lot. He knew what H.E. would do to a tank at point-blank range.

They were all silent, eyes fixed now on the line of

81

petrol cans stretching up the far hill; only the sway and
the stones running from the wheels marked their progress.
Then from the right there was the sound of another
engine, revving, and the blare of a horn, short—long—
short. He looked across, to see a scout car, driven fast,
cutting diagonally towards them; there was a figure
standing in the turret, waving its arms.

"Better stop," said Anson.

The scout car circled them and then came up on the
left; a tall fair lieutenant jumped down and walked over.
He was a gunner.

"Good morning," he said. "And where the bloody
hell do you think you're going to?"

Anson felt in his pocket and produced the message
form. "To Alex," he said.

The lieutenant stared at them all in turn. "You're
crazy." Then he unfolded the paper and read it. "And
the bloke that signed it is crazy too." He stopped and
peered at the signature. " 'Dangle-toes', I might have
known it." There were not many in the fortress who
had not heard of the brigadier.

Anson spoke very patiently, "Crazy—or not, I've got
them. And I'm going to carry them out. And no one
this side of hell is going to stop me."

"That would be about the place——" the subaltern
broke off and then grinned. "The only thing that sur-
prises me is that the brig isn't sitting on the bonnet,
waving that bloody cap of his, and roaring at Jerry to
clear a path through the minefield for him and have a
hot bath ready by six. They'd probably do it, too."

Anson said, "He won't any more. He bought it this
morning. Direct hit on a staff car. We saw it happen."

The lieutenant said, "God! I'm sorry," and there was
a silence. Then he looked at Anson again. "These
sisters—do they know the risk?"

"Yes. They've agreed. And I don't want them disturbed now. We know that path through the minefield, anyway. We've done it before."

The gunner was scratching his chin, he looked at Zimmerman. "What about you, Captain?"

Zimmerman, sitting there, legs straddled out on the floor of the cab, the two packs resting on his knees with his hands folded on top of them, said, "It's all right with me."

Tom had been staring at him through all this. He was wondering what could be in those packs, apart from that bloody gin . . . especially in that big square one that had not been opened yet . . . that looked so heavy . . . and was handled with such care. The first dislike had gone —after all, he could not have known, be expected to know, of the problem of booze. But he didn't want him . . . didn't trust him . . . however good he might prove to be in the pushing in soft sand.

He came back to the present to hear the gunner saying, "Is there anything we can do——? We're dug in all along the top of the ridge."

"Nothing—except not to fire—even if they do."

"Our O.P. says there's nothing on the far slope of the minefield, although there's a lot of dust kicking up over the skyline. There's no air report yet—but their R/T is very active."

"Thanks."

"If I were you I'd bear pretty sharpish south-east, if —when you get through the field. Well, I'll get back to the blower and tell our people you are coming."

He turned on his heel and walked a few steps back towards the scout car. Then he looked over his shoulder and said, "But I still think you're quite crazy." Then he climbed in and the car jerked forward to circle round and return in the direction from which it had come.

When they reached the second crest, they almost ran over an old embrasure that now housed a Bofors with its long barrel sticking out through the camouflage netting. For a moment, Tom saw the shine on steel helmets, the glint of field-glasses played on them, then they were past and running down the steep slope towards the mine-field.

"When you get to the bottom, Tom, turn right along the wire. I think I'll spot the old gap. We'll stop and check it on the bearings I've got on the map."

"O.K., sir." As he eased her down the slope, he looked across the field and then up the ridge on the far side. There was nothing; no movement, no sign of vehicles. No sound above the noise of their own passing. They were alone.

The wadi, though broader, was the pattern of them all; the steep rocky walls, shading grey to brown in contrast to the flat bottom of softer yellow sand. It looked like a river against the sides, the illusion heightened in this case by the ragged, rusting coils of wire that gave the impression of banks. Between, the ground had the look of weathered untidiness, a cross between a neglected garden and a scrap yard; on the pocked sand and among the patches of camel-thorn were rusting and blackened piles of metal, the burnt-out wrecks of lorry and tank that had been caught. Everything was still—and, somehow, the more menacing in its stillness. With nothing to see, there was a feeling of being seen.

They kicked up a cloud of dust as they ran fast down the slope and then skirted along the edge of the wire. One gap . . . two . . . and then Anson said, "That's it, Tom. I'm sure. Stop and I'll take a bearing."

He watched him get down and then move a few yards out of the ambulance's magnetic field before putting the compass to his eye and then taking a bearing right and left on landmarks on the opposite ridge. He came back to the car, sitting with map-board on knee, drawing with protractor and ruler.

"That's it." He walked round to Tom's side. "I'll walk in a bit and see if any old tracks are there—or any sign of re-laying." He looked up at Tom and smiled and said, "I'm sorry about that drink this morning—I could do with it now." Then he turned and started to walk down to the gap in the wire. As Tom swung the car round in a half-circle so that they were facing down towards him, his heart was sick with pride . . . and something more. . . .

Zimmerman did not move, he did not speak. Both sat quite still watching the slight figure dwindle as it walked out into the field.

It was an odd sort of walk, slow, with one foot placed in front of the other like a tight-rope walker, head bent forward as if he were searching for a valuable lost at yesterday's picnic on the sands. When he had gone about twenty yards, he stopped suddenly, took a jump of a few feet, turned left again and came back towards them in the manner he had used going out.

Zimmerman shifted. "What the hell's he doing?"

"Found an old track—walking along it to see if there were any signs of re-laying. Then he jumped to the opposite one—and he's doing the same thing back along that." Tom spoke through gritting teeth.

"Man—he's got some guts!"

"Yes." He wondered how long he would be able to say that.

When Anson reached them, he was almost cheerful. "It's all right to the first sharp turn. The tracks are very faint, but there is no sign of re-laying. But I think we had better walk the whole thing, though."

"But that will take hours, sir."

Anson looked up at the ridge opposite. "No one's objecting to us yet. And, with the girls, it would be better to be sure—than sorry."

Zimmerman stirred. "Look—if one was to walk the other track at the same time, it would halve the time, wouldn't it?"

"Yes. But—I can't ask you to do that. You're heavier than I am."

Zimmerman put his packs down, then swung his legs down at the side of the cab and stood up. He grabbed the biggest pack, slinging it over his shoulder. "A Springbok can go as far as any bloody Englishman," he said. "What do I look for?"

"Take the left-hand track, watch for any place where the ground has fallen in, or the marks of the tyre do not follow on. Go slow, and if you see anything you're not sure of, give a shout, and I'll hop over." He turned to Tom. "And don't you follow up closer than ten yards."

"O.K., sir." Tom looked at Zimmerman. "Wouldn't you like to leave that pack in the cab, Captain? It will make it easier for you and be quite safe."

Zimmerman gave him an odd smile. "No, they're my valuables. I'd rather they went with me than with your ambulance."

The path through the minefield ran zigzag, always with the longer legs down the length of the field. The turns were the worst for him to follow on their path, but in a way it was relief to have them come back close and guide him round foot by foot. In the other time, there was nothing to do except watch the two figures as he crept along behind them, in bottom gear, intent on Anson's slim back, expecting any moment to see it disappear in a cloud of smoke and flame and shattered flesh. The sweat was pouring down his face now; salt, smarting in his eyes so that he could not see. He brushed it away with the back of his hand, but more came to take its place.

They were in the middle—at a turn—when the first intrusion came into their lonely battle. Droning high overhead in the wide bowl of sky came a single plane circling before it went away, then from the far side, the German side, came a faint crackle of automatic weapons and the soft sighing of something passing overhead. But he dare not turn to see. Then, the two in front stopped suddenly and looked back to the way from which they had come, lifting their heads and shading their eyes.

Zimmerman shouted, "Three star shells—two white and a red between."

"Good boys——" Anson's reply was fainter, "—they're trying. It's the best they can do to signal the red cross."

There was no more firing and they went on, creeping, feeling for each step. It was on the last, longest leg, when the sweat was so blinding that he had to stop for a moment, that the door opened behind him and Diana came out of the cab. She came quietly and quickly, and he did not know she was there until she spoke. "I just couldn't stand it any longer in there," she said.

He could not look round. "We're in the middle of the minefield. You get back."

"I know we are. I've been trying to look out through that little side window. I couldn't stand it."

"The captain will be livid. You get back, miss, like he said."

"Not miss—Diana. Isn't there anything I can do?"

"The sweat in my eyes—I can't see. There's a hand-kerchief in my trouser pocket. Can you get it out and wipe my face?"

He felt her hand groping down against his leg and then the relief came of the mopping of his forehead. "Thanks," he said. "I wouldn't like to muck the whole thing up—on account of a little sweat—after he's done so much——"

"I think both—are doing wonders."

There was silence for a moment. "Too good to last," he said.

She was crouching beside him now, wiping gently, steadily. The sweat was still flowing, he could feel the trickle of it between his shoulder-blades, but it didn't matter any more.

"You love that man—don't you?" It was very soft. When he didn't answer, she said, "Sorry—I'm putting you off."

"No. I like you talking. If you don't mind me answering when I'm not at a tricky bit." There was silence again before he said suddenly, "It was at Sidi Rizegh—we were with ambulances then—and at one dawn we got overrun by Jerry tanks. I think it was a mistake—in that light they couldn't see what we were. We got shot to hell. In the confusion, I was left, without my truck."

Another pause while he swung the wheel, staring intent on the slim figure walking in front, then he said, "I was just standing there, the stuff cracking all round, wondering whether to dive in a slit-trench or run, when the captain swans up in his truck—as cool as a bloody cucumber. All he said was, 'Morning, Mr. Pugh. Want a lift?' And he hauls me in—about four hundred yards from the leading Mark IV—and we go lickety-spit after the rest, with bullets clanging into the back of us all the time. Then he said, 'How careless of you not to arrange transport, Sergeant-major,' and a bit later, when we had a bad burst from them, 'Do you think we are showing them the most lady-like view of our arse?'—sorry, Miss Diana—but that's the sort of man he is, really. I wish I had a son like him——"

"And you have no son, Tom?"

Silence. Another turn and the last short leg of the path that reached to a gap in the wire before the steep rock slope of the wadi. The two figures had gone farther in front again, walking their tight-rope, treading that dusty path of death.

"No. And it's too late now. I'm rather glad."

"You're married?"

"Was. Plymouth blitz. She was only there for that one day, visiting her sister——"

"Oh, I'm sorry."

"No need," he said, "I don't mind talking about it now."

There was a dream-like quality about their movement over those last few yards—a feeling that something must happen, that they could not be through. Then they were through the break in the wire, on harder ground, with the walkers waiting for the car to pull up to them. In silence, they all turned to look back at the silent yellow river they had crossed.

Zimmerman leaned against the side of the cab, wiping his arm across his face. "Man—I'm sweating." He looked back across the field. "But I don't believe there's a bloody mine in it, now."

"There were," said Anson, "—plenty."

The girl got up. "I'd better get back. She was showing the first signs of coming to." She went through and closed the door.

When she had gone, Anson gave one look up the silent empty slope that stretched on towards the skyline in front of them. "We had better take it diagonal; south-east, like that gunner said. I don't like it—too damned quiet."

"You drive, sir?"

"No. My legs are too shaky. Carry on for a bit, will you, Tom?"

89

Zimmerman said, "What about a drink, first?"

Tom, cursing silently, inwardly, watched the eyes light up and one hand come forward, then hesitate and fall back to his side as the expression on his face changed. "No. Make it later—we must get on."

They piled into the front of the cab and started moving off up the slope.

The diagonal course was long and fairly steep and there was no chance of seeing what lay beyond until they had reached the crest. They moved steadily, and were about half-way up when the noise came breaking over the sound of the engine and the rumble of the tyres on the rocks. It came from the air, the sound of aero engines that changed to the scream they had heard over the harbour.

"Dive-bombers——" Tom did not know who shouted it first, but the car was stopped and they were running away from it, scattering. Then he remembered the girls, turned on his elbow from where he had fallen flat to see what had happened. There was only Zimmerman, ten yards away, on the far side. The captain must have gone in the back, but it was too late to do anything about it now.

The noise was falling on them and above he could see the glint of the bombers: there were eight. Their dive steepened and in the moment of their release the bombs were plain, like clusters of black eggs. But they were not the target; in an instant he had rolled to his knees, looking down the wadi.

In a pattern, far down beyond where they had crossed, he saw the ochre fountains spew up across the minefield, the smaller blobs that rippled out in strings from their bases as the mines exploded by concussion. So that was the way they were going to get through.

The noise came, thunderous; the bombers climbed and

turned, heading back to the east. Far away, there was a dry crackle of machine-gun fire and then one dark spiralling plummet staining the sky. There were no more sounds, no second wave coming for the moment. He got up, dusted himself and ran back to the car.

Anson was already in the driving seat, shouting, and the engine was running as he and Zimmerman climbed on board. "Come on—for Christ's sake. You know what that means. They're going to attack." Then they were bumping on, accelerating up the hill.

Zimmerman turned to him. "So—it was live, after all?"

"Yes. It was nice of you both to leave me flat when those birds arrived. We could hardly hold that stupid bitch—had to tie her down."

Nearly at the top now, Tom silent and ashamed. Then Zimmerman started to say, "Man, that was a fine bit of navigation across——" when his voice died and they were all staring at the sight of the plain that was opening up to them over the crest.

The sun was high now and the mirage had started, but, whether they showed as thin black rods, far to the south, or sprawled like fat slugs on the nearer fringe, there was no mistaking what they were. Widely dispersed, but with the nearest squat, square turret showing plainly the white cross, they were running at an angle towards a laager of German tanks, ready to go into the attack and at a range of about a thousand yards.

Anson swore horribly, put his foot right down to the floor and the engine snarled as they turned a few more points to the east. The going was better now they were on top, hard gravel and clumps of camel-thorn replacing the rock. They ran diagonally, like a hare before the guns at a corner of a field, jinking and swaying as the captain cut in and out of the patches of green. Tom watched the speedometer needle hovering over the forty mark and even at this time the engineer came to the fore. "For Christ's sake, sir, watch for holes—you'll bitch all the springs. . . ."

Anson did not answer and beside him Zimmerman, crouching, peering past his shoulder, called, "They're coming to cut us off." Behind, in the back of the car, Tom could hear screaming, then he too, beyond the captain, could see the plumes of dust trailing out behind two trucks that had appeared from among the tanks and were heading directly towards them. Something whined over their heads and then came the cracking of giant whips all around him and he knew that the fire was coming straight at them.

"Turn your stern towards them," he shouted.

"No. The girls——" Anson swerved, but did not alter course.

Then another noise came—a deeper, angrier sound. It went 'wacker-wacker-wacker-wack' like a great stick being scraped along a paling. The body of the car jumped and shook and he knew they had been hit, and cried out to stop, but he knew that the captain would not heed him. Then the door behind pushed hard against his back and as he rolled to one side his heart turned over in terror as he saw the red stickiness on her hands. She was crying, "Stop, stop—for pity's sake! It's Denise," and for the first and last time he overrode the captain. He bent forward and cut the ignition switch and the engine choked to nothing, but Anson did not try to start it again. There was no more firing and in the silence as they coasted in a wide circle to face the oncoming trucks, her sobbing voice went on, "She went mad . . . tore off those bandages we had tied round . . . I tried to hold her down . . . but I couldn't. Then the bullets came . . . she's been hit . . . in the stomach. . . ."

They had stopped now and the two trucks were fanning out to close on each side. They were open and he could see the grey mushrooms of the steel helmets and the yellow dust rolling away behind. The girl said, "I had better get back—and see if there's anything——"

Zimmerman was on the ground now, and his voice had a different tone; there was authority when he spoke. "I'll talk to them. Don't say a word—except to me."

Without waiting for an answer, he shouldered the pack and walked round the ambulance, slow and unconcerned, towards the leading truck with his hands held high above his head.

Tom felt in his pocket. "Cigarette, sir?"

"Thanks." Just before they lit up, a puff of hot air brought the scent of crushed camel-thorn towards them. With it—that unforgettable, bitter-sweet smell—came back to Tom all the times, the good and the bad, that they had spent together in the desert. Perhaps the captain was thinking the same, for he said suddenly, "Sorry, Tom. I've made a balls of it—as usual."

"No——"

They lit their fags and drew on them, sitting quite still, side by side, watching the distant group of figures, one towering out of the mass of khaki and grey. Anson said suddenly, "Where's that bloody pack of his?"

"Captain Zimmerman's?—he's got it on his shoulder."

"No. I mean the other one. There's one bottle of gin in it, I know."

"It's on the floor here, sir—but don't——"

"Give it to me."

When Tom had handed it across, he ripped the flap open and pulled the bottle of spirit upright from among the medley of socks, shaving kit and cigarette cartons. Then he put it back on the floor beside him. His eyes drifted back to the group breaking up and coming over to them. Zimmerman, surrounded by the Afrika Korps. "If we are going in the bag," he said, "I'm going to drink the whole of his bloody gin, now. If——" He stopped suddenly and gripped Tom's arm. "Do you see the way they are holding their guns? Quite loose— they've dropped the muzzles. He may have pulled it off . . . it's just possible. . . ."

They were close enough to see the faces now, and they were wary, not hostile.

Anson's voice went on, it was different, held a far-away, dream-like quality. "If he has . . . I'm going to tell you something right now, Tom. It will be a sort of peace offering. Do you know the next drink I'm going to have——? A beer, Tom. A bloody great, tall, ice-cold glass of Rheingold in that little bar off Mahomet Ali Square in Alex . . . and I'll buy you one, all of you one, because I'm bloody well going to get you there. . . ."

He could not bear it. He said, "Shouldn't one of us go in there—to help?"

"You go, Tom."

They were very close now, the Germans. He could hear the crunch of their boots on the gravel as he slipped through the door into the back of the ambulance.

III

IT was only in the middle of the minefield, when she could stand it no longer and she had come out into the cab to talk to Tom Pugh, that Diana had begun to try so desperately to remember those long-forgotten prayers.

Before that, the chain of events had been no more than alternate discomfort and annoyance. The trip to Tobruk had started as an adventure, spoilt only by being put in charge of that stupid little bitch by matron. When Denise had panicked in that raid on the harbour, it had been a sweat to go and find her, there had been the discomfort of being left with only a medical haversack and a handbag; having to sleep in her clothes. After that, the bore of having to stay in the back of the car, trying alternately to cajole or bully Denise into some form of self-respect, before being forced back on the last remedy of morphine. But now, for the first time, there was fear, not for herself, but for the others.

She had thought a lot about her escorts—Zimmerman she classed as a passenger—and though she had liked both from the start, she understood one far better than the other.

Anson was the replica of hundreds she had danced with, dined with, and fought off with good-natured firmness in the backs of staff car or taxi; and the greatest tribute to her honesty in this was that none of the escorts ever bore her the slightest ill-will afterwards. Yes, Anson was the pattern—but with one great difference, they had been in the Delta, relaxed, with trouble behind them, or far in the dim future that did not matter; he, with too much sun, too much sand, too much of everything to bear. She thought of a band of rubber, stretched so tightly that it twanged transparent; now the cement of alcohol was taken away, it was liable to break any moment.

The warrant officer, Tom Pugh——? She could not quite understand herself there. She did not know many —none well—and there was therefore no yard-stick to judge by. Yet she knew he was far above the average of his kind and something of his withdrawn feeling had touched her from the very first. And now, as she came out and saw him there, crouching over the wheel, jaw clenched, sweat pouring down his face, the fixed agonised concentration on the slighter of the two figures ahead, there had been fear—for him, for all of them. And beneath it, something deeper, a stab of jealousy.

While she crouched beside him, mopping his face with that sodden handkerchief, while she had been listening and talking, her mind was groping back desperately into her childhood, trying to find the right words.

She couldn't remember. The ones that she did were no use . . . "Please, God, make me a good girl . . ." but she didn't want anything for herself, only for the man walking ahead, and the one who steered behind in the cleared tracks. What else used she to say? "Please keep Mummy and Daddy safe and well. . . ." But she had not heard—did not care if she did—of her mother for three years, and Daddy, dear inconsequential Daddy, was dead.

She smiled in the middle of wiping, as she thought of him; the little professor of the Midland university; his agnosticism—how he would laugh at her now—and his lapse.

Even as she listened to Tom Pugh, half her mind was remembering the day he left; suddenly, without a scene, with a lady snake-charmer he had met first through the gift of a complimentary ticket to a visiting circus. Happy ever after . . .? She remembered her mother's pursed lips and the sneering, "He'll be back," but he hadn't. She had visited the den of sin unknown to her mother, to find it clean and comfortable, the old man looked after and laughing for the first time in years; later, saw the girl's performance with the python, that she thought vaguely disgusting. But there were only four years between them, daughter and mistress, and a deep bond

96

grew up, through common affection for the professor. The more she saw of them, the farther she drifted from her mother; at last a job away from her home—nursing —had been the only answer. And when the war came, and she had heard, in the North, of the bomb that had brought down the theatrical digs in a welter of brick and plaster to bury the snake-charmer and Daddy and the python for ever, she had dried her eyes and applied for overseas.

Now she was in the middle of a minefield, wiping the face of a strange warrant officer who would call her 'miss', with a fierce, unreasoning jealousy in her heart, searching for the things that Daddy had not believed and Mummy had had no time to teach . . . not for herself, but for them . . . not to save them from pain, but fear of their own fear. . . .

It was easier when they were through the field and she had gone into the back again, to sit and watch Denise begin to come round, muttering and plucking at the blankets. It was when the bombs had come that she had started to struggle and scream and she did not think she would have been able to hold her if Anson had not been there. When they started off after, she had been quieter, still under the blanket and the bandages with which they lashed her down. It was only when the ambulance had began to go very fast, bumping and swaying, that she started to go mad.

She broke free, screaming again, clawing at the walls as she tried to reach up them; Diana had her by the knees, gripping tight to bear her down, to get on the floor as she had been told, when it happened.

The noise had started—that awful 'whacking' noise— and Denise had jerked and gone limp against her as the red dripping stain had spread on the shirt above the waistband. The inside of the car was a dancing pattern of sunshine from the row of jagged holes that ran up and across the side above the bunk.

After she had put her down and run to the door and begged for the end of movement so that the slaughter might stop, it had become the numb concentration of routine. She had torn up the dressings from the medical box, making pads from shell dressings, bandaging round from the purple bruised hole above the navel to the worse torn mess of the back. There was so little there to satisfy those terrible demands and soon, as she worked, she knew it was to be no use. But it was her job, and she went on working on it methodically, not conscious of anything outside except that they had stopped. There was no thought of capture until Tom Pugh came through the door and closed it behind him.

Denise was lying flat now, covered by the blanket, eyes open, staring at the roof. She did not make a sound. Tom did not speak either, but stood looking down at her. Recognition came back in her eyes and she said suddenly, quite normally, "I want a drink."

His hand was on the screw top of one of the white water cans before Diana caught his sleeve. She turned so that her body shielded both of them from the bunk, then shook her head and pointed to her stomach.

"I'm thirsty." The voice came clear from behind her and she turned to look down. Denise was crying, soundlessly, the tears just running down her cheeks.

Tom did not look again. He just stared at Diana and said, "We are in the bag. They're just coming over to us. That Zimmerman—he's been over to talk to them. The captain thinks he may have worked something— but I doubt it. So I came in to say—'sorry'—from us all. And see if there was anything I could do. . . ."

They were standing close and perhaps the thing that made her feel better than anything was the way he had said 'that Zimmerman'. She agreed. She said, "Don't say 'sorry'. You've all done so much—it makes me feel ashamed." Then she let her eyes slide down to the bunk. "But there's so little we can do for her," she was almost whispering, "she must not drink—just moisten her lips."

He held the water can and tipped it over the wad of bandages she got ready; she knelt on the floor beside the bunk and started wiping her mouth. She said, "Does it hurt, darling?" and the voice came back, faint but petulant, "Who kicked me?"

They were still in the same position when the door opened quickly and a Hauptmann of the Afrika Korps came in with Zimmerman close behind.

She did not move, stayed kneeling, holding Denise's hand, feeling for the feather of the pulse, keeping her eyes fixed on the badge of palm broken by swastika that was in the front of that grey long-peaked cap. He did not look in the least like the blustering bully that was always depicted to her as a Hun. He was oldish, dark, very pale, the cheeks had a sucked-in look and there were dark rings beneath his eyes. She wondered how long it had been since he had had a good night's sleep.

He gave her a little bow and clicked his heels and there was nothing she could do in that position but give a silly bob in answer. He ignored Tom and turned back to Zimmerman. A stream of German passed between them. She thought, 'Perhaps it may have done the trick —I don't understand a word, but he certainly speaks it well.'

Zimmerman's voice was quite impersonal.

"The captain says that he bitterly regrets this accident, Sister. The Afrika Korps do not shoot women. If the red crosses had been more easily distinguishable, if we had asked for a safe conduct, it would never have happened."

There was nothing to do except nod again. More meaningless, guttural words, then, "He wishes to know if she is badly hurt—and if they can do anything."

What was the use of telling him she would be dead in an hour or two—that nothing could be done? There were others, the ones that had the chance to go on living, to be considered. It might depend on what she said—whether they were allowed to go on.

"Tell him she has an abdominal wound—it's not too serious, but she should be taken to hospital as soon as possible."

The Hauptmann nodded, then leant against the end of the bunk as a few more sentences passed between him and Zimmerman. She had found Denise's hand again, and suddenly, as they were talking, the cold fingers gripped hers, unbelievably strong; she looked down at the face and the eyes were open, filled with entreaty.

"What is it, Denise?" She soaked the pad in water again and started to moisten the mouth.

The Hauptmann had walked past her now, still ignoring Tom, to start a perfunctory search. He opened the medical lockers and lifted one or two of the cans stacked at the back. After kneeling to peer under the other bunk, he gave her another of those funny stiff bows and walked out of the door into the front of the cab.

Those open eyes, so sunken and ringed with purple now, lifted up over her head; she turned to see Tom bending forward, staring.

"What is it, miss?" The soft Devon burr sounded so persuasive. Now the lips were opening and shutting slowly. She was trying to talk.

Diana went on sponging, seeing in pity how that full mouth she had always admired was shrinking, cracking, some flecks of lipstick still hanging loose like flaking paint. She bent close and said, "I know you're thirsty—

but you mustn't have a drink yet." The lips moved again, but even with her head right down there was only a faint rattling at the back of the throat. Fighting the instinct of years of training, she picked up the mug and let a trickle of water fall down into the open mouth. And then she knew she could not stand another moment of it without a break.

"Tom—I must have some more dressings. I'll go out and see if I can scrounge any."

"I'll stay here, then. Is there anything to do?"

She shook her head gently. "No. Not now. Just be near."

When she had got up he slipped into her place. At the door, she turned to see him kneeling as she had done, chequered in sun and shadow from the gashes in the wall of the car, one big hand engulfing the little one, the other reaching up while the blunt fingers stroked up and down the forearm.

Her eyes were blinded by sudden hot tears as she went out into the still sunshine of the cab.

DENISE

"Please, please, don't let it happen.

"I know that something has happened already . . . after I got frightened . . . and then I went to sleep . . . and then the noise started all over again. I thought I was back in the nursery and started to try and get out of bed. Then someone hit me . . . in the stomach. And now I'm so thirsty . . . but they won't give me a drink.

"I'm not surprised that snooty bitch Murdoch won't—she would stop anything that I wanted, but that man, the big one with the grey hair and the blue eyes, he would. I'll ask him in a minute . . . and tell him about that other thing. . . . He'll understand.

101

"*There's a great cold weight lying on my middle and I can't feel anything below that . . . but when he comes closer, I'll tell him and he'll take it off and get me that drink. After that, I'll tell him what I heard.*

"*There's so much to be sorry about now . . . but it's always too late to be sorry. I couldn't help having the body I was given . . . and men liking it . . . and I liking men. I knew what everyone thought . . . particularly the women . . . but I couldn't help it. And then, after the last time, when matron said she was sending me home . . . though I hated it . . . I knew she was right to send me up here.*

"*But why with Murdoch? She never tried to understand . . . always looked down her nose. And when the noise started, she was bloody . . . swore at me . . . smacked my face. But she's gone now and there's only this man, closer, holding my hand. So it's the chance to tell him.*

"*Can you hear me . . . nice man with your grey hair and your crinkly eyes? . . . You must, because I'm shouting at you. Those other two that came in . . . did you hear what they said? . . . but perhaps you don't understand German. I do, nice man . . . and it was bad for you . . . bad for all of us. Something about Cairo. That big one . . . with the orange on his shoulders . . . he's no good.*

"*So watch out . . . watch out for us all. That big one . . . he's not what he pretends to be. He's a NAZI.*

"*Did you hear? I think you did, for you're coming closer. There's a strange look in your eyes . . . all the understanding I always wanted . . . and never had. Go on stroking my arm . . . I'm so tired . . . and so thirsty. . . .*"

After she had come out to the cab and brushed her sleeve across her eyes, Diana jumped down on the sand beside Anson and Zimmerman, who were leaning against the side of the car, smoking.

The Hauptmann had disappeared, but they were

surrounded by a ring of the Afrika Korps, khaki and grey, with their automatic weapons crooked loosely under their arms. She saw the ripple of interest pass round the circle and wondered how long it was since they had seen a woman; it would be something to talk about in the canteen, something to write home about, if they were allowed to. There was no enmity in their look, only a curiosity; she returned it in the same spirit, wondering that they looked so young, so tired, and why hadn't someone done something about those dreadful desert sores. Then, deliberately, she had turned her back and taken a cigarette from the packet held out by Zimmerman.

Anson said, "I think Zimmerman has fixed it." He spoke very softly. "The Hauptmann has gone back to his truck to radio for permission for a safe conduct."

"What did you say, Captain Zimmerman?"

"The truth, dear lady, except that I implied the captain and the sergeant-major were—medical officers."

She did not speak again but stared past his head at the slanting line of holes that ran across the canvas and the red and white paint. Which one of them was Denise's? ... Probably the third along. ... They didn't look so spectacular from the outside.

She came back with a jerk. "Captain Zimmerman, I must have some more dressings. Do you think you can do anything?"

"I'll try, Sister."

He moved past her and walked over to the nearest Feldwebel. Anson looked round at her and said, "How is she?" hopefully, but she shook her head.

Zimmerman and the Feldwebel had gone over to the remaining truck and presently came back with a square grey package. "That's all they can manage," he said.

The other truck was bumping back towards them from the direction of the tank laager, and because she could not bear to hear the verdict out there, she took the package and said, "I'd better get in," and climbed back to the inside of the car.

Tom was in the same position as when she had left him, kneeling, holding the hand, but he was no longer stroking the arm. There was trouble in his eyes as he said, "She tried to get up—and she said something. But she hasn't moved since."

The sun was still low enough to throw a speckled pattern from the ragged holes across the floor. There was plenty of light to make the quick examination, even down to the formality of holding the mirror from her handbag before the lips. There was nothing.

"She's dead, Tom."

Quickly she got a hypodermic from the haversack and laid it on the blanket, then folded the loose arm underneath and closed the eyes. She turned and gripped Tom fiercely by the shoulder. "But to anyone else—until we know what's going to happen—she's asleep. I've given her an injection."

"If you want it that way."

There were voices outside and then she said suddenly, "What did she say?"

"I couldn't really hear—it was only one word. It sounded like 'nasty'."

"Poor kid," she said. "But I don't think there was any pain."

There was a soft tap on the door this time and then the Hauptmann came in again, followed by Zimmerman. The South African said, "The captain has orders to escort us to a point south of German operations. They are taking Captain Anson with them in the truck to ensure we follow. You are to drive the ambulance,

Sergeant-major. They would like to move as soon as the sister is ready."

She said, "Now, if you like," and the Hauptmann looked down at the bunk, his eyes expressionless, before he turned to Zimmerman and spoke softly.

"He wants to know how she is."

"Asleep. I gave her an injection."

Her voice seemed to come quite naturally and the German nodded and went out of the car. As Tom passed her she managed to press his arm and whisper, "Not yet."

When they had started she did the few things that had to be done and then sat on the opposite bunk, holding Denise's handbag, watching the pattern of light from the bullet holes dancing on the floor as the car swayed. She had bent over and pulled the blanket up over the face opposite before she remembered that the German might come in again. So she folded it back as before and then went out to sit in the cab with the others.

They were almost at the far cliff that they had seen for a moment when they had first come over the escarpment. There were no tanks near them now, nor any transport that she could see except the one grey truck ahead of them, a cloud of dust trailing away sideways from behind it. She could just make out Anson's head, sandwiched between two grey caps in the back. In their own cab, Zimmerman was lounging in the passenger seat, the pack balanced on his knees; Tom, upright, hands loose but sure on the wheel, driving.

She shut the door and sat down with her back against it, feet stretched out straight in front of her across the floor. She shook her head, without speaking, at the cigarette offered by Zimmerman, then turned to watch Tom.

Though she did not drive, she knew in a moment that

she was being driven by an expert. It was difficult to know how she knew, except that there were not any bumps. Everything was anticipated: a turn of the wheel, and the hole they would have jolted over passed harmlessly just to the side of their track; if there was a gully, he sensed it yards ahead. There would be a check on the brakes, a loosening of them at the critical moment to let her roll over easy, then the quiet pick-up in a lower gear. There was never a fault. 'And he's had six hours at it already,' she thought.

Now the truck ahead had reached the foot of the cliff and was nosing along it to the east. Presently it turned sharp right between the boulders and up the thin crack of a wadi.

They followed in and at once the going was rougher. She said, "Take it slow, Tom—just as you would if——" She stopped, remembering that Zimmerman did not know.

She turned to where he sat, still, staring straight ahead, with that heavy pack on his knees. She wondered what was in it.

She said, "Sister Norton is dead. I didn't say anything, because I thought—well—it might prejudice——"

He didn't answer, but nodded, not looking at her, pulling at his bottom lip. The car crept on up the wadi behind the truck, the noise of the two engines echoing back from the steep rocky walls. Ahead now was the straight line of blue sky where they would gain the next level of plain. The Germans would be leaving soon and there was something else to say before they did—and Anson came back to them. And because she knew there was no time, she said it badly.

"Captain Zimmerman, I want to ask you a favour. Captain Anson had had a pretty bad time, before you met us. He—was drinking, quite a lot. He's probably screaming for one now. But we all depend on him, absolutely, for navigation. So please keep that gin of yours out of sight."

He was silent for a moment. "What do I do—if he asks me for one?" he said at last.

She searched the clipped English for sarcasm—and decided there was none, but before she could answer, Tom's voice cut in fiercely from the other side, "He won't—he'd rather die than do that. But help him—don't let him see it, or offer him one."

"I'll do my best," said Zimmerman.

They were at the head of the wadi now, coming out on to another flat brown plain, with the same kind of low cliff far to the south of them. A hundred yards in front, the grey truck had stopped and the Hauptmann and Anson were standing beside it, waiting.

They pulled alongside and then Zimmerman jumped down and went over. Tom and Diana sat watching the group while Zimmerman and the Hauptmann talked.

Tom broke their silence suddenly. "After we left the water point—where we picked him up—did we pass anything on the road?"

"I don't know, Tom—I was in the back."

"Of course you were—I must ask the captain."

"Why——?"

He did not answer and she saw the three men were walking back towards them.

Zimmerman looked at the Hauptmann, standing a little apart, then said, "We are now well south of their operational axis—at least for the first part of their attack. The captain is leaving us here, but advises us to go farther south, in case of a chance meeting with one of their patrols. He is sorry he cannot help us with petrol or water, but they are short themselves."

He stopped for a moment and stared straight at Diana, "—and he asks how the sister is."

"Still asleep," she said.

Zimmerman turned to the Hauptmann and there was one last exchange of words, there was a quick jerk of his head and then Anson and the South African came over to the ambulance and climbed on board.

The German stood close to them, stiff, with the background of his truck and the faces of the troops in it, all heads turned, staring curiously. He looked all round— at the dull brown and olive of the shimmering plain, the full blue bowl of the sky, the emptiness of both; when he looked back at them there was a flicker of expression on his face, and somehow Diana knew exactly what he was thinking. That it was one of the times when it didn't much matter whether you had the red desert rat or the broken palm painted on the front of your truck, because ahead of you were hundreds of miles of loneliness and soft sand and rock, the doubt of thirst, the danger of error in navigation, or the chance of a stray mine.

He drew himself up and gave a funny little military salute. As they passed by and he slid back out of their vision, he shouted something.

The ambulance gathered speed and there was only the open desert in front of them now, and silence among them for a few minutes. Then Anson said, "What did he say, Zimmerman?" and the South African, looking straight ahead, answered, "Good luck," and after that no one spoke for a long time.

It was very crowded with four in the front and she thought that it might be a good idea for someone to go in the back and have a rest. There was no question of who it should be, for at close quarters Anson looked pitiable. The face was shiny and white and the sweat showed in little beads through the stubble of his chin.

She had never seen anything so exhausted as those red, ringed eyes.

She said, "Don't you think it would be a good idea to take turns to lie down for a spell? Why don't you start, Captain Anson?"

She saw the gratitude in his eyes, and then he said, "But I'll disturb her," and she remembered that he was the only one that did not know and had to tell him that Denise was dead.

He looked older, even more tired, when she had done and for a moment she was sorry she had ever thought of the idea. But Tom's voice came the other side, "Yes— you go on, sir." There was distaste in his face even then, so she said, "I'll go first—and get things ready." As she went through the door, she heard him say, "All right. Another twenty miles on this bearing—and then stop for a brew-up."

There was only time to pull the blanket over the still white face and unstack those on the other bunk before he stumbled in after her. He almost fell across it and she had knelt and taken off his desert boots and swung his legs up before she realised that he was already asleep. She pulled a blanket over him and stood for a moment looking down, smoothing the dark hair away from the temples, thinking of all the lost and lonely little boys she had ever seen, while all the earlier jealousy drained away. Then, softly, she closed the door on the living and the dead and went out to the cab.

There was more room now. They sat in the same order, silent save for an occasional call from Zimmerman, who held the compass. She moistened her mouth from the water can and passed the mug in turn to the others. The tiredness was coming back, heavier, more urgent. There was no sound but the hum of the engine and the steady hiss of the tyres against the gravel, soothing.

The ambulance went on, a minute dot in the immensity of the desert. That far low cliff seemed to hang at the same distance on the horizon. As the sun climbed higher, the mirage grew and closed in on them. Sometimes they were running into a great shining lake that always moved on; then chains of mountains or fairy castles would sweep in majestic procession across the sky; once the gaunt timbers of a shipwreck that melted when they drew near to the bleached ribs of a long-dead camel.

Nothing was real—or lived. It was getting hot now and soon she was tired of watching it and turned to look at Tom. The greying hair, the firm jaw, the eyes shadowed by sun-glasses. She noticed the long white scar on the tan of his cheek and wondered how he had got it. . . .

KATY

My official name is A1079654, ambulance, Austin, K2. I have a six-cylinder, overhead valve 29.8 H.P. engine, four gears, and I weigh about two and a half tons. But I have always been called KATY.

Not KATY II, or KATY III . . . just KATY, which shows the measure of care I have had from my one and only driver. He drew me from the depot at Slough, brand new, and drove me and maintained me until yesterday; he painted the name on my bonnet in England, just before we set out on that awful cross-country journey to Swansea in the winter of 1940; then I lost him when we were loaded in the dark. I was deck cargo on a superannuated tramp that took me round the Cape, smothered in salt spray in the Atlantic, grilled across the Equator. But my driver was there for me at Suez and he took me back to the camp and cursed and sweated until he had got the brine and the rust off and had me back in good nick.

And then it was up into the blue. Up and down, up and down that strip from Matruh to Benghazi; boulders and soft sand, shale, gravel and solid rock—my wheels have hardly touched a road. And with it, the strain of the banging and the twisting and the bumping, however careful he was.

They say that machinery can't speak. But it can, through little subtle sounds that are different, or the flicker and fall of a needle on a dial. The ones that know these things—that think of us in terms of straining muscle and pumping artery—they understand. The one that's driving me now—he knows. I can tell by the way he lets me ride a bump. Brakes off at the last moment to let me roll; just half the strain on the springs.

Springs . . . that's one of the things I'd tell him if I could. I was never designed for this kind of war; on the drawing board, they were thinking in terms of the continent . . . roads. But for me it has been sand and rock all the way, and I've taken my fair share of punishment, and got through eight sets of springs to date. The trouble is that the replacements—they're not so good now, not from England, but tempered by Wogs in the Delta. And something has started to happen to mine, the rear ones, right at this very moment. In the main leaves, the important part that is the only connection of axle to body—and takes all the weight. Cracks are starting, hardly cracks yet, for only a microscope could find where the crystals are forming in the texture of the metal. But it will get worse, with each jolt, however hard he tries, until they break. And then two tons comes straight down on the back axle.

There's another thing, but I think he'll see that in time. Just as my springs were not made for the desert, so my engine was not designed to run all the time in a temperature of 110°. I run too hot, but there's a water pump that circulates the stuff that keeps me cool, and it's as vital to me as a man's heart. In that pump there's a washer, made of carbon, to stop the water escaping past the spindle. It is starting to crumble . . . soon the water will leak past . . . the water that is essential to stop me seizing . . . and more precious here than petrol itself. But I think he'll spot

*the drips when they start. It's only an hour's work to strip the
pump and put in a new washer . . . if he's got one. . . .*

*There's nothing to be done about the springs, nothing to see,
until they go. So take me easy, driver, and I'll do my best. Only,
I hope you spot the first ooze of water from behind the fan. . . .*

IV

ZIMMERMAN sat in the passenger seat, clasping his
heavy pack on his knees, staring out over the shimmering
desert, thinking. There was so much to think about, and
as he was a methodical man, he divided the agenda into
separate compartments of his mind. He would think of
them one by one. There was plenty of time.

The past . . . but only as much of it as was safe to
remember.

The directive had been explicit. The MUST of
delivery to the Delta and the joining up with P9. Then
the secondary—'if possible'—task of making trouble in
Tobruk before he started on his way.

He had always known that the most dangerous part
would be the getting there. Not in Tobruk, not inside
the Delta, but the passing out of one security net, the
blank between, and the getting through the other. It
was curious that he had felt and would feel safest when
he was surrounded by them; it was the emptiness between
—the lone South African making for the Delta, the
chance, casual meetings, the check posts on the way—
that worried him most.

Afraid? . . . No, he had not been afraid before he
jumped. But he had tried not to think about it too much,
it would be better to trust to opportunity. Any thought-

out plan always involved some consideration of failure, and he knew what had happened to the ones that had tried before . . . he was not going to follow Brünner and that other fellow—what was his name?—Schmidt, to their stone walls at dawn. He would not think about it, be very, very careful, and something would turn up. And it had—beyond his wildest dreams, just at the right time.

He gave a little secret smile as he thought of that swinging drop into blacked-out burning Tobruk the night before, hanging to the ropes of his harness as the flak and tracer came up to meet him in orange streams, the burying of the parachute and the shouldering of his packs. With his clipped English, the genuine South African uniform and identity card, it had been simple to get shelter for the night on the excuse of a ditched truck. He had moved on at first light, looking for a means to escape east and implementing the minor part of his mission.

But there was no need for the second, no point in wasting precious time in fomenting something that had burst into flower already. There was enough alarm and despondency in Tobruk without his bothering to work on it.

So he had gone from camp to camp, unchallenged, searching for the truck that was to carry him east, the sooner the better for him while that flood of transport was still streaming out along the Bardia road. In each place he had managed to slide in some little thing, a nasty remark about British to South African, or vice-versa; some may have stuck, done a bit more of the good work, but he had not borrowed a truck. He had waited by the water point as a likely place and within a few minutes all his difficulties were solved in one stroke by the arrival of this ambulance.

It was almost too good to be true. A party, with written orders to go straight to the Delta. The danger of their method had been no worry compared with the relief that all gates would be open to him now. Alone, his story and his papers might—probably would have—got by; as a passenger, with the others, genuine, to vouch for him, it was certain. He would be the passenger, sit tight, help where necessary to convince them. That was the most important, then they could do all the talking.

All of it? . . . He smiled again as he thought of the irony of that meeting with the Panzer Group: remembered with gratitude the quickness of the Hauptmann in spotting the sign and transmitting his code number to headquarters. It had worked, these English had swallowed it, but he would not care to have to do it again.

Zimmerman . . . his mind lingered over his new name, then jumped back over the time he must not remember to what had happened before. All those years in the Union and South West-Africa . . . so busy, so long . . . the fluency of his English and Afrikaans making him almost forget his native tongue. The homesickness and then his return to the Fatherland just before the war.

That was the time he must not think about, the war; not until the day the real Zimmerman, dying, was brought in to their lines after a skirmish near Bir Hakeim. There had been no likeness between them except in size, but someone must have said something, and then Intelligence were on it. His papers were vetted and he had had to admit his knowledge of the Union, his English and his Afrikaans.

And now he was Zimmerman . . . in dead Zimmerman's clothes. They had asked him to volunteer—he smiled again—for one was not usually asked to volunteer in the Wehrmacht, and of course he had said, "Yes." Not for love of the Fuehrer—he despised him, though he

114

was always careful to say the right things at the right time—but the simple calculation of the war being nearly over and won. When it was, there would be the reward, the pickings for such as him back in Africa.

And all he had to do was to complete the job and stay out of trouble. It was dangerous, but he was better equipped than most. The part he liked least was the heavy pack that lay across his knees.

Just keep out of trouble . . . that brought him to the present . . . and his companions. He glanced sideways for a moment at the girl and the sergeant-major, then stared out over the desert again, trying to weigh it all up.

So far, so good. The captain had hardly glanced at his identity card, had accepted him, it seemed. But had the others? It was too early to judge yet, but they might be more difficult. It was lucky they were all British, though. When in difficulty, he could always fall back on talk of the Union. He doubted if their combined experience would add up to more than a few days at Durban or Cape Town.

He looked across again. That girl . . . he thought he understood her. She should have been a German, that type; strong, capable, attractive. *Ein kamarad*. . . . No, he must not do that—even think in anything but English. 'A pal'—that was the right phrase. He went on thinking about her, grudgingly, liking her. He must make her like him.

The one that was driving. He could not see the face, only the arms resting on the wheel, the brass coat-of-arms on the leather strap on one wrist. The Unteroffizier —no, sergeant-major. There was a different one, he could not fathom him, he was so totally different from his German counterpart. He and the captain were friends, in an easy natural way that would be impossible in the Afrika Korps. . . . Yet, all the time, he was—

correct. Be careful there, Zimmerman, that one says little but sees a lot.

Last, the captain. He made a contemptuous noise in the back of his throat. Those lectures they had had were right. There, in the back now, was the living example of the decadence, the morale propped up with gin. He hadn't believed it, but it was true. He would admit he had courage of a kind—he had shown it in that mine-field—but that was different. The moral fibre had gone, and now the captain was deprived of his drink, he would crack altogether. But not before he had finished his use-fulness. He was the only one to navigate—then let him take them back to the coast the other side of the frontier. Then let him sign the movement order that would send him and the girl back to the Delta. After that, he would not think of them . . . or care. But he had the means with this captain, it had been stupid of the others to mention the gin . . . a carrot to any donkey was better than a stick . . . he would feed it to him, in secret, in small doses, as long as there was the need. He knew that type. They couldn't hold out against it.

Yes, that was the way to play it. Feed the captain, make up to the girl, watch the sergeant-major. It would be simple. There was nothing else to worry about for at least two days.

Or was there? A little frown crossed his face . . . were they quite so simple, so easy to bluff. He remembered the one disturbing thing . . . when he had come back with the Hauptmann to the ambulance and found his other pack opened and disturbed. Had they been searching? His hand tightened on the big square pack on his knees. At all costs, they must not get at that, it must never leave him. It would not be a question of not getting to the Delta then, but being up against the same wall as Brünner and Schmidt. Be careful, all the

time, don't underestimate them. Especially at night . . .
when he had to carry out those special orders. . . .

He eased the pack on his knees and stared out over
the heaving plain, brooding.

V

TOM said, "What's the reading on the bottom row of
figures on the speedometer, Miss Diana?"

She leaned forward and read them back, "Five . . .
seven . . . eight, on the yellow one—no, that's just coming
up to nine."

"Good enough." She watched his hand come forward
to cut the ignition and then the car crunched on across
the desert until it came to a halt. There was no particular
point in the place he had chosen to stop, just a patch of
pinky-brown gravel, bounded on three sides by low
coarse sage-green scrub.

"That's the captain's twenty miles," he said, "now we
brew-up." He turned in the driving seat and started
rummaging behind it. "And if I know anything about
Driver Grimes, there'll be enough tea somewhere here to
start a café. Ah——" He tugged and strained and then
his hands came away with a square biscuit tin. He pulled
off the top and looked inside. "Half full," he said.

When he had jumped down, he looked over at Zimmerman. "You'll find the tins under your seat, I think, sir."

She looked at Tom and said, "What can I do?"

"I don't want to go blundering into the back, waking
the captain yet. Do you think you could slide out
another tin of water—and a jerrican? Mind that one,
it's rather heavy."

117

She turned with her hand on the door. "I'm pretty strong," she said.

Anson was still asleep, so dead to the world that she stopped by him for a moment to listen to his breathing. When she came out with the cans, Zimmerman was just walking round the front of the car with two cut-down petrol tins, both blackened on the outside. Tom was ripping the wood from one of the cases he had lifted out from under the dash.

"Thank you," he said. "Could you put the sand in, sir?"

"Sand——?" Zimmerman stood quite still, a tin in each hand, staring at him.

"Yes." Tom had a puzzled look on his face. "Sorry— I thought all the Union troops brewed-up in the same way as we do. Don't worry, I'll do it."

He took the tins, smelt them, and then turned one over on its side to scrape sand in from the ground. When he had got enough to cover the bottom for about three inches, he righted it and walked out to stand it well away from the ambulance. "Always down-wind," he said. Picking up the jerrican and a splintered stick from the packing case, he poured petrol on the sand, stirring it until there was a consistency of porridge. Then he moved the remaining petrol away, struck a match and threw it at the tin.

It ignited, almost exploded, with a soft 'wooshh'; the first flare had died down as he filled the other tin with water and placed it on top, leaving a little gap at one side. He handed the stick to Diana. "Now you watch it. If the flame gets low, just stir the sand, and more petrol will come up to the top."

Zimmerman was standing, watching them. "Anything else I can do, Sergeant-major?"

"Open up the biscuits, sir. And find the sugar. It

should be in another biscuit tin, behind the driver's seat."

She sat by the fire, absorbed in her job, poking the sand as the flames died, watching them flicker and rise again. Once she turned, to see Tom at the front of the ambulance with the bonnet open and the tool kit strewn out beside him. The fire had just been tended, so she got up and went over.

It all looked so terribly complicated, those copper tubes and the wires and the thing that looked like a tea-pot with warts on that she believed, vaguely, was the carburettor. The thing that surprised her most was that it was all so clean.

She leaned over, watching him. "I wish I understood it all."

Her eyes stayed fixed and intent, but he smiled. "Not so difficult, or different from your job. They're like humans, really. If you give them the right food and drink—a dose occasionally—and don't overwork them, they obey all the rules." He was moving the fan blades to and fro, feeling with the other hand behind it. "The only trouble—and difference—is they can't talk. So that by the time you know they have a pain, it's usually too late."

She ran her hand down the hot, smooth olive of the bonnet to where the name was painted, so beautifully, in white.

"Has KATY got a pain?"

"I don't think so—yet. But she's got what your docs would call a 'constitutional weakness'—and I've got to watch it."

He was whistling through his teeth now, as he man-œuvred his hand under the fan while he moved the blades left and right. Then the hand underneath, cupped, came out and there was a small drop of red water in the palm.

119

The whistle died suddenly as he stared at it. "You had better go and watch that fire," he said.

When the tea was made, it was hot and very sweet and the best drink she had ever had. There were only three mugs that they could find, and Tom said, "One for you —I'll share with Captain Zimmerman—and one to go in to the captain."

She could see from his eyes that he didn't want to go in there, so she said, "Can't we leave him in peace?" But he shook his head: "No, he must eat." So she took the mug, and a cigarette that she lit and put in between her lips, and climbed into the back of the car.

Anson was deep, deep down in exhaustion still, so that she had to shake him. When he had opened his eyes and remembered her, she put an arm behind him just like a patient and helped him sit up and gave him the tea. When he had swallowed, she took the cigarette from her mouth and passed that over as well.

"Tom's done your twenty miles," she said, "he's getting some grub now."

He had another drink from the mug and then drew hard on the fag, letting the smoke trail out through his nose. "I feel better," he said, and she thought that he looked it. He moved a little sideways and patted the empty space on the edge of the bunk. "Sit down for a minute, Sister."

She said, "Please call me Diana—the others do."

"—All right, Diana. I wanted a word with you, before I talk to the others——" He looked across to the other bunk and his eyes clouded; she thought how she had forgotten for the moment what was there—and felt ashamed.

He said, "First—I don't want you to think we are— unfeeling—in not doing anything about that, yet, but it will be hard work, and we're all very tired. I would

120

rather get on as far as we can today. So, last thing tonight, or first thing tomorrow morning—will that be all right with you?"

"Of course."

"Then, when that's done—I want you to have the back of the car, for your own, for the rest of the trip."

She said, "I wouldn't dream of it. I want us all to share. I'll come in with any of you—all of you—except Zimmerman."

He blew out another long trail of smoke. "You don't like him?"

"No. Do you?"

He ignored the question; he said, "He's useful. He got us right out of the last mess—and, I realise now, we wouldn't have had a hope on our own. And he's strong. We may need that."

Both were silent for a moment. "Anyway, Diana, I'll work out some sort of rota—two sleeping, two awake—and fix it so that you're never paired off with him."

"That's nice of you. Now come and have your grub. You must be starving." But he held her arm. "There's one more thing—and I must say it. I've had a pretty bloody time lately, and I'm afraid——"

She put a hand to his mouth. "You don't have to say anything."

There was gratitude in his eyes. "I won't, then. But I have told Tom, so I must tell you. The next drink I have—is going to be in a certain bar in Alex. I don't suppose you know it—just a little place off Mahomet Ali Square. There's a marble-topped counter, and high stools, and they serve the best and coldest Yankee beer in the Delta. And when we've got this lot sorted out, I'm going to take you and Tom there, and buy you one. And it will be my first. So don't tempt me before that."

She said, "I won't—and I'll dream about that bar."

They went out and ate their bully and biscuit. The bully wasn't like any she had had before, it came out of the tins almost liquid, greasy, like a half-set jelly. It was nauseating to have to push it on to the biscuit and swallow it like that, but no one made any comment, so she kept quiet, assuming that it was always that way.

When they had cleared up and were ready to move off, Anson said, "Your turn for a kip in the back, Tom." But his eyes had moved away and he said, "I'm all right, sir." There was a long silence before Zimmerman said, "—If no one else wants to, I will," and he went through the door into the back, taking his two packs with him.

Anson took over the driving, Tom in the passenger seat, Diana on the floor between them. In a moment the atmosphere had changed and she leaned back, eyes closed, listening to the flow of talk that passed over her head. She heard calculations of food and water and petrol; gathered they had plenty of all for their trip to the 'wire' and then back to the road. There was only one time when their voices held a serious tone, something about, "—if that bloody pump holds——"

Tom said suddenly, "I meant to ask you, Mr. Anson. Do you remember that drive along the road in Tobruk—after we had picked up——" he jerked his head backwards—"*him*, at the water point?"

"Yes. Why?"

"Did we pass any truck—that was abandoned?"

"No, not that I remember."

"No. Nor can I—but *he* said he had run a big end there."

"It could have been farther on, you know, beyond where we turned on to the track."

"He must have had a long walk, then," said Tom.

The talk turned to other, more comfortable things. Of the 'hay-box' that had been found in the back and speculation as to whether it worked. She opened her eyes to ask what it was and was told it was a sort of giant vacuum flask. She looked at Anson. "Do you mind me asking questions? There's so much I don't know—and want to. I don't want you to think of me as anything different—a woman—a liability."

Anson smiled, swerved to avoid a gully, and said, "Ask away."

"Well, when we brewed-up. There was no one keeping a lookout for other vehicles. Wasn't that risky—when we're still so close?"

"We were listening all the time. It get's automatic. You can hear a truck long before you can see it in a mirage. And the next——?"

"Where are we going now?"

"I was going to talk to you about that. I'm turning slowly east—running diagonally towards the escarpment, that cliff you saw before the mirage came down. Then we'll skirt along the base until about six. Run into one of the wadis then—snug for the night and we can have a good rest. Then——" he hesitated, "—see about Sister Norton."

His voice was very gentle as he went on. "You see— out here in the open, we can't be absolutely accurate as to position. It might be very difficult to find afterwards. A wadi on the edge of the escarpment is much easier— we can mark the edge of the cliff above with a cairn of stones."

There was silence for a moment and then he went on, "Then tomorrow, head for the 'wire', and when we hit it, turn north-east straight for Sidi Barrani. That's about the drill—what do you think, Tom?"

There was no answer and she turned to see that he was fast asleep, his head nodding on his chest, swaying in his seat to the movement of the ambulance.

"He's asleep," she said.

"Good. But for God's sake see he doesn't fall out if I have to swerve. Hang on to his belt."

She slid a hand up between it and the top of his slacks and was comforted, strangely, by the warmth of him and the easy rise and fall of his side in the slow breathing. They went on steadily with the engine monotonous in its even beat. The sun had fallen away behind them now and the square shadow of the ambulance was creeping farther and farther away ahead on the sand. The mirage had quite gone, there was a luminous purple tinge staining the brown of the sand, and on their right the cliff was close and clear, with the dark jagged cuts of the wadis showing like valleys on a coastline. Nothing else but their tiny moving speck on all that broad horizon. They talked in spasms, of the Delta, of home—that other life. Tom slept on.

The shadows were long when they reached the foot of the cliff, and after they had nosed their way along it for about a mile, Anson said "I think this will do." He swung the car in towards a narrow cleft, twisting round boulders and bumping over rock slab. Tom woke up with a start and apologised and she was sorry to have to leave off holding his belt. They were cut off from the plain behind them now, going up the twisting channel of the wadi bed with the rock walls rising steeply to each side. The going became easier again, the flat bottom of hard-baked clay covered with tinder-dry camel-thorn. They went on until it widened into a sort of dell and then Anson turned the ambulance sideways and cut the engine. A deep compelling silence fell over everything.

They got down, stretching and rubbing their eyes. Anson said, "I'll wake Zimmerman and start the brew. Tom—to save time—will you go up the side of the wadi and back to the edge of the cliff? Have a look round, and then put up a little cairn. It needn't be big—just a marker."

She said, "I'll come with you."

The climb looked steep but she was past that sort of tiredness now, light-headed, almost floating.

When they had made the slope, the top was hard and level, another flat brown plain stretching away to the southern horizon without a break. There were plenty of loose flat limestone slabs about and soon they had made a pile about four feet high on the edge of the drop to the level below. As they finished, a breath of wind came suddenly from the north, infinitely refreshing. Tom eased his back and then turned through the full circle of the compass, staring at the desert and the sky.

He said, softly, "I've lived in green hills all my life. But here—at this time—it always gets me. . . ."

The ambulance was hidden by the angle of the wadi, there was nothing but the two of them standing under the wide bowl of heaven that ran through every shade from pink to lilac, with the blue curtain of night sliding up from the east. The red tip of the sun was going and the plain below a moving, changing sea of orange and slate-blue. They were the only two people in all the world. She moved closer to him. Then he said, "We'd better get down."

The petrol fire was flickering pale in the shadows of the wadi, with Zimmerman squatting in front of it, stirring. When they came closer, a delicious, unbelievable smell wafted towards them and then Anson walked round to them from the back of the ambulance. Though his voice was steady when he spoke, she saw his face was deathly pale.

He said, "Driver Grimes will either go on a charge—or get an extra week's leave—when we get together again. I've never seen such a scrounging b——. He's got everything except the kitchen stove on this car. I found a sack of spuds and onions under the stretchers. Most of them are in that stew now." It was ordinary, but breathless, and she knew he was talking because he had to.

"Anything else happened?" she said.

As he looked at her, his face changed. "No—except I've cleared out the cans at the back and opened the doors. I thought it might be a good thing to get her on a stretcher and take her out of there now." Then he added, very slowly, "Unless you want to scrounge a drink first."

"A drink——?"

"Yes. A drink. Zimmerman's been flashing that bloody bottle of his. I expect he would spare you a little one."

"Did he give you any——" It was Tom, the voice very low.

"Why should he—if I didn't bother to ask him?" There was a sort of smile there and the voice sounded brittle. Then he turned away. Faintly, she heard Tom's breath go out in a long hissing sigh.

They went to work without another word and it was easy to lift her down on to the stretcher they had put between the bunks because she was so light, almost impossible to avoid the dark stain that was left on the mattress beneath her. When the two men had run out the stretcher and carried it over to the far side of the wadi, Anson said, "Fix the back up, will you, Tom?" and they were left alone together.

She said, "I'm terribly sorry——"

"About what——?"

It was so difficult to put into the right words. "—That Captain Zimmerman upset you——"

"Upset me—why should that fat bastard swigging gin

upset me? I'm tired, that's all." Then his voice changed completely, "Sorry to have to talk about these things, but have you got her identity-discs?"

"I've got one in my bag—and I put the green one round her neck. Is that right?"

"Yes." He was staring down at the long dark shape on the stretcher. "Would you think it awful—if we postponed this till first thing tomorrow? I don't feel too good —I don't suppose any of us do."

She said, "I was wondering—couldn't we take her with us—to Sidi Barrani?"

He shook his head. "We can't be certain how long that will take. It's the top of the summer now—might be grim, and then we would have to do it anyway . . ." His voice trailed off to nothing.

"Tea's up, sir." Tom's voice came from behind them.

"Tomorrow morning, then," she said, and they all walked back to the ambulance.

The stew was very good, and though they could only find one plate and two spoons, they finished it to the last drop. She sat back with the plate, watching the three of them sitting cross-legged round the tin, bending forward to fish in turn, just like those men with hammers who hit crowbars into roads. She should have been revolted by the sight of the poking and balancing with fingers of bits of stew on biscuits, but somehow it seemed quite natural.

Then came the tea, sharing mugs, and she saw the rest of it being poured into the big cylinder with the bolt-on top that she now knew to be the hay-box. After they had sipped their tea in silence for a time, Anson said, "Now, orders. It's eight o'clock and Diana has agreed to my decision to do the digging at first light. So we'll divide into two shifts. You, Tom, and Diana, have a sleep from now until twelve-thirty—then, Zimmerman and I will carry on till five. That gives us four hours each. Then

127

we'll be fresher to get cracking with it—and then on for the dash to Barrani."

Tom said, "Do you think we'll do it—in a day?"

"If all goes well—yes. We should hit that old ambulance track near Piccadilly by sundown, and it's a cake-walk to the road on that, dark or no."

Zimmerman spoke for the first time. "Wouldn't it be as well to wait for the light—and make sure who is in Barrani?"

Anson stared at him. "Do you mean Jerry? Hell, man, Barrani is half-way to the Delta."

Zimmerman shrugged. "It's your party." Then he said, "If sister doesn't mind us coming in the back with her—why don't we rack up the top bunks, and all get a good night's rest?"

The last of the light had gone so quickly that it was impossible to see their faces now, but she knew that Tom and Anson were looking at each other. Then Anson's voice came quietly: "Someone must watch—there might be wild dogs—and Denise——"

Zimmerman broke the silence. He got up, swinging the bigger of his packs on his shoulder. "It's O.K. by me. See you later." He went over to the ambulance and she heard the scrape of the spade as he lifted it from the retaining straps; it showed in silhouette against the night sky as he walked off up the wadi with it tilted over his shoulder. The grate of his boots faded in the darkness.

"What on earth is he doing?" she asked.

There was a pause before Anson answered and then a hint of laughter in his voice. "Lavatory. In the desert, you never ask anyone where they are going with a spade."

"Common to both sides——" It was Tom's voice coming from the direction of the fire; she heard the rustle of scattered sand and then the last flicker of flame died.

The silence fell on them again, heavy and foreboding. No one seemed inclined to move. She thought, '—If I offer to sleep on the bunk she was on, Tom will be offended. He'll insist he does—and I know that he won't like the idea any more than I.'

Anson solved the problem for both of them. He said, "Before you two buzz off to bed, I want to tell you a story, Diana. And remind you of one, Tom. It won't take long, and I want to—because, when you go in there, you'll be thinking of things . . . and I want to tell you of something else that happened in this very car. . . ." She could only see the change of shape in the pale oval of his face as he turned towards Tom. "Have you forgotten the piano?"

There was a faint chuckle from the darkness. "Of course. It was this one—and Driver Grimes. I'd forgotten."

Anson's voice went on, "It was a year ago. The first time we took Benghazi. This car was attached to—I think it was, the Royals—when they went in as striking force. There wasn't any fighting, the Ities had gone, so the driver, Master Grimes, was told to come back and report to us in the desert at first light.

"In the meantime, there was some pretty terrific looting going on in the town, so, human nature being what it is, Grimes and his medical orderly helped themselves. After they had collected a silver tea-set and some nice lace table-cloths, they came on a very fine upright piano in an empty house. Then Grimes thought of his poor commanding officer—me."

He paused for a moment. "I try and think I can play the thing," he said.

"He does—very well," came Tom's soft voice.

"Well—somehow, and I didn't probe too deeply, naturally, they managed to get it down the stairs and into the back of the ambulance. It just fitted between the bunks. Then they pulled out of the town to have a few hours' sleep before starting off to where we were, right in the middle of the bulge of desert that's east of the town. Everything was fine when they started off down the ten miles of road before they had to turn off into the blue, but when they had done about three of them, they saw, to their horror, that an M.P. check post had sprung up in the night, swarming with red-caps, searching all the transport going out, on account of the looting. They couldn't turn back, they couldn't dump it in sight on the open road. The only chance was to bluff their way through.

"They coasted up to the post very crafty and slow. When the red-cap sergeant came out, the orderly—who was just as bad—put his fingers to his lips and said, 'We've got a bad case for the field ambulance in the back, Sarge. It's urgent.' When Grimes told me afterwards, he said there was only one lie in that. Really it was a good case—rosewood."

Another chuckle from the darkness; she could sense the flow of warm intimate feeling between those two, the bond of so many things seen and done.

"The sergeant said," Anson went on, " 'All right, boys. Just pull to the side for a moment, while I look at your pay-books.' Grimes said afterwards that it was sheer bad driving, but, as he eased her over, the back wheel went over a rock, and there was a bloody great 'doiinngg' from the strings.

"The sergeant said, 'Christ—what's that?' and the orderly said, very quick, 'He's groaning, Sarge. He's terrible bad. *Tussis alcoholica*—we've got to get him to the doc pretty sharp.'

130

"The sergeant fairly threw their pay-books back at them and then he said, 'Just one second, boys,' and went running back into his tent. He came out with a young corporal and he said, 'Corporal, there's a very sick man in the back there—get up on that ambulance and see they have absolute priority down the road.' And off they went. Grimes said he nearly wet himself laughing: there was the copper sitting on the bonnet, waving his red hat and blowing his whistle, shouting to all the stuff coming up to get out of the way, and all the time behind them, the old joanna bouncing on the bumps, going 'dooiinngg, dooiinngg, dooiinngg'. They made the end of the road in record time and dropped their escort and thanked him, saying that they would be sure to tell the patient all the M.P.s had done."

Now she was laughing too. "I shouldn't approve—but it's very funny. Did you get your present?"

"Tell her what happened, sir," said Tom.

"Well, they cut straight across the desert, and when they were right in the middle of sweet nothing, they had a puncture. It was a place just like where we were this afternoon—a brown plain stretching in every direction to the horizon, with just one ambulance stuck in the middle. Only, being winter, there was no mirage.

"The ground was a bit soft, and Grimes didn't fancy all that weight on his jack, so they got out some bits of plank they had in the back, and ran the piano down on to the desert. Grimes got under to change the wheel and while he was doing it he said, 'Let's have a tune, Charlie,' because he knew that the orderly could play—one of those arpeggio boys. Grimes said he never saw anything so funny as that bloke, sitting on a pile of jerricans, with nothing round him but sand and sky and a piano, playing 'I dream't I dwelt in marble halls' with all the twiddly bits.

"The trouble started when he had finished the wheel and they tried to get it up the ramp again. It was too heavy for them. They cursed and sweated, but it was no good. Then, to cap everything, there was a cloud of dust coming up on the beam, a big convoy from the east that would pass close. They couldn't do anything except wait until they had gone past, pretending that nothing was there. But a truck and a three-tonner broke away from the formation and raced over. There was an officer and he said, 'What the hell are you doing with that bloody piano?' and Grimes said, "Found it here, sir. We were trying to salvage it—to save deterioration.' The officer said, 'I'll stop that right now—I'll give you ten pounds for it.' Grimes said that they had their workshop lorry over and had it up on the crane and he was left holding the money before he realised properly what was happening."

"So you never got your piano?" She found herself resenting the soft laughter that was coming through the darkness, and was ashamed at once of resenting it.

Anson said, "No. I'm sorry to have kept you up with a silly story. But when you are in there—instead of thinking of other things—remember a piano going 'dooiinngg' beside you."

She got to her feet and said, "Thank you. I thought it was a lovely story—and I won't forget."

Tom was standing too, she could see the dark height of him against the sky. "Time to turn in, then."

Anson said, "Sleep well, you two," then, petulantly, "Where the hell has Zimmerman got to?" and the two of them groped their way to the square bulk of the ambulance looming against the stars. Then they had climbed into the back and she had flopped down on *that* bunk and pulled the blanket up over her before she realised—and then didn't care any more.

In the darkness, Tom said, "Would you like a last cigarette?" and she had said, "No, but I'll have a drag at yours." They lay there, separated by the narrow gap of the alley, with the glowing tip of the cigarette passing to and fro; each time she took it, she felt the touch of his fingers. When it was smoked right down and he had said, "I'm stubbing it out now," her hand had strayed back again and found his still there.

It was nice to go to sleep like that, surrendering to the waves of tiredness she had been fighting for hours, touching him—and with the ghost of a piano going 'dooiinngg, dooiinngg' beside her.

VI

WHEN Zimmerman walked off up the wadi, he had gone straight along the bed for about fifty yards and then turned sharp left to start the scramble up the steep wall. Slowly, carefully, with his desert boots making only the slightest noise with the loose stones they dislodged, he made the top in a matter of minutes. Then he moved away from the edge, ten yards on the hard, level ground, dropped the spade and lowered his big pack to the ground. He turned it on end, looking at his watch before he started to fumble with the straps.

It was the worst, most dangerous thing of all—the part that he hated; to make it worse, in his opinion the most futile as well.

He knew that they had to be got to the Delta—that they were too new, too advanced, to risk being dropped by parachute; he could understand the necessity of the orders, "Singly—by safe hand," but not the added danger of testing them on the way. If they wanted strength and range data, they had the whole of Tripolitania to do it in; why add to the risk in ordering him to do this, when they must know he would be in the position he was now—watched or in close contact, all of the time? But those were the orders. He wondered bitterly if the same sort of thing happened on the other side. . . .

Well, he had better do it. They had been explicit. Each night, between eight and nine—only call-sign unless there was anything vital. He looked at his watch again as the flap fell open . . . only eleven minutes left. He had better hurry.

Now the shirt had been pulled aside from the mouth. No need to see anything. Feel was enough. He grunted as his fingers touched the little knob, twisted and pulled, and then the thin rod of the telescopic aerial jerked its way up into the dark. He felt along the panel and there was a click and a tiny light glowed. Another inch to the left, and he found the key. It made a faint clicking noise as he started to transmit.

GMX . . . GMX . . . GMX. . . . Over and over again, the thin crackle of his call-sign went out into the black æther, the faint ghost fingers of it reaching out over the desert, groping for his headquarters, hoping they would detect, get the strength and make a fix. There was nothing else to transmit, nothing to tell them. They would know he was on the way, would not be interested in details of dead English nurses.

GMX . . . GMX . . . GMX. . . . He went on steadily until the luminous hands of his watch showed nine exactly. Then he switched off, lowered the aerial, replaced the shirt and strapped up the pack. Slinging the spade over his shoulder, he scrambled down the side of the wadi and made his way back towards the ambulance.

·   ·   ·   ·   ·

To Tom, it only seemed a second before he was being shaken by the shoulder and Anson was standing over him, holding a mug of tea. From the other bunk there was a faint blur of movement as the girl slipped out of her blanket, the open square of the door at the back showed only a difference in the texture of the darkness. The moon must have gone down.

They changed places in silence, there was only Anson's quiet, "Call us at first light and then we'll get on with it," before the bulk of Zimmerman slid in behind them and the door of the ambulance closed. They walked round to the front of the car, drawing the blankets they had kept tight round their shoulders, and then leaned back against KATY's bonnet, sipping the tea in turn, silent, looking up at the sky.

The night was so still, so beautiful. The strip of sky that showed between the banks of the wadi was like a glittering river with the stars so bright and close that it seemed you had only to reach up your hand to pull them down. The sides of the wadi came down dark and uneven in contrast with the pale grey of the scrub. He tried hard to avoid looking at the long dark shape that broke the smoothness of it on the far side.

The girl was still looking up. She said, "I never dreamed there could be anything like that."

"No. When we get home, we'll be missing it—longing to be back here again."

"I suppose so. As now we long for those other things —that seem so remote and past."

"Just a few of them," he said. "Not many—with me."

"What do you miss most, Tom?"

He said, "Haddock," quite seriously and without hesitation and when she had stopped laughing went on in the same tone, "Do you know, often when I wake up out here—and think of that bully again for breakfast—

my mouth starts to water, I almost sweat, when I remember a great wedge of golden haddock, properly done in milk, with a poached egg on top."

Her voice was still full of laughter as she said, "—But you can have the eggs——"

"Eggs? Do you call those things eggs? The size of marbles and no taste at all. Do you know the official rate of exchange for them with the Bedouin? It's in general orders—a handful of tea for each one. I call it encouraging robbery——"

He broke off suddenly, running over to the far side of the wadi, circling round the stretcher, kicking the scrub. As she joined him, she said, "What was it?"

"I thought I saw a dog."

"I didn't believe that was true—would they——?"

"Not if there was anyone around. They're very timid."

They were standing close to the stretcher now and he did not think that she liked it, so he made a move to go back to the car.

"No. Wait a minute, Tom." She stood looking down at it and the starlight was so bright now that it shone on her hair. She was quite still and he could not see any expression on her face. She said, "Don't think me silly—but I can't bear to think of her—covered up, on a night like this." And without waiting for him to reply, knelt down and folded the blanket back off the face. Then she got up and took his hand and walked back to the ambulance without looking behind her.

They sat down close, their backs against the front wheel, and she said, "Will it take long—tomorrow?"

"It depends—some places are easy, at others you hit solid rock two feet down. It's all trial and error. But I'll find a likely spot as soon as we can see and start right in."

"Cover her up before the others come," she said.

There was a long silence after that. He tried to ease it by pulling a couple of cigarettes from his packet, lighting them and passing one over. She drew on it eagerly, staring out into the shadow of the far side of the wadi; she said suddenly, "She wasn't a friend of mine. I hardly knew her. I was just put in charge of her for this trip. She was a silly, man-mad little bitch—and useless as a nurse. But I feel worse about it than anything else that has ever happened."

"You weren't to blame. Our fault—if anyone's."

She said, "I wonder what she was trying to say to you——"

"I don't know. Nothing to me, really, I expect. She may have thought I was someone quite different." They were quiet again, each locked with their own thoughts, then he said, "Captain Zimmerman—he shouldn't have done that."

"No. Not after we had asked him not to. But we weren't there, Tom, we don't know what happened. And—perhaps he may have taken notice already. He took the pack with him when he went off—with the spade. And I saw it slung over his shoulder when he went in to bed, just now."

Tom snorted. "It isn't in there—it's in the other one."

"How do you know?"

"We looked—when he was over talking to the Germans, and you were in the back——" He got up and moved back to the cab, there was a fumbling and a faint scraping. Then he came back swinging a pack by its straps. "He's not so careful about this one," he said. "It was lying on the floor."

He stood swinging it, listening. There was no sound from the back of the car. Then he said, "I'm a very careless man, Diana, clumsy. After I had to get up in the cab, when I jumped down, I tripped on Captain Zimmerman's pack and knocked it off——" He shortened his grip of the strap and brought it down hard on a rock that was by his feet, there was a faint brittle sound above the thump and then he lifted the pack again, feeling the under-side carefully. "I'm afraid I broke his bottle of gin," he said as he put it down again, "so you must remind me to apologise first thing in the morning."

When he came back and sat down beside her, he added, almost defensively, "The captain's got over it now—but perhaps it will make things easier."

She said, "He's probably got some more—in that other pack."

"Then I'll drop that too—or run over it—if I get a chance——" He stopped suddenly, jerking his head round. "Hush . . . Listen!"

The sound came to them, suddenly and very clear, perhaps because they were fully conscious of it for the first time. 'Plop. . . .' A little sound, a cross between a ping and a splash. It came from directly behind them, underneath the bonnet. She started to say something, but he said, "Hush", again.

It came a second time at an interval of about ten seconds. 'Plop. . . .' He cursed and turned, burrowing his head and shoulders underneath the car; when he came out, he dragged a shallow tin after him.

"That bloody pump," he said, "I thought it had begun to leak at lunch-time. So I put this tin underneath tonight to check. Look—it's half-full already."

"KATY's constitutional weakness," she said.

"Yes—and it might be serious. It's the washer that's gone. I haven't got a replacement—and if you try to tighten this one to stop it, it might break up altogether."

"What would happen then, Tom?"

He tried to explain a little of it, but gave up as soon as he realised she hadn't got a clue. He put the tin back and, to stop thinking of the wound that dripped behind —that could use up their water so fast that there might not be any left to drink, started talking of other things, far-away things.

Of the garage, of the village and what his life had been like so long ago; in turn, he heard of her father, the snake-charmer, what had happened in the blitz.

Quite suddenly the stars were gone and a faint luminous greyness was creeping into the dark of the night. He said, "First light," and got up stiffly and went to the other side of the wadi and pulled the blanket back in place. When he came back he said, "If I light the fire, will you watch it while I find a place to start?"

He left her crouching in front of the tin, stirring the sand, then went and got the pick and shovel from their clips and cast round in the bed of the wadi until he found what he thought was a likely place. He started with the pick, swinging slowly and rythmically until he had broken the surface in a space two feet by six. As he stopped to lift the spade to clear away, he stopped and stared for a moment at the bright, clean blade. Captain Zimmerman must be very particular to have cleaned it after use in the dark last night . . . or perhaps he had not used it at all. He went on with the shovelling.

It was when he had got down about two feet that he came on trouble. The point of the pick started bouncing back with a hollow sound, the shock jarring up the handle to his hands. Rock. He tried all along the narrow trench, but it was all the same.

It was clear grey light now. He straightened as the girl came over with a mug of tea in her hand. "I've wakened the others," she said, "—and broken the news of the accident to Zimmerman. They're just coming over."

"What did he say?"

"Nothing."

He stayed, leaning on the pick, until they walked over. He said, "I'm terribly sorry, sir. Knocking that off the step in the night, I'm afraid I've spoilt everything."

Zimmerman shrugged. "An accident, Sergeant-major, it can't be helped. Most of the cigarettes are all right—and my socks will dry." He looked down into the trench. "How are you getting on?"

"I'm not. I think we'll have to start all over again. I've hit rock."

Anson said, "Solid—or a layer?"

Tom let the pick bounce off it once again. "It sounds hollow," he said.

Zimmerman stripped off his bush-shirt and spat on his hands. "Give me that thing."

Tom watched him, standing in the trench, the rippling play of the muscles of that great back as he swung the pick high and brought it down with terrific force . . . 'About twice as hard as either of us could hit,' he thought. Zimmerman was hitting always in the same spot and now little sparks were beginning to fly, then there was a sharp crack and the pick point went on through. He grunted as he levered up a slab. "The rest should come up easy," he said. He went on lifting and shovelling, while Tom watched the swing of his arms, the red and green identity-discs hanging against the matted black hair on the chest. He wondered if he had been wrong in all those half-formed thoughts, was ashamed of what he had done last night. There was only one thing certain, neither he nor Anson would have had the strength to break that rock.

When the captain had taken over for a spell he went back to the lee of the ambulance where the girl was opening tins of bully and a second batch of water was near the boil. He talked at random, trying to keep her mind off other things, but the chink of the pick and the dry scrape of the shovel kept on breaking in through their words. Then the noises stopped and he looked over the bonnet to see that they were walking over towards the stretcher.

He said, "Look—I must try and fix the pump. Will you help me while we're waiting for them?"

"Of course. What do you want me to do?"

He spread a blanket beside the car and tipped out the entire contents of the tool-kit box on it. "Look through all those little bits—the nuts and bolts—and see if you can find a black washer, it will feel sort of soapy." He had looked earlier and knew there wasn't one.

Then he wriggled under the sump. "And pass me the tools as I want them."

He lay on his back, fumbling, listening to the shovelling noise that had started again, delaying as long as possible to keep her on the ground beside him where she could not see. Only when the sounds from the far side of the wadi had stopped and she had reported that there was no washer there, did he wriggle out, pulling the tin after him. "Over a pint gone," he said, "and I've tightened as much as I dare."

As he straightened, to pour the water from the tin back in the radiator, he saw the two men walking towards them from the far side of the wadi, carrying a folded stretcher.

They all tried to be terribly normal while they ate, the conversation ranged on anything except the last thing that had to be done. The words got steadily more stilted, more brittle, and at last he could stand it no longer. He looked at Anson and said, "Shall I try and make something up, sir?"

Anson nodded, so he got up and ripped two strips of wood from the top of the case that held the tinned milk. He took a bit of the binding wire and got it red hot in the fire and bored holes through each and then bound them together in the form of a cross. He searched his pockets but he only had a pen and that wouldn't take on the wood. None of their pencils were indelible and they could not think how to do it until Diana said, "My lipstick's supposed to be water-proof—and I don't want it any more."

So he printed with that—her name, her number—which Diana got from the other identity-disc—and the date. Then Anson got up and said, "We'd better get it over. We must get on our way."

As they walked over to the long mound, the sun came over the lip of the wadi and it was hot already, with the first dust-devil spiralling along the edge of the cliff, the scrub at the bottom beginning to shimmer in waves. Zimmerman had put on his bush-jacket but had not buttoned it up. Tom thought, 'He might have'—but at least he had left that bloody pack behind.

They stood two on each side while he pushed the wooden upright hard down in the sand and banked some stones up round it. Then Anson had said, "I'm sorry—I don't know the service. Does anyone?" But Zimmerman shook his head and Diana turned away.

And not because he was in any way a religious man, not for the dead Denise, but for the living Diana, he felt he must do something. Slowly, the soft Devon voice stumbled out in the words . . . "The Lord is my shepherd . . ." He got half of it wrong and dried up after a few verses because no one else had joined in. Then he said, "I'm sorry—that's all I know," and they all stood silent, looking at the ground, before the noise came to them for the first time.

It started as if someone was shaking a chain, softly and a long way off. It went away for a moment and then came back louder, more clanking. He looked up at Anson and the knowledge passed between them, then they were all running back towards the ambulance.

The noise got louder as they began to throw the kit on, but then Anson said, "No good. If we move, they'll spot the dust. Douse that fire quick, Tom. And stay still." As he shovelled sand on the fire, he looked across at Diana and said, "Tank—probably theirs."

The clanking came up the wadi to them in gusts, but there was nothing to be seen because of the bend towards the mouth. It stopped for a moment and then started again, coming closer. Anson whispered, "Christ!— they've seen our tracks."

It was very loud now, echoing off the rocky walls, sounding like a scaly dragon crawling up to meet them. They stayed together, quite still. Then round the corner came the long grey shape of a German half-track and Zimmerman had cursed and started to run down the wadi towards it with Anson close behind.

He stayed where he was, leaning against the car. Diana was very close to him, and somehow his arm had gone round her. The haze jumped and shimmered over the tangle of scrub and the grave.

VII

ANSON could feel the sweat running down between his shoulder-blades as he pounded after Zimmerman. There was no question of catching up, as the big man had had a couple of seconds start and was running very fast. All he could hope was to be at that meeting as soon as he could . . . he wanted that very badly.

The half-track had stopped and the troops in it had jumped out to form a semi-circle in front, their automatic weapons crooked under their arms; between them, leaning back against the radiator, arms crossed, with a big Luger held loosely in the right hand, was an officer, a lieutenant. He looked young and tough and arrogant. 'Not a hope in hell, this time,' thought Anson as he came level with Zimmerman's shoulder.

It all happened so quickly that, afterwards, it was difficult to sort out the order in which he noticed things. Perhaps, first, the way the lieutenant was looking, not at Zimmerman's face, but his chest, his eyes not hostile, but wary—just as they had been the time before. Then, Zimmerman's hands, the way they were up on his chest, just as if he was buttoning his jacket, the speed with which they cut away as he realised Anson was at his shoulder. Last, the tone of his voice.

There was no diffident explanation there, it was intense, almost commanding, as question and answer went to and fro; wishing desperately that he spoke the language, he watched the circle of hard eyes under the steel helmets.

At last Zimmerman turned to him. "Twice is bad luck. They were on patrol. They saw our tracks and followed them. I have told him we have a safe conduct from 15 Panzer Group but——" he spread his hands, "—there is nothing written and I do not think he believes me. He says he cannot check our story as there is wireless silence. I think he suspects a trap— for he says he will search and question us all before he decides what to do." He stopped for a moment and looked very straight at Anson. "He tells me that they entered Tobruk at certain points last night—and that the whole fortress surrendered this morning without a fight."

It made him feel sick—physically sick. He said, "I don't believe it," but in his heart he knew that it was true and if that had gone there was nothing much left. Matruh? . . . he remembered that sham fortress, how its minefield looked so impressive on paper, how, only last year, he had led a convoy over the fringe of it by mistake . . . and not a single mine had exploded. Someone had said they had been filled by a civvy contractor in the Delta . . . probably with sand.

Zimmerman's voice cut through his thoughts. "He says to go back to the ambulance."

As they walked back to the car, he heard the crunch of the steps behind of the soldier who was covering him; watched others climbing the walls of the wadi, slipping and scrambling up the sides like grey beetles, then standing at the top to sweep the horizon with binoculars Then he heard the faint call of, "*Nein, nicht*——" float down from one side and the other. At the ambulance Tom and Diana were standing close together. Even in this moment he envied them, thought for a fleeting second of Ariadne . . . then Paul. Where was he now. . . .?

The questions, passed on by Zimmerman, were confined to the simple name, rank, number and the details of the shooting up and Denise's death. It was when the Germans made the search of the ambulance that he saw the other small thing.

It was only because he was watching—intent on every little movement now, that he spotted it. The lieutenant was rummaging in the clutter on the floor of the cab when his hand moved towards the square pack that Zimmerman had rested on it while he leaned against the windscreen pillar. It never got there, that hand, because in that instant the South African's eyes and the German's caught and held and something sparked between them. The hand hesitated, and moved on to another object. No one else saw, he would not have seen if he had not been watching for it. Perhaps it was imagination. But now he was so nearly sure . . . and being sure would make it all the more difficult.

After he had finished, the German gave a jerk of his head to Zimmerman and they went over to the grave together and they saw him copying the inscription into his field pocket-book. Then Zimmerman came back alone.

"He says we may go. That the Afrika Korps do not bring women into fighting areas—and we should not either—but he cannot be bothered with her. But we must go farther south. Their armour is already through the 'wire' as far down as Maddalena. They will have cut off Matruh in two days. He says we must start now."

They threw the rest of their gear on, watched by the stiff circle of grey figures in the shimmering heat. When it was done, the lieutenant gave a signal with his arm and the circle drew back. They moved off, passing close to him as he stood, stony-faced, by the grave. They climbed on up the slope of the wadi bottom and the walls fell away to nothing and then they were on the last stretch of endless brown plain, heading south.

Anson was driving, Zimmerman in the passenger seat, still hugging that pack, the other two had gone into the back of the car for a rest.

Anson felt in his pocket and pulled out the compass, he passed it over without looking round. "Keep her on 170°, Zimmerman."

"O.K., man."

Except for his clipped directions to keep them on the course, they did not speak for the first half-hour. Once

146

or twice Anson glanced at him, sitting there, hunched over the compass he had balanced on top of the pack. Then his eyes went back to the way ahead.

It was brown and dead. No camel-thorn here to make any form of pattern, only coarse gravel like Demarara sugar, and as the sun got higher, the mirage took on a new form. It was as if the edges of the horizon were drawn up into the sky all round and they were floating in the bottom of a brown bowl, with only a small circle of blue sky directly overhead. The going was good, so smooth that they did not seem to be moving at all, they were stationary at the bottom of this dun sea and the gravel was sliding by them in a quiet dry crackle.

At last he said, "So you got us out of another jam."

The voice came back, tight and clipped. "Man, I don't know how. He was a bastard. But with Tobruk gone—they had more important things to do than to round us up."

"You believe that—about Tobruk?"

"Yes."

Another fifteen minutes . . . another 7.2 miles on the clock. But they were still at the bottom of that brown bowl, did not seem to have moved at all.

Zimmerman said suddenly, "What's the plan, Captain?"

"I was going to talk about that when we stop to brew-up. But do you know the lie of the land this far south?"

"No. Only what I've read."

"Well, if it is true they are through the wire—and I don't believe a word of that cock about outflanking Matruh—it won't be wise to try and make the coast road west of there. That means we'll have to keep on bearing south-ish, to give the coast as wide a berth as possible, until we hit the Masrab that runs along the top of the Depression, when we can turn north up the

Garawla track to the sea." There was a pause and then he said, "—But it means another hundred and fifty miles."

Zimmerman did not say that he understood the geography; only, "There's plenty of petrol, isn't there?"

"Yes. That's not the trouble. It's the bloody water pump. Did you hear the sergeant-major swearing at it? We lost a quart of water last night, though of course we can save that. But we can't when we're running."

"Can't it be tightened—or disconnected?"

"No. There's a carbon washer—it's wearing. If you tighten too much, it will crumble altogether—and then we're done. I don't think you could disconnect the pump anyway—and if you did, she'd boil like a bitch in this heat."

"So——?"

"So there will be an increasing drain on the water—and always the chance of a bloody long walk."

Silence again, floating on the bottom of the brown sea, with the gravel rushing under them in its quiet sound.

Anson said, "I was attached to your div. for a bit."

"When?" There was a hint of sharpness in the question.

"Oh—let me see—about nine months ago. When they first came up. I was with supply services. They were a bloody good lot."

"I wasn't up with them then. I only came up from the Union last January. I'm afraid I haven't had much to do with the supply side."

Nothing could have been more negative. He said, "But you must have heard of some of them—old Kramer, the colonel—he was a character."

"Kramer—— Yes. I did meet him once. I can remember him."

"And the general——?"

"Dan Piennaar?—Yes."

148

"Do you remember . . .?" Anson embarked on one of many tales that surrounded the legendary figure of the commander of the 1st S.A. Division. While he was talking, his voice seemed to come from outside him, from someone else. He could even listen to it while he was thinking . . . 'You managed to get one name right, Zimmerman. But anyone would know about Dan Piennaar. Kramer, though . . . you have met him . . . the colonel of supply services. There's only been one head of supply services, and his name was not Kramer . . . it was Maggs . . . Eugene Maggs. And he was such a well-known and loved type . . . you must have heard. . . .'

His own voice finished, "—And he put it in orders, that any gun troop that fired at a range of more than eight hundred yards would be court-martialled, or castrated, on the spot—whichever was the most convenient."

Zimmerman did not laugh. He was pointing through the screen. "What's that ahead?"

Something was showing on the edge of the bowl ahead of them. At first it looked like a row of thin black columns, then the mirage cleared and it was a low rusting barbed-wire fence that stretched across their path from horizon to horizon.

"The 'wire'," he said, and leaned back and pushed open the door to the back and shouted, "Wake up, Tom, it's the 'wire'." They were quite close to it when Tom came out from the back, rubbing his eyes. "That's pretty good, Captain Anson. Where are we on it?"

"Unless we're a lot adrift—about two miles north of El Washka—you know, where there are those two palms, and a gap. I'm going to turn south and find it."

It was four miles to the south of them in fact, but still he was very pleased. They ran that distance down the edge of the fifteen-foot-thick fence. Diana was peering out through the door now and Anson told her how it had been put up for the 180 miles from Sollum to Siwa by the Italians, to keep the Senussi in Libya for not too pleasant purposes. Then there were the two stunted palms, the gap, and they were bumping over the flattened coils. The brown plain looked exactly the same as before. Only now it was Egypt.

As if to welcome them home, the going altered within ten miles. It was rougher, with flat grey stones jutting from the ground, the smaller ones rattling away from under the wheels, but ahead the flatness had gone, weird mountains and terraces were floating now in the mirage, that resolved to low flat-topped hills at closer range.

"Where to now, sir?" Tom was still looking out from the back.

"I'm going 15.2 miles on 152°, Tom. That should hit Bir Bayley. We'll brew-up there—and see if the well is worth digging out. We can't drink it—even if there is any—but it will help for the radiator." He looked across at Zimmerman. "It's a well we dug out two years ago—but God knows what happened to it since."

The desert was as empty as it had been all day, the going got steadily worse. Now there was bare rock on the ridges and in the hollows between patches of cracked mud. The sand was taking on a reddish tinge.

He drove on until Zimmerman said, "Fifteen up," and then stopped and climbed up on the bonnet with the glasses. The mirage was bad, but nothing like that of the morning. He swept the lenses round the dancing hills that seemed to come towards him and then curtsy away; at last he found the little yellow pimple that jutted out from the side of a ridge. "There it is—half-left. We'll go over and brew-up there."

. . . . .

Diana had never seen anything that looked less like a well. After they had come through the 'wire', and she had got up from the bunk to tidy up, Tom had told her about Bir Bayley. She knew that 'Bir' meant 'well'—in this case having, presumably, refreshed or been discovered by a Mr. Bayley—and even if her imagination did not reach as far as lush grass and bubbling springs, at least she thought she was in for a few palms.

There was nothing. Just a mound of yellow sand on the lee of a hill, and in the bare rock beside it a small square pit with more sand drifting up to one lip. She stood in the cab looking at it while the others jumped down. "Where's the water?" she said.

Anson turned from unstrapping the spade. "Five . . . ten . . . fifteen feet under that lot. We've got to dig to find out." He turned to Tom. "It looks a lot worse than last time, but go down a bit in that corner and see if there's any dampness. Then we'll decide. I'm going to do a bit of thinking—and plot the next course. Diana, will you start up the brew?"

She put out the tins and the water and the petrol, was proud and grateful that he sat in the driver's seat, the map-board propped up on the steering wheel, without attempting to help or interfere. When it was going, she looked over towards the well and there was nothing but Zimmerman sitting on the edge smoking and the bright blade of the spade flashing out of the hole at regular intervals, each time dropping off a gout of sand. She walked over to it.

Tom was still digging. He was stripped to the waist and it was the first time she had seen him like that. She watched with pride and it was a personal, possessive thing.

He had not the spread of Zimmerman, but he was brown and supple and smooth, the sunlight flickered over the play of muscles each time the arms swung up and winked on the brass badge strapped to one wrist. Then she looked at the other man, sitting there, watching lazily, smoking. And she was full of a hot resentment.

Tom threw the spade down suddenly and knelt in the bottom of the hole, feeling with his hands. He turned and looked up at them. "It may be wishful thinking— but it feels dampish to me. Will you take a spell, Captain Zimmerman?"

"Sure." He stood up and stripped off his shirt and laid it carefully on top of the pack that was by his side. Then he jumped down to Tom. "What do I do?"

"Just dig, sir. Until you hit real wet sand." Then he said, "My God! I've forgotten that bloody pump—it's been dripping all this time. Must put a tin under it." He climbed out of the hole, grabbed his shirt and almost ran back to the car.

She stayed for a moment, looking down at the great shoulders that were making the sand fly. Then she bent down to reach for his bush-shirt. "Shall I take these back to the ambulance for you?"

He stopped in mid-stroke, with a jerk that spilled the sand from the side of the spade. His whole body went rigid.

"No, thanks. I'll bring them myself."

"Very well." She turned on her heel and walked back to the car.

Tom was standing beside the captain, who was still fiddling with ruler and protractor. She said, "Captain Anson, I want to talk to you."

He looked up from the board and she saw that through his tiredness his eyes were wary. "So does Mr. Pugh, Sister. I imagine, on the same subject. Don't you think it can keep? I may think the same—but listen . . ."

He held up his hand and in the silence there was that

little sound they had heard the night before. 'Plop . . . plop . . . plop . . . plop.' Water dripping into the tin. Only now it was coming five times as fast.

He said, "I don't want to frighten you, but that is far more important." He looked towards the well, where the flash of the spade still came regularly. "Whatever we think—let's keep it as thoughts. Until we can do something about it. He's strong. We're going to need him."

Then he turned back to Tom. "What happened to his haversack last night?"

Tom, wooden-faced, looking straight back at him, said, "I had an accident—I dropped it."

"All right—you dropped it. But we don't want any more—accidents like that."

The tea was made and the bully opened by the time Zimmerman came back to them from the well. He lowered the spade and opened the other hand; on the palm was a pile of sand, darker than they had seen before. "That's from the bottom," he said. "I've gone down another three feet."

Anson took it and crumbled it and put a fragment to his lips. He spat. "Hardly damp—and salt as hell. We might go on for hours, and then get nothing. Let's eat, and talk about it after."

The bully was tepid and almost poured out of the tin. It made her feel sick but she knew that she must eat it. The sun beat straight down on them now, very hot, and they crouched in the little strip of shade at the side of the car. The mirage heaved and swirled outside the narrow circle round them. They were alone in the middle of it and they talked because they had to—of anything that would shut out that background noise that was in their minds all the time now. The steady, fast dripping of water into the tin under the pump.

153

She said, "Flies—I've only just noticed. There aren't any. But there were clouds at Tobruk. Why?"

Anson spooned another gob of bully out of his tin with a wedge of biscuit. "No human beings, Diana. Flies only go with man and his filth. This desert—no one ever comes to it—for nothing has, or ever could, live here. So there are no flies." He munched for a moment. "How many times have we been up and down between Matruh and Benghazi, Tom?"

"Five—no, six, counting this swan."

"It was different there," said Anson, "though we always tried to keep it clean. It's funny—though all the desert looks the same you get a fondness for certain spots, and always go back to them if you can." He took another bite of biscuit. "We had a notice made —Tom did it beautifully—a lovely big board painted in the correct German. When we had to retire, we stuck it in the ground. It said, 'We are coming back —leave the desert as you found it.' Twice when we came forward again, we found it turned round the other way, and they had written, 'We have—and so will we.'"

Tom said, "And they did—always left it like a new pin. The Ities, that was different." He looked at Zimmerman. "Did you find the same thing, sir?"

Zimmerman didn't answer for a moment and then he said, "I can't remember us—ever leaving messages for Jerry."

While they were clearing up, Anson said, "The water, Tom. Check every drop, and then we'll talk this out." He sat on the step with his map-board on his knee, with the others beside him, waiting for Tom to come back. Then he cleared his throat.

"Well, how much?"

"Ten full tins—and a drain in the one we're using."

"That's twenty gallons. And how fast is that thing leaking?"

Tom shrugged. "It's difficult to say. Perhaps a gallon to every four hours' running. We can't save that."

"Say, three gallons a day—at the top. We've been using four for cooking and other things. So there's three days' water."

"Can't you tighten it up at all?" It was Zimmerman.

"No. Tom tells me another quarter-turn and the washer will break. All he can do is to keep it packed with grease—and we haven't much of that.

"Three days . . ." Anson repeated, "—and there are two—no, three alternatives. Have a crack at digging that out——" he jerked his head towards the well, "—in hopes of getting enough to fill some cans for the radiator only. It will be undrinkable—too brackish. But we might not find any, and waste the time and be consuming water ourselves, just the same."

Diana said, "What are the other two?"

"The first—to disregard what our German pal said, and go straight from here to Matruh. That's not more than 150 miles. Easy. But we would be converging on the coast all the time, and it would be awkward if he was right. The other way is to stick to my original plan and skirt round the longer, safer camel road at the top of the Depression and then up the Garawla track. 270 miles—all of three days and about our limit."

He was silent for a moment. "Of course—there is one other. Go south from here to Siwa or Qara Oasis, where we know there's water. Fill right up and then go straight across the Depression itself——"

It seemed as straightforward but equally as incomprehensible as the other plans. But there must be something different about it, for she saw Tom's face—and it was as if his C.O. had made rather an improper suggestion.

155

"You wouldn't do that, sir."

"Why not? I've done it before. I know the distance is greater, but we would be filled up, and certain not to meet anyone."

Tom said, "I didn't mean that. The other time—it was training. You had light stuff—and there were planes to keep a check on you. But alone—and in this crate, no."

It was completely beyond her, so she said, "What is this Depression?"

Anson got down from the driving seat and propped the map-board up against the bonnet. "Come here, Diana—and you, Zimmerman. I'll try and show you." She peered over his shoulder while his finger moved over the face of the map.

"From here, east, the desert proper funnels down until it's only forty miles wide at a place called Alamein. The sea is the boundary to the north and this Depression comes up to meet it from the south. It's a salt marsh—and to understand it, you must try to think of the lie of the land sideways. From the sea, the desert rises up in shelves——"

"I know—escarpments. Like those yesterday."

"Yes. And the ground rises gradually between them, so that here we are at about six hundred feet. It goes on south of us to eight hundred or so, then drops a thousand in one big cliff to the Depression—which is below sea level. There is a track across—but the going is—very bad. That's what Tom meant."

She was watching his pointing finger. It rested now on a great area that was coloured grey-green, a faint dotted line wandered along its length, almost uncertainly. There were words printed in places beside it . . . 'Bad going' . . . 'Soft sand'. In one place, just '???'.

Anson said, "I think I could make it." Then he looked

round the group. "Well—there you are. Direct to
Matruh, or the Garawla track, or across the Depression."
No one said anything, so he looked straight at Tom and
said, "Then it will have to be like a court-martial, junior
first. You, Tom?"

"The Garawla track, sir. And—somehow—I'll make
that pump last."

"Now two pips. Diana?"

"The same as Tom."

"Zimmerman?"

He said, "I've heard about that Depression. No, the
same as the others."

Anson did not make any comment. He just said, "The
ayes have it," and then he looked across at the well. "At
least, we haven't wasted much time on that caper.
Might dig for a week for nothing. One order before we
start, though. No more washing or shaving——" he
rubbed his beard, "—we've left part of it a bit late, anyway."

He looked across at Diana. "We'll try and spare you
a drop. Not more than a pint a day, I'm afraid. We
must keep the tea ration up if we can."

She said, "Put that in the tea. I don't want to be
different. If you don't shave—then I don't wash."

He said, "Good girl," and threw the map-board on
the driver's seat. "Well, let's get cracking. Nuts to you,
Bir Bayley—some other b—— can dig you out. I'm
going to get a taste of that Rheingold soon. Tom, will
you take over? Sixty miles on 115°. Then call me. I'm
tired." He went into the back of the car and Zimmerman, with his pack, followed him.

When Tom had emptied the tin back into the radiator
and poured in a good deal of one of the cans beside, they
set off into the emptiness ahead; the only living moving
object in a thousand square miles. But they had made

their decision. They were moving on a set course towards their destination. . . . For four miles—to be exact, 3.8. Then on a bit of level going, suddenly and without reason, the left rear spring went.

There was a sharp crack and the car lurched and seemed to sag backwards and sideways. Tom swore horribly and braked gently to a halt. As they jumped down, the other two piled out of the back.

She could only stand and watch, feeling useless. But there was one thing she noticed at once and it did not seem strange to her: without a word being spoken, Tom had taken over control. He had gone straight to the back, squatting, sucking his teeth as he looked at the bright, broken end of the main leaf of the spring where it jutted out beyond the shackle. Then he crawled underneath and came out dusting his hands and looking quite cheerful.

"Not too bad. We can fix it. Get a lot of flat stones." Then he looked at her as if she was an orderly: "You, Diana—put that tin under the radiator like you saw me do it last night. And make sure the drips are falling in it."

Meekly she went, and when she had finished crawling under the sump and went back to the others, the wheel was off already and the jack supporting the chassis. While Anson was going out in the surrounding desert and bringing in flat slabs of rock, Zimmerman was underneath the car making a pile beside the jack. Tom looked up from his work on the axle, pausing to wipe his hands and smile at her.

"Best know what we're doing, Diana. It's got to be done in two stages with only one jack. We put her up— make a pile of stones under the chassis, then let her down on that—so that the jack is free to work the spring in."

"Work the spring——?"

158

"Yes. You've seen the spare ones tied on the front. Well, when there's no load on them, there's too much camber—bend—to let them reach the shackles, the bolts that hold it to the car. So we fasten the front end, then press the spring up against the weight until it is flat enough to reach the back. Then we bolt up, put the wheel on, kick away the stones and let the whole lot down. Simple."

"It all sounds as if it will take a long time."

"All of two hours," he said, "but there's nothing we can do about it." He went on with the task of unbolting the broken spring from the axle.

She wandered round, watching them; Anson was underneath with Zimmerman now, helping to pack the stones. At last he said, "That seems firm enough. Let her down gently, Tom."

She watched him leave his work on the spring and go round and twist the lever of the jack. Slowly, the body of the ambulance sank down on to the stones, there was a grating noise, a gentle rock, and then no movement. Tom slid the jack clear.

When it happened, it was so quick that she had no time to gauge the disaster before it was past. Anson was coming round from the front with the new spring, Tom was lifting the old one clear, Zimmerman, apparently resting, still underneath the back, when there was a brittle cracking and puffs of dust jetted out from underneath the chassis and the ambulance started to slide down while the stones slipped out of the pile in a rattle.

Tom shouted, "Christ!—she's going. Captain Zimmerman—try and hold her—just for a second——"

While he was shouting, he moved, and she had never seen anyone move so fast in her life. He dived down, the jack in one hand, pumping at the lever with the other while he stuffed it into position. But, before the pile

159

disintegrated entirely, before the jack took the strain, before even Anson was under there to help, Zimmerman took the strain. Zimmerman, on hands and knees, grunting, joints cracking, held the body on his own for five long seconds. . . .

VIII

HE had not been resting underneath the car, only thinking. It was in the shade and as good a place as any, had the advantage that no one could see his face. He was beginning to wonder how much they were watching him. . . .

So, when he had finished piling the stones and Captain Anson had gone out to get the spring, he had just stayed where he was, working the whole thing out.

It was not going as well as he had hoped . . . it had been damnable luck to run into his comrades twice . . . and that second one had been so aggressive, so slow, that the Englishman had almost seen. Or had he seen? . . . there was the accident to that other pack of his . . . but that was before. Had they been searching for something . . . or was it just to sabotage that gin? There was only one thing certain, that it was no accident. The bottle had been smashed to fragments.

He had looked out sideways, at the bottom half of their legs moving about as they worked, then on to the flat dun heaving plain of the desert. He supposed they must be 180 kilometres from the coast now . . . a long way. He thought for a moment about what it would be like, that 'long walk' the captain had spoken of . . . quickly turned his thoughts to what now lay ahead. He was glad they had not chosen the short way back to Matruh. It would be the certainty of walking into his own, having to start all over again. Equally relieved that the Depression had been ruled out. They had had lectures . . . he knew their General Staff had assessed it as impossible for transport in their plans for invasion of Egypt. So it was the middle way—three days, if they were lucky. Could he keep them satisfied for that time? He had to, they were his only chance of getting into the Delta.

Then the cracking started and he had turned on hands and knees before Tom shouted. He had locked his arms and his legs and heaved up, taking the intolerable strain while the cross-members of the chassis ground down into his spine, the terrible tearing moments, with the twisting pain in his guts and the thudding, red haze before his eyes. He had taken it, and there had been no thought of his mission, of the war, as he had done so. Only that long walk there would be for all of them if he failed, the unending waste of sand that would divide them from other humans, the thirst, the sunstroke. There was only one enemy in those seconds. The desert.

Then relief came and they pulled him out. He sat on the sand, unable to get up, drained of everything except that awful pain in his guts. When he could see properly, he looked up and they were grouped round him, staring down in a peculiar way. The girl said, "Are you all right, Captain Zimmerman?" and he couldn't answer for a moment and when his voice did come it did not sound like his own. "I've hurt my back—I think I'll lie down."

She said, "Let me help you into the car," but the captain said, "No, not until we've finished the job. There's some shade on the side now, put him there." Then, louder, looking round the circle, "That was one of the most bloody marvellous things you have ever seen. If she'd come down hard on the axle—we would have been done."

They got him under the arms and walked him round and it hurt like hell. When they were in the strip of shade, the girl said, "I can manage now. You get on with the job." As the two of them had walked away, he heard the sergeant-major say, "He must have stood up to all of a ton—perhaps more." The tone was awed, but it didn't help him much . . . didn't take away that pain. . . .

The girl had got a blanket and spread it out, then she helped him move on to it. "My pack," he said, "it's still under the car—could you get it?"

"Of course."

She came back at once holding it by the strap and he knew there had been no time to open it. She put it down beside him. "Would you like a drink?"

"I would, but mine's broken."

"Wait a minute." She went to the front of the car and fumbled in her haversack, she came back with a flask he had not seen before and held his head while he tilted it back. It was Scotch whisky and made him feel better. She knelt beside him. "Where does it hurt?" she said.

Something in her attitude irritated. "Everywhere. I think I've twisted my guts. But if I've ruptured something—which is what you think—there's nothing to be done about it, is there?"

"Nothing," she said.

"Then give me a cigarette—and go and help the others. We don't want to be here for ever."

When she had gone, he lay quite still, flat on his back, watching the thin spiral of smoke twisting up into the hot air, regretting everything.

.   .   .   .   .

It took them three hours to complete the job. They worked slowly with a double check on each stage, and this time there were no accidents. Diana's part was the selection of the smoothest, flattest stones, and she thought afterwards that she must have walked at least five miles in her circling of the ambulance looking for them. They had made her loosen her hair to hang over her shoulders as protection against the sun. Secretly, she thought it silly, for it was not so hot now, a deathly stillness coming with the cool. The sun was sinking away behind them now, getting redder with each degree it dropped down the sky. The mirage had gone, the low flat-topped hills clear and steady on every side.

When she came back from one trip she went up to Anson and held out her hand. "I thought you said nothing lived here?—where did this come from, then?" On her palm was a dry white empty snail shell.

He looked up from tightening the rear shackle. "So we're getting near that part. Tomorrow you'll see millions of them—the ground is just covered. Don't ask me how they came. No one really knows, though there is a theory this desert was a sea-bed once." He gave another couple of turns with the spanner. "How's Zimmerman?"

"I keep having a look at him. He's asleep—and a much better colour. I don't think there's anything—vital—hurt. He's just played out."

When they had finished, they let KATY off the jack and stowed away the tools. Anson looked at the slanting rays of the sun and said, "Not worth it—before dark. We'll brew-up now and get Zimmerman in the back, then wait till the moon comes up and I'll have a crack at some night-driving." They got Zimmerman into the back without much difficulty, it was just as if he was rather stiff and tired. They brewed-up and took his share into the back of the car and he seemed grateful, but uncommunicative. The sun vanished soon after they had finished clearing up, suddenly, twisting the purple shadows in a moment to blackness. Anson looked at her.

"Tired, Diana?"

"No, not particularly."

"Well, take the first stretch with me and let Tom have a spell. We'll be off with the moon and drive while it lasts. Tom, I'll call you at midnight."

After Tom had gone into the back and they waited for the moon to rise, Anson said, "Sit down—or walkabout?"

"Walkabout."

They wrapped the spare blankets round their shoulders and started a slow circle of the black square of the ambulance. They were out of earshot, but she spoke very softly: "I picked up Zimmerman's big haversack this afternoon," she said.

"So what——?"

"It was heavy—and it didn't feel like bottles. I thought you ought to know."

He stopped in his tracks and swung round towards her. "Do you know he saved us all—completely—this afternoon? If she'd come down on the axle, we'd have been bitched, had to walk a hundred miles—probably straight back into Jerry hands."

"That's not the point," she said.

"It IS the point, Diana. Look, I think I know what he's got in there——" he peered at his watch—"and if something happens soon—I'll have proved it."

"If what happens?"

"—Regardless of his twisted guts, or his stiffness, Captain Zimmerman will continue his regular habits before nine."

It was ten minutes to the hour before they heard the sounds coming from the cab; when they had circled to that side, it was Zimmerman, standing on the ground, unclipping the spade. They moved over to him.

"Are you all right, Zimmerman?"

He turned, leaning heavily on the spade. "Yes. I won't be long."

"Don't be. The moon will be up any moment, and I want to move off at once."

"All right." He turned away and shuffled off into the darkness.

She waited for Anson to speak, but he just resumed his leisurely pacing. She said, aghast, "But aren't you——?"

"NO." It was fierce. "Whatever's wrong, he can't be doing any harm *yet*. And he's saved us three times already."

He wasn't long. When he had come back out of the gloom with that slow shuffling gait, the tip of the moon was just beginning to show over the hills to the south. "He just made it," said Anson; "now, let's get moving."

He climbed into the driving seat and gave her the compass and showed her how to use it. There was deep satisfaction in being for once rather important, and she held the heavy roundness of it clasped tight on her knees, peering at the swing of the needle's luminous point against the pre-set mark of 95°, giving him the direction when he veered off course. As she got more used to it, she could relax and they talked in spasms. Once he said, "That shell you brought in—it reminds me of a story about these parts."

"Tell me—I love hearing of the desert."

"Do you like it?"

"Yes."

"Well, I hope you still do when you've finished with it." There was a silence while he concentrated for a moment on the dim moonlit way ahead and then he said, "It was two years ago. I had been sent down here

165

from the coast—to dig out that bloody well we were at today, as a matter of fact--and in those days anywhere within twenty miles of the 'wire' was the front line, and you had to be careful. We were a bit east of here—country you'll see tomorrow—even more desolate than this, just red sand spattered with gravel on top, and millions and millions of those white shells lying about——"

She cut in, "Right a bit, George—a bit more. Now, steady as you go."

He picked up the new course and then went on. "We were trundling along quite happily—until we came on some other tyre tracks. Now, you learned to know all the patterns made by our vehicles and theirs, but these weren't like anything I had ever seen, thin and narrow. I was wary, but curious, because they looked so new; where they had broken the gravel crust, the edges were as sharp as a razor. Anyway, they were leading in the right direction, so we followed them. They led south to one of these flat-topped hills—they call them Quarets—and then turned off to the west. But on the side of the hill, 'they', whoever they were, had stopped and made a fire. And then I was even more wary, because the charred bits of wood left balanced on each other and the ashes looked so new that I expected them to be hot. But they weren't."

The moon was sinking already, the faint grey light fading so rapidly that now there was no horizon for him to take a mark on any more. Anson said, "Another couple of miles, and I'll have to stop."

"All right—but go on telling me."

"Well, having felt the ashes, I was happier—but not quite sure, so I thought I had better climb to the top of the hill for a look round. There were other footmarks going up the sides and I had the queer, rather frightening feeling that I was going to find something at the top.

There was—but not in the least what I expected. Laid out in a pattern of the shells like the one you had today was a message and a date. It said, 'LONG RANGE DESERT CAR PATROL. 21st NOVEMBER 1916.'

"That was why we had not recognised those tracks— they were 'T' Model Fords, and they and the fire had been made almost exactly twenty-five years before. But there's no wind here, it never rains, and so they had stayed as sharp and new as the day they were made. We were the next people to chance that way."

"What did you do?"

He laughed. "Just put our unit and the new date underneath. But I don't suppose anyone will ever see it —unless they start another war in about 1970, and some other poor bloody fools have to come mucking about in these parts." He bent forward and threw out the gear lever. "That's the lot—my eyes are getting sore."

When they had coasted to a halt he struck a match, shielding the flame as he looked at the speedometer. "Twenty-one miles farther east—that's good. Anything should be behind us now."

"Behind us?"

"I didn't like to say anything before, but if that Jerry was right and they're through the 'wire' and striking at Matruh, they must come south and occupy Giarabub and Siwa—or be outflanked. But now, they'll pass well behind us."

"Giarabub, Siwa—they are just names to me. Tell me, I want to know."

He jumped down from the driving seat. "Come out from under there—and I'll do my best."

After they had gone through the routine of putting the tin under the bonnet and wrapped the spare blankets round them, they sat on the sand with their back against the front wheel. For the first time, she saw the full sweep of the night sky and it was even more beautiful than the night before. Wistful, almost angry, she wished that Tom was beside her to share it.

There was the dome of black velvet, so riddled with stars that there seemed to be more light than dark; they did not twinkle like the pin-points of a northern sky, but glowed, each enormous, hanging just over their heads.

"Oh . . .!" she whispered.

"Yes." His voice was just as soft. "The deeper you get in the desert, the better it is. They'll look so pale when you get back to Alex. Look—there's Cassiopeia . . . and the Plough, over there to the west. Those two stars—the pointers—follow them through——" his finger moved dark against the blaze of light, "—and the next bright one is the Pole Star. That's got me home, many a night."

She said, "I think I could watch for ever."

"Yes—if you had the right kind of things to go with it."

"Such as——?"

"Oh, the right kind of music—Beethoven, and the right kind of girl." Then he said quickly, "Sorry—that wasn't meant to be rude."

"I'll forgive you, George." She was laughing. "Tell me—have you got a girl?"

He made an uneasy movement with his shoulders. "I don't know. Sort of—but it's all rather complicated."

There was a silence and then he said, "But you wanted to know about the desert. Well, you see the Pole Star? Keep that over your left eyebrow and walk about a hundred miles, and you'd hit the coast at Sidi Barrani, going down-hill over the escarpments all the way."

"Yes, you told us about that this afternoon."

"The other way—south—you'd climb a bit more, and then break your neck over the thousand-foot drop to the Depression. Siwa and Giarabub are on it, at the western end. Oases—real ones, lush, plenty of trees and water."

"This Depression," she said. "What's it like——? Why was Tom so dead against crossing it this afternoon?"

"It's a salt marsh—a bog, if you like. It's shaped rather like a pear, stalk up and tilted over to the right. It's two hundred miles from end to end and a hundred across the broadest part. It's all below sea level and water seeps through the deep rock strata of the desert and comes up from underneath it. But it never rains, so the sun dries out the top in a sort of crust, thickest in the summer, of course. But the whole issue is floating, really, and if you break through the crust, you've had it."

He was silent for a moment. "There's one track down the middle—I suppose the ground may be a foot higher than all the rest and dries out quicker and thicker. It's marked 'safe for vehicles', but it's difficult to follow. If you don't——"

There was another pause and then he said, suddenly, "I did it once. There were two blokes in a jeep with the convoy. They started fooling around, wouldn't keep to the track—went arsing off on the mud at the side. And it went through—God!—it was like a bloody submarine diving. We got the blokes out with a rope. But the jeep —it had gone—completely—in a minute."

She said, "That's why Tom didn't fancy crossing it?"

"Yes. And he's right. This ambulance is far heavier than the trucks we had."

"Could we go round to the south of it?"

"No. The Great Sand Sea is there."

"What's that?"

He turned his head towards her and the starlight showed he was smiling. "You're a devil for punishment," he said. "I'll try to describe it. But it's difficult —I've never been there—only seen it once.

"Can you imagine rows and rows of sand dunes, all running due north and south, each about five hundred feet high and a mile from crest to crest? Bright yellow sand, soft—and the length of them—no one really knows, but at least six hundred miles. You can't cross them, only run down the troughs. It would be all right if we had enough petrol and wanted to get to the Cape."

"So we must keep to the top of the cliff?"

"Yes. It's wisest."

He pulled out his cigarettes and lit two carefully, turning towards the ambulance to shield the flare of the match with his body. "Half an hour—and then I'll wake Tom."

She said, "You're very careful about lights."

"Better be safe than sorry. They might try a night dash for Siwa—and you can see a match the hell of a distance."

"They . . ." Her thoughts turned abruptly to other things. "Zimmerman," she said, "he——"

"Skip it, Diana. I'll talk to you and Tom about that later." Then his voice changed and became very casual, so casual that she knew the question was important. "Can I—talk to you about something completely different? Ask your advice—as my big sister, if you like?"

"You're not very flattering, are you, George? But if that's the only way I qualify, I suppose I'll have to."

"I've got eyes in my head," he said; she blushed and hoped the starlight was not bright enough to show it.

"Go on, little brother."

"It's a question of the woman's angle, and it's rather complicated. You asked about girl friends. That's the trouble. I don't know what to do."

"About what?"

He said, "Paul Crosbie—my best friend—he's with the

170

company, and he was left in Tobruk. We've always done everything together—leaves, and things like that. We always used to go to Beirut. And we met a girl there, always went about together as a trio——" It was coming out in a rush now, but he would not look at her.

"What's her name—and which of you does she like best?"

"Her name's Ariadne—and I don't know. That's the trouble."

"So——?" she prompted.

"I am terribly fond of her—but I was never sure about Paul. It was the one thing we never discussed. But things seemed different after we came back from the last leave—and then I had to take over the C.O's job, and I started hitting the bottle——"

For the first time, he looked at her. "It seems so stupid —but I was so bloody tired—all the time."

"That's finished," she said, "and anyone who thinks at all can understand. But go on with this problem."

"An officer had to be left in Tobruk. I had no say— the brig detailed him personally. But I know Paul thought—because it was him—that I was ratting."

"And now——?"

"Paul's in the bag—I'm certain of that. At the moment, I'm outside. If I stay out, and get a chance to write to her—or go and see her, what do I do?"

She said, "You don't understand women, George."

"How do you mean?"

"You think that because you're free, there might be an unfair advantage—that your nearness might tip the scales?"

"That's the rough idea."

"Well, all I can tell you is that if your Ariadne's a real woman, she will know already just what she wants—if anything. If it's neither of you—there's no harm done.

If it's Paul—nothing you can do will make the slightest difference. So I would write to her, George. Tell her what's happened. If there's no answer, tip your cap and walk in another direction."

"Do you always know what you want?"

"Always."

"Right now?"

"Yes."

He said, "Let's talk about something else. . . . Beer."

"But I thought that was out."

"It is—until that date in Alex. Do you know—I've been thinking about that one particular drink all day. I've told you about the bar, haven't I? But that Rhein-gold—it's so bloody cold that there's a sort of dew on the outside of the glass. I always run my finger up and down—to make a sort of trail—before I have my first swallow."

"And what will you do then?"

"Oh, have a bath and pull the lavatory chain about six times—to hear running water. Then take your advice, I think."

She said, "After the desert—the oasis."

"Not any oasis," he answered softly, "but Zerzura."

"What's that?"

He did not speak for a long time. Then he said, "I'd better call Tom."

"No. Give him a few minutes more. Tell me."

He looked up at the slow turn of the blazing lights round the Pole Star, then he said, "I've never talked about it before—though I've read all there is to read. It's the lost oasis. The name means, 'The Place of the Little Birds'."

"Please tell me."

"There's not much to tell. The story goes back seven hundred years—an oasis, somewhere down there—" he

172

jerked his head back towards the south—"that's never been properly discovered. It comes up again and again in the old chronicles—with always the same detail: palms, a white city in the middle, a wall and a door with its handle carved like a bird. Inside there is a treasure, and a king and queen, sleeping."

"How lovely—go on."

"There's not much else. Up to thirty years ago, there were old men that remembered seeing it, but that's all gone now. But the point always was, it was only ever found by someone who was lost themselves—or looking for something that had been lost, like a straying camel. And afterwards, they could never find it again."

"Did it really ever exist?"

"I don't know—I'd like to think so. Some Europeans still believe in it, passionately. They've spent most of their lives trying to find it. Personally, I think Ralph Bagnold has the truest idea. It's the wish-oasis. That when you are in danger—desperate—there's always something left to discover a little farther on, something difficult, but nice, if one has the guts to carry on and look for it. Perhaps, not even a physical thing . . . an idea. . . ."

His voice drifted in silence. Then he said, "You must think I talk an awful lot of drivel."

"I don't—and nothing has ever been discovered?"

"Not a thing. And with planes—and the war—the possible area has shrunk to nothing. I'm afraid it is just the echo of that idea started by the Bedouin long, long ago."

She looked up at the stars for a minute. "Still—I hope you find your Zerzura, George."

"And yours——" he said.

"I will."

As if in answer, there was a bumping and a scuffling

behind them and Tom Pugh came out of the cab to jump down on the sand.

"I woke up, sir." The voice was reproachful. "It's an hour past your time."

"Sorry, Tom. We were nattering. How's Captain Zimmerman?"

"Still asleep. I didn't like to wake him."

"No. Let him go through." He looked at Diana. "Would you like a spell?"

"I don't have to drive. I can sleep any time. I'll keep Tom company."

Anson got to his feet stiffly. "Well, I could do with it." He stretched. "Don't do anything I wouldn't." Then he started to climb up into the cab, stopped and looked down at them. "Are you sure he's asleep, Tom?"

"Yes. Snoring."

Anson got down again. "Then we had better get it sorted out—once and for all." He came and squatted close to them. "Both of you—at one time or another— have come to me to complain, or comment, on Captain Zimmerman. I wouldn't listen to you. Now's the chance to get all of it off your chests. You first, Tom."

Tom looked down at his feet. "Well, sir, he just appeared from nowhere—said his truck had broken down up the road, but we didn't see it. Then, when we went through the minefield, and they fired on us, he was swearing—and I'm certain it wasn't Afrikaans. He hadn't a clue as to how to make the fire—yet all Union troops brew-up the same way as we do. And—excuse me, Diana—why does he always go out to the—lavatory —at exactly the same time—and what's in that other pack—the one he keeps so close, and never lets anyone touch?" He ran down.

"Diana?"

"The same as Tom—I've never liked him, but it's

174

more than that, there is something phoney. I haven't told anyone before—but after he had been over to the Germans, had been talking to them, he came back and called me 'dear lady'. Isn't that rather near German—not South African form of address? That pack, too. I'm the only one that's touched it. It's heavy, solid, as if it was just one thing, not a collection." Then she said, "And why should he snap at me when I tried to pick up his bush-shirt?"

Anson answered them very softly, "I know all of that. But, for the last time, whatever it is that's wrong, he can't do any harm—now. The most important thing is that he shouldn't know. We want his help—there's enough on our plates without having trouble with him as well. We need him. So, ignore it, try not to think about it. I don't want any more 'accidents'. But if you see anything, just let me know on the quiet."

Then he said, "That's an order. Understand?"

Tom said, "Yes, sir," and as she did not quite know what to say, she said nothing. Anson swung himself up on the step again and melted into the shadow of the cab. The door to the back of the car shut with a click.

They sat on under the silent, circling stars, they talked of many little things but afterwards she could not remember any of them. The only jarring note was the noise of the pump dripping into the tin behind them. It was faster, and she hoped that Tom had not noticed. She did not want to spoil a moment of it, she was still thinking of Zerzura.

IX

IT was the most wonderful thing in the world . . . this soft warm feather bed of sleep, and it was infuriating to be dragged back from it, to be shaken and see Tom Pugh standing there, a mug of tea in one hand.

"First light, sir. That pump—it's much worse. Almost running out now."

It all came back to him and he turned, propped on one elbow as he took the tea, looking back over his shoulder out of the open door, seeing that the darkness had changed to pale grey.

He said, "Damn the bloody thing!" and then swung his legs down and rubbed a hand over the stubble on his face and into his hot eyes before he leant over to the other bunk, looking at Zimmerman.

The big man stirred and muttered in his sleep, but Anson could not hear what he said; he reached forward and shook the big shoulder and then Zimmerman rolled on his back and opened his eyes.

"How do you feel, Zimmerman?"

"Rested, man." Then he groaned as he tried to sit up. "But stiff—bloody stiff."

"Take this tea. I'll get some more outside. We must get going as soon as we can."

Zimmerman sipped. "I'll be all right. When I've had a walk round and limbered up."

Despite himself, Anson was listening to every word now, trying to weigh up the clipped English, trying to remember if the Afrikander did speak like that.

They were away by seven, with Diana going into the back for her sleep, Anson driving, Tom in the passenger seat and Zimmerman sitting on the floor between them, which he said was the most comfortable. They took a course a little south of east and soon were in the shell country. They were littered everywhere, stretching to the horizons, covering the dark gravel like white flowers on a black field. They heard the crunch of them under the wheels, the softer hiss of the gravel flowing on in between.

By noon they had made sixty miles, with three stops to top up the radiator with water, and it was taking nearly a pint at a time now. Their course wound in and out of the flat-topped hills, with nothing to see but the red sand, the black gravel and the white shells; as the sun rose in the sky above them, the curtain of the mirage started its weird writhing dance.

As he drove, he kept on glancing down at Zimmerman. The long hairy legs in their brief shorts were straight in front of him, the square pack balanced on the thighs. It looked so square, that pack, almost like a box, and at one corner the canvas had started to fray. Was it wishful thinking—or was that a gleam of metal beginning to show through? His eyes strayed farther to the left and he found that Tom Pugh, from the passenger seat, was looking at it in exactly the same way. Their eyes met for a second and then flicked away. Tom's voice came quick and guilty. "Two points to the left, sir." He kept his eyes fixed on the plain ahead after that.

The desert was opening out in front of them now, the hills falling behind; far to the south, through the mirage, a yellow tinge stained the sky. He pointed. "Reflection of the Sand Sea—we're getting close to the cliff now." Then there was a thin column dancing in front of them, so that they were afraid for a moment it was a vehicle, but it cleared to a single conical hill.

He said, "That's Qur el Laban—we should cut the Masrab just beyond it bearing north-east. We might as well stop there and eat, then crack on hard for the rest

177

of the day." All the time now, his mind was reaching out in calculations—water lost, time spent, miles to be done.

The hill was only about fifty feet high but it looked greater because of its loneliness. Behind it, the ground went on level to the horizon, only it was a nearer, clearer one than they had seen before, without mirage. They stopped on the east side of the hill and he unhooked the glasses from the back of the door and said, "I'm going up to have a look." He had scrambled half-way up the slope when he heard a shout from behind him. It was Diana. "Can I come up with you?"

Soon they were standing on the hard level top, about the size of a tennis court, littered with the white shells even on this older level of the desert. He swept the glasses to the north, but there was nothing but the mirage; south, about a mile away, was a faint wavy line running across in front of them; scattered near in several places were lumps of white, far larger than the shells.

He handed over the glasses. "There you are—straight ahead. Do you see those faint lines, with the white things beside?"

"Yes."

"That's our track."

"What are those white things?"

"Camel bones—probably hundreds of years old. It's a Masrab, an old caravan route. There will be bones marking our path all the way now."

He saw that she had lifted the glasses farther towards the horizon. "What can you see now?" he said.

"It looks like the edge of something—the cliff, I suppose. Then a haze—the most wonderful colours, blues and greens. Then, far, far off, something yellow and knobbly, like the backbone of an animal."

"The colours are the reflection of the Depression—and

you, lady, have joined the select band who have seen the Sand Sea. That's the dunes, end-on to us."

She said, "This Depression—I wish I could see it."

He looked at her gravely. "I don't think you'll miss much."

A faint call came up from below and they both turned to see the ambulance the size of a matchbox, the pigmy figure of Zimmerman, crouching by the fire, Tom standing by the open bonnet, waving his arms. "It's that damned pump, I suppose," he said, "I had better get down."

"Can I stay for a bit? I'll never see it again."

"Not too long—without anything on your head. The sun's right on top now."

"What about you lot? You walk about in it all day without a hat—even a shirt."

"We've had two years of it," he said, "we're kippered." Then he started to scramble back down the slope.

It was the pump, and now the leak was so bad that Tom had wanted his permission to risk another tightening. The two of them became absorbed, Anson holding his breath as Tom coaxed with the spanner, only relaxing when he said it would be all right, but could not be touched again. Only when they were wiping their hands, and Zimmerman came over to say that grub was ready, did he realise that the girl had not come down.

They all shouted and it was some time before she appeared at the edge of the slope; she was waving her arms and shouting back but they could not catch what she said. Then she came down the hill in a sliding run towards them.

"I heard a plane," she gasped.

"A plane . . .? Hush. . . ."

They all stood quite still: only the sound of the occasional crack from the cooling engine and the steady dribble of water into the tin. Outside their own world, nothing.

"I heard it—I swear I did," she said. "Very faint. It went away—and then came back, louder."

He said, "You've had too much sun. I told you not to stay up there. Get into the shade of the cab at once."

She went without a word and he was sorry in the instant that he had spoken to her like that. When food was dished out, he said, "Let me do that, Tom," and went over himself to the cab with the plate of stew and the spoon. "What else did you do up there, Diana?"

She looked a little better now, not so white. "I hope you don't mind—but I was thinking of your story of the shells, and I arranged some as our names—and KATY's —and the date. I hope someone sees it . . . one day."

He said, "I doubt it—but if you want to tell your grandchildren, the name of the hill is——"

Behind them, Tom said, suddenly, "Listen."

They all heard the drone now. It got louder every second, coming from high up and the north-east. Diana made a move to lift the glasses that were still slung round her neck, but he pushed her hands down. "No. The sun might catch the lenses."

They stayed frozen, looking at each other, not the sky, while the noise got louder and louder. Then, with the tight roar of a power dive, the plane came straight down at them from out of the sun.

In the last seconds they scattered a yard or so, crouching. There was that awful split-second of shattering sound and the dark shadow flicked over them like a bird of prey. Anson turned on his elbow to see the plane banking to climb away, and his whole being filled with relief at the sight of those stubby wings with the curved tips, the roundels.

"Spitfire——" he yelled and was running out into the desert. "What's the bloody ground to air recognition sign?" They were running after him and through it all he heard Tom—"a 'Y' in white strips, I think."

"We haven't got any strips—we'll make one ourselves. You, Zimmerman, go out about ten yards. Tom, thirty beyond him. I'll get out between and behind them—Diana, you get back directly behind me." As he ran out to his position, he shouted, "And wave like b——"

The pilot was very careful, he came past low in long runs four times before he climbed and headed away to the west. The noise faded.

Anson looked back from where he was standing to Diana. "Good boy, that. Didn't stay stooging around for too long—in case he attracted attention to us. But it means——" He stopped suddenly.

"Means what——?" She had walked close up to him now.

He looked at her for a moment. "That something, he doesn't like, could be very close."

They had only just picked up their food when the sound came in from the west and he was coming in again low, flaps down. Before he got to them, there was a flash from the cockpit and a bundle of coloured streamers tossed behind in the slipstream, to float down behind their metal container and bounce on the desert. Tom ran out for it and had unscrewed the top and pulled out the message before he got back to them. The writing was uneven, in places almost indecipherable, but Anson remembered with gratitude the difficulty of writing on your knee while trying to watch your plane, the ground, and the sky all round you at one and the same time.

The message was brief and to the point.

MATRUH BYPASSED. JERRY ARMOUR
STRIKING TWO-PRONGED DABA AND BAGUSH.
NOTHING YET SOUTH OF LAT 31° 2', EXCEPT
COLUMN RUNNING DOWN WIRE NOW AT EL
WASHKA. OUR TROOPS FALLING BACK TO
ALAMEIN. DO NOT REPEAT NOT ATTEMPT
COAST WEST OF THERE. IF UNDERSTOOD
CIRCLE VEHICLE CLOCKWISE.

They heard him coming back, high this time, directly
overhead. Anson said, "Tom, get in her quick, circle
wide, right hand down." When he had done it they
waited again and the Spit came back for the last time,
so low that he seemed to be touching the desert. For a
second they saw the open cockpit hood, the helmet, the
goggles and one bare arm raised in salute. Then he was
gone, spiralling in a victory roll, while another bunch of
streamers fluttered down towards them. The message
was very short this time. WILL INFORM ALL GOOD
LUCK.

The plane was high again now, dwindling to a speck
in the blue of the north-east. The noise thinned and
faded to nothing. They were alone again and no one
spoke for a long time.

Tom tidied up and refilled the radiator automatically,
but all the time he was watching the captain, sitting
there, hunched in the driving seat, scribbling furiously
on the corner of the map-board. He knew what that
message meant to them; that hard look had come back
into Anson's eyes and he did not like it.

At last Anson laid the map down and said, "Con-
ference, chaps. And then we'll be off."

When they had gathered round, he said, "I'm not
going to muck about with this. It's come down to a
simple time and motion study. We are here——" his

finger pointed at the map—"this column on the wire is there, and to the north, Jerry has reached there." Then he smiled, "—At least, according to that bird-man. They tend to exaggerate, but as we're grateful to him, we'll take it as truth. So you see—on the coast, Jerry is a hundred miles ahead of us already, and because of the lie of the land, the farther we move east the nearer we must get to him. Within forty miles, near Alamein, we must be right in it."

He paused and looked towards the north; Tom looked after him, over the flat dun plain, knowing that they were both thinking the same thing, that somewhere out there, unseen and incalculable, was a grey stream, flowing east. Like a tide on the shore, it might check for a moment, but a thin feeler would move out, turning to find another way. Then the whole would move on.

Zimmerman broke the silence. "So——?"

"The cliff route is out—the odds are too great. Even if we don't meet anything, we could not last to Alamein on our water."

"Then——"

"Yes. It must be the Depression—the whole bloody way."

No one spoke.

"I'll have a crack at it—if you want me to." He said it very quietly and again no one answered.

"We know we can leave Qara Oasis full up with water —probably food and petrol as well. Now the only danger there will come from this column moving down the 'wire'—and that's where time and motion come in. El Washka to Siwa, which they must occupy first, is a hundred miles. Give them twenty miles in the hour— that's top going—and they would get there in seven hours——" he looked at his watch—"that's nine tonight. Now we are only twenty miles from Qara here. Say two hours, because we've got to get down the cliff—which makes them five hours behind—apart from the seventy miles they still have to do between Siwa and Qara. A fair start."

"What do we do then?" It was Diana, speaking for the first time.

"Pull out ten miles from Qara tonight—that's to the edge of the soft stuff—and get cracking as soon as it's light."

"Couldn't we push on tonight—supposing they follow us?"

He gave a short laugh. "Even for a prize like you, dear, they wouldn't risk their vehicles on that stuff—and I wouldn't move an inch on it at night."

Zimmerman said, "I don't like it—supposing——"

Anson stared at him. "Yes. Suppose that. It would mean we'd had it. But there is a chance of getting through. The other way——" he jerked his head to the north, "—is a certainty of walking into the bag. Do you want that?"

Zimmerman didn't answer.

"Well," said Anson, "there it is. In my humble opinion, a certainty with Jerry—or a chance against the marsh. There's only one other thing I must tell you before you decide. You won't be able to change your minds. Once we're down that cliff, it's too high and steep for KATY to climb out until the far end."

Tom saw the eyes fix on his and he stared at the ground because he did not want to let the captain down, let him see the doubt in his face. He heard the voice go on quietly, "Diana? . . . Zimmerman . . .?" but no one answered. He understood for the first time in full measure how they would be lost without the captain, and that he knew it, realised the loneliness—the responsibility of leadership.

"So I have to decide . . ." Anson was staring at the board, skin glistening tight on his cheek-bones. "Well, it's the marsh. And tomorrow—or the day after—when we're bogged down to the axles, and the water's gone, and we're a hundred miles from anywhere—you can spit in my eye."

It was a silent party that started to pack up to move; while they were doing it, Tom saw that Diana had gone quiet and was very pale. "All right, Diana?" he said as he poured the precious water back in the radiator.

"No—I feel sick. Got a bit of a headache."

His eyes met Anson's behind her back and he touched his head and looked up at the sun. "You silly girl," he said, "you have got a touch of the sun. Go and lie down."

When they were ready to move, he said to Anson, "Why don't you go in the back with her for a bit, sir? You'll want all the rest you can get before tomorrow." He knew who was the only person to do the driving then. But the captain smiled and said, "It wouldn't be quite the same thing, would it?" So he went and sat on the edge of the bunk and made a compress with bandages and the tepid water, bathing her face and neck, not caring how much he wasted; sat on, wiping gently, holding her hand between whiles, not talking, not wanting to. Soon he felt the first jolt as the car hit the furrows of the track, the rocking as they turned south along them. She was asleep now, and he went to the door for a moment, looking out at the grooves worn by generations of plodding camels, the white bones of the fallen gliding by on either side. Then he went back to his watch.

He was drowsing, nodding over her, when a jerk told him that the car had stopped. He went out into the cab, but there was no one there, and ahead on the desert, where the track dipped out of sight between two spurs of rock, he saw the little figures. It must be the edge of the cliff and they had gone on to spy out the land.

He went back into the car and she was still asleep. He shook her shoulder gently and said, "Diana—we're at the top of the cliff, I think. The others have gone on to have a look with the glasses to see if the coast is clear. Do you mind if I go and join them?"

She didn't open her eyes, just said, "Tom, darling——" and took hold of his hand and turned over on her side with it against her cheek. Then she made a little soft noise and went to sleep again. So he did not go, but stayed, watching her through the still, hot afternoon.

The two captains were sweating but cheerful when they came back. The report was that they had had a good view of the oasis and that there was no sign of transport there. Anson said they must move down as soon as possible.

"It's a rough track, Tom. Steep slab stuff. Will you take her down—dead slow, in bottom? I'll walk ahead and try and find the best path." Then he looked towards the back and said, "How is she?"

"Asleep. I don't think she's got it bad. Be all right tomorrow."

Zimmerman was unslinging his haversack. "God, I'm thirsty. Can I have a swig of water, Captain?"

Anson said, "Only a mouthful—until we're sure. Don't forget the water we take on will be bitter—not too good for tea."

Tom was looking at the square pack. It lay on the cab floor where Zimmerman had put it while he tilted the water can. That split in the canvas was bigger, he could see the gleam of metal quite plainly now. How long could they possibly go on without a showdown?

They entered the rocky defile and were soon creeping,

186

almost hanging, to the steepness of the tilted slabs of white limestone that fell away in a giant staircase over the thousand-foot cliff.

Tom took it dead slow, with eyes only for the figure walking in front, ready to twist or stop according to his signals. Zimmerman was in the passenger seat, silent as usual, and then the door opened behind him and he knew it was Diana coming to join them.

He said, "Better?" without looking round, and was relieved by the answer of, "Yes." Then she said, "Oh, Tom—it's beautiful."

"I can't look—tell me."

As they banged and bumped their way down she tried to describe it all, the magnificent sweep to the bottom of the Depression, with the evening shadows coming up to smother the blues and greens of it, the Sand Sea behind, the humping backs of the dunes already slanting orange and purple; then Qara itself, over on the right, the palms in a hollow with the curious white rock rising from the centre that swelled out from its base like a mushroom and had the mud village sitting on top of it.

As they went lower, the air seemed heavier, sticky. Then the smell of the oasis came, dank, like moist rotting grass.

They drove straight to the outside fringe of palms and it was a strange feeling to be under the shade of anything again.

Anson said, "I'll go off and scout round—see what I can fix. Zimmerman, will you come with me? You had better keep quiet, Diana, and in the shade, with Tom." Zimmerman slung his pack over his shoulder and the two of them walked off into the trees.

Tom made her sit quietly as he put the tin under the radiator and lit the fire for their tea. When it was going, because she said she felt, and looked, a great deal better, he agreed to go for a little walk, circling the car. There was no one in sight; underfoot, a coarse grass, and everywhere, between the tufts of it, flakes of encrusted salt gleamed; over them, the palms rustled dryly, secretly as the sunlight slanted through the fronds. There was no other sound—except when they were close to the ambulance, and then there was the reminder of that constant dribble of water into a tin.

Once, through a gap in the trees, they had a glimpse of the white rock, and she said, "It's like a dwarf's house on top of a toadstool in a picture book."

"The captain was telling me. It's the wind that's worn it like that. They live on the top for fear of raids by the nomad tribes."

"But why build so high?"

"They can't expand sideways—they're up to the edges already. So if another house is wanted, they just slap some more mud on top. Siwa's the same—only bigger, and really fertile. There's real gardens, and wells. One built by the Romans—about twenty feet across—and you can bathe in it. The water bubbles up from the bottom like a fizzy drink."

"Have you been there, Tom?"

"No. But the captain told me. He has."

It seemed a long time before the others came back, but they were accompanied by a silent, ragged Siwan, riding a skeleton donkey.

Anson said, "They are pretty scared here. A British convoy came through from Siwa early this morning, probably the garrison. They went east very fast along the edge of the Depression. Must have been making for the one track up the cliff that leads to Daba. Probably sorry they tried it now."

Tom was thinking of two things: first, this news—and

Zimmerman standing there listening—what price was his potential harm now?—then Anson, having made the hardest decision, was so much more like the old captain, treating even the most serious things with a sharp flippancy.

He was speaking again. "We can have all the water we want—free, as is the oasis custom. But he'll charge for his moke to bring it here—and make us pay through the nose for our own petrol that was left in a dump. And some dates—and perhaps a few eggs."

They loaded the empty water cans on the donkey and, while they were waiting for the man to come back, had their tea and food. At last the donkey appeared, laden high and followed by a procession of the curious from the village. They stood at a distance, silent, staring, while the water cans were counted, the four-gallon tins of petrol laid out beside them with a slab of dried dates and a cloth containing twelve tiny eggs.

"Will they take money?" said Diana.

"I doubt it—we can try. But it will have to be re-inforced with tea and sugar, I'm afraid."

The Siwan squatted opposite Anson, wrapping his robe close, eyes dark and watchful. "Come on. Divvy up your cash——" the captain was looking round at them, "—we can't hurry this, but we must be away as soon as possible." They felt in their pockets and Diana emptied her bag and the piles of notes and coin grew beside Anson. Tom noticed that when he thumbed through his own money, he pulled off three green pound notes and put them back in his pocket.

He looked up and smiled. "Rheingolds are fifteen ackers each, Tom. That's sixty a round. Three rounds, with tip—two pounds. The other one for luck. We'll be drinking them the day after tomorrow."

The Siwan looked at the money that was pushed over

189

to him and shook his head. Anson sighed. "Get out the tea and sugar—and a few tins of milk."

They put out handfuls of the first two on the cloth beside the eggs, the tins of milk near the dates. The Siwan watched carefully. All the time the sun was slanting lower through the palms above their heads. At last, without a change of expression, he made a gesture to indicate his side of the collection was theirs. Then he scraped the tea and sugar into bits of rag that he produced from odd parts of his person, stowed the money, and collected the tins of milk. He got up and turned on his heel without a word, leading the donkey off through the palms, while the sightseers faded away behind him. They were alone again.

Anson looked at his watch. "Six. They can be no nearer than forty miles to Siwa. That gives us a hundred start. Don't let's waste it."

Zimmerman said, "What are you going to do now?"

"Push off for the first ten miles—to the last ridge before the marsh. Then on again at first light, without waiting to eat."

"Wouldn't it be better—to push on a bit farther tonight?"

Anson just looked at him. "In the dark? I wouldn't move an inch on that stuff then—with all the hounds of hell after me."

They topped up the radiator and moved off, out from the shade of the palms. As they went east, skirting the edge of the cliff on a faint wandering track, the air seemed to get even more breathless. At Tom's suggestion, they clipped back the rear doors of the car, so getting a little relief from the wind of their passing.

Anson's voice came back through the open front door suddenly, as Tom sat opposite Diana on a bunk in the back.

"Ladies—and gentlemen. We are about to begin the passage of the Masrab Mahashash. The old camel road by which all bloody fools—since Alexander the Great—have returned from Siwa."

Diana looked across at him and smiled. "He seems so cheerful—so different."

He leaned forward and took her hands. "Yes," he said, "we're going to be all right now."

When they reached the last slope of the hard ground, it was in the grace of the last few moments before the sun went down behind the cliff and night descended like a curtain. In that little time, there was nothing to see ahead but a mysterious purple flatness that stretched to the horizon, flanked on their left by the diminishing perspective of the cliff buttress.

Anson made no bones about the next move. "As I have done it once before—and as I made the choice, I propose to do all the driving while we're on this lot. So I'm going to have a proper night's rest. I think Diana ought to have a full spell too—make certain that head of hers is right. You blokes can sleep all day tomorrow." Then he looked straight at Tom, "Let's have a shufty at that pump before I lay me down."

There was no point, there was nothing to be done to it, only look, but he opened the bonnet and waited till Anson came round on the other side. "I don't know there's anything we can do——"

"No, Tom—I just wanted a private word with you. I must get some rest before tomorrow—I'm not feeling too good," he was almost whispering it as they bent, heads together inside the bonnet—"but I rely on you—Zimmerman must NOT take one of those walks tonight. Whatever happens."

"But how can I——"

"Use your loaf, man. Do the same thing at the same time."

Then he had straightened and said, in that mocking, half-serious voice of his, "The curfew must not ring tonight——" and they had walked back to the cab; there had been a few directions, a watch to be kept for lights and noise, the eggs they had bought to be hard-boiled at the first brew, and then he had gone into the back of the car with Diana.

It was a difficult, uneasy watch. They had agreed to sit on the back of the ambulance, facing the direction of Qara, so that it would be easier to watch for lights, listen for sounds. The darkness was complete now, a blanket round them, the only noise came when a breath of wind bore back the noise of the dripping water from the front. But he didn't care any more, there was plenty of water now . . . plenty of everything. And he didn't mind that his captain was just behind him, asleep there in the dark, close to his girl.

He thought of her like that now, had done since the moment she had whispered in her sleep and rubbed her cheek against his hand. But he didn't know what she really thought . . . for a moment his mind jumped forward beyond their lonely battle . . . to what would happen afterwards. A warrant officer . . . and a nursing sister. Too difficult . . . there was nothing he could say.

They sat there huddled in blankets, silent. Suddenly, Zimmerman said, "What's that?" sharply. He got to his feet and peered round his side of the car.

"What, sir?"

"A noise—listen. . . ."

"It's only that water dripping."

"No, it was louder than that. You have a look your side—I'll take this. It came from the front of the car, I'm sure."

He walked down his side and up past the radiator, stopping to listen, but hearing nothing but the monotone of the dripping water. When he got back to the rear of the car, Zimmerman had disappeared.

He cursed softly, ran a few yards out from the car and went flat on his stomach, swinging his eyes round the level of the skyline, it was an old desert trick: there was always a little difference in the dark of ground and sky, and anything on the first would show up against the latter.

Over to the left . . . yes . . . there was something, a vague humped bulk jutting from the ground. He stared until his eyes smarted. Was it imagination—or was that thing beside it real, a thin dark line that was jerking up against the stars? . . .

"So that's it," he breathed and, regardless of noise, got up and ran towards it.

Zimmerman was standing up again when he reached him and it was too dark to see his face, or note anything more than that the pack was slung loosely over one shoulder.

The big man was peering about him. "I heard something—I swear it. Out near here."

Tom played for time. "Would you like to scout round a bit and see, sir? As long as we don't get too far from the car."

He looked at his watch as he walked, never more than a few yards from the captain. Nine o'clock—so it must have been about 8.55. He must tell Anson that. They made a wide aimless circle and then went back to the car. They sat on the step, huddled in their blankets, leaning back against the door, waiting. Soon there was a soft sound beside Tom and he turned to see the big head nodding forward on the chest, the hands falling limp from where they had been folded across the pack. Captain Zimmerman was going to sleep.

He waited, almost holding his breath, for a minute, then reached out gently towards the dark square on the other's lap. In the same instant, there was a grunt, the head jerked up and the body stiffened, just as he pulled his hand back in time. Zimmerman, yawning, said, "Mustn't do that, must I? Supposed to be on watch."

Tom said, "Yes, sir," and laughed.

"What's the matter?"

"Nothing, I was only thinking of something."

He couldn't tell him that it was about the certainty that neither could go to sleep for the fear of what the other might do. Only, it was going to be an awful long time before the dawn.

Zimmerman lay on his back, staring at the white ceiling above the bunk, feeling the gentle sway of the ambulance as it moved, hearing the creak of the body, the steady soft snores from the sergeant-major opposite. He was lucky to be able to sleep—Zimmerman could not. They had been two hours on the road, it was starting to heat up already, but there was no let-up, no peace for him. He lay there, dead-tired, yet wide awake, sweating . . . and thinking.

Were they very clever . . . or complete stupid fools? His mind dodged back over every incident . . . how they had reacted . . . how his own varying moods of contempt and wariness had pulled him this way and that like a straw in the wind.

Last night . . . had that been deliberate or an accident . . . when the sergeant-major had come blundering at him out of the dark, before he had even got the aerial right up and had had no chance to transmit? Was it coincidence that it was the only time there had been anything to transmit—that Siwa was undefended. And what had he been thinking . . . the rest of the night, as they both struggled to keep awake, so correct, only speaking when spoken to, but even then with a barrier of reserve he could never penetrate?

There was something else that made it all the more difficult. Increasingly, he liked them—and it was dangerous to like those you had been taught to despise.

The girl. He thought of her for a moment, she had not cried or argued, done all she had been told—as much as any of them. And she had been kind to him when he had hurt his back. Anson?—there was only increasing respect now. The decadent Englishman of those lectures had gone, he had risen to the occasion, shown himself the leader not only by knowledge, but by authority. There was no question of taking orders from a vacillating drunkard now. He had seen a new man born.

It was an alliance, he supposed—a subconscious, growing challenge between them all against the worst the desert could do. He remembered the first time he had realised that, accepted it in those tearing seconds when he had held up the car. It had not been for them, or his mission, only against the thought of a long, cruel walk. And so—he had been committed, would keep it that way: help, and not think of his job until he had been brought safely through the net. Well, perhaps not quite . . . this was a personal thing, because he had been foiled last night. This evening, to show he could do it, though he doubted if the strength would reach them, he would send his call-sign only out for the last time.

He smiled. But he would remember them . . . and all they had done. He would keep their names, numbers, if he could get them. And when the Afrika Korps was victorious in Cairo, he would do what he could. . . .

No use trying to sleep now. He swung his legs to the floor, pulled on his boots and went out softly to the front of the cab.

The girl was in the passenger seat and she turned and smiled at him. "Sleep well? And how's the back?"

"Better, thank you—still just a little sore." He crouched down between them and stared out over the plain ahead.

There were no purple and brown shadows like those that had masked the Depression the night before; in their place, a dead flat mottled expanse, smooth, shading from patches of brown to yellow, grey to almost blue. Everywhere, it twinkled with flaking salt. There was no rotting vegetable smell of the oasis now; something else hung in the hot sticky air—clinging to everything, sour, metallic, like brass polish.

He looked to the south and far, far off the yellow haze of the Sand Sea just broke the horizon. To the other side, the great cliff hung like a curtain in folds, shadowed light and dark with valley and headland.

"What a place," he said.

The girl let her eyes follow it round. "I've just told Captain Anson it reminds me of a mouldy rice pudding." Anson, driving, laughed, and he joined in politely, although there seemed little point.

"Twelve miles in the last forty minutes," said Anson. "We're safe from behind now. Actually, I doubt if they would be half-way from Siwa to Qara yet."

"How's the track?"

"Easy for the first ten miles—lots of new tyre marks, that lot of yesterday, I suppose. Then they branched off towards the cliff as I expected, but I managed to pick up the other way. It's faint—it would be after two years, but I can just see enough."

"Is it straight all the way?"

"For the next forty miles—more or less. Then there's a fork, and we'll have to watch that. It's marked '?? White Stone ??' on the map. Helpful—but if we turn the wrong way—to the right—we'll land up hundreds of miles to the south, in the Bahariya Oasis."

While he was talking, Zimmerman had been looking at the ground ahead and to the sides of them. The track —and there were faint lines, like a road where the tram rails had been taken up—stretched straight on to the horizon. But that was not the only mark of the way they were following: there was a slight, subtle change in the appearance of the ground. For about the width of an ordinary road, it curved up, lighter in colour, more gravel-strewn, the salt flakes closer, sometimes showing as solid blocks. On each side, the ground was smooth hard mud, cracked finely into an octagonal pattern, it went on unending, only changing in the shade of colour. It looked so firm and safe. He wondered if Anson, or his own General Staff, knew what they were talking about.

The air was getting hotter, damper. He found that he was beginning to pant. He looked down at the girl beside him, and there were the dark stains of sweat spreading down her shirt from under the arms, then he felt the first trickle of his own running down between the shoulder-blades.

Anson jerked suddenly from his crouch over the wheel, sniffed, and bent forward, listening intently with his head cocked sideways though his eyes were still on the track.

"That engine's getting bloody hot," he said. Then he bent forward and switched off and, as they coasted to a halt, another sound was coming above the noise of the tyres. A rumbling bubble from the front of KATY. When they had stopped, the front of the bonnet was wreathed in billowing steam.

"What is the matter, sir?" It was Tom, pushing past him from the back.

"Boiling like a bitch—but we topped up before we started. I can't understand it."

"Must be something to do with no wind—and the density of the air. Don't forget we're below sea level."

They jumped down and came round the bonnet as Tom opened it, showing no longer a clean engine, but caked sand and oil and spattered rust. While they were waiting for her to cool, Anson said, "No walking sideways off the track—everything fore and aft from now on. Diana, you take the back stretch—we'll keep in front."

It took a long time for her to get cool and when they topped her up, they found they had lost three pints.

They went on and this time it was only ten miles before she boiled, the next time seven, the next four. Hotter ... hotter ... the sweat pouring off them now, the plain heaving in steady waves, the northern cliff fading and then shooting forward again in the mirage. There was nothing else but the brassy sky that seemed almost filled by an ever-growing sun.

They hardly spoke. He did not ask, could not ask, if they felt as he did, that raging thirst, the lack of any desire for food, the feeling of being pressed down into their own little world as they crept across hell. Hotter ... the cliff had gone now. Nothing but that heaving mottled plain.

In turns they went to the back to lie on the bunks, panting at the stream of hot air that drifted by in the speed of their passing. All except Anson. Zimmerman wondered how long Anson would stand it—sitting there mile after mile, hunched over the wheel, hands slipping in their own sweat as they clenched the rim, all through that endless morning. He felt an odd surge of pride—in what he did not understand—when, after the sergeant-major had said once, diffidently, "Let me take a spell, sir," he was turned on with a savage, "Jesus Christ, Tom! I got you into this—and if anyone is going to make a final balls of it, I will."

At last something came out of the mirage in front of them and did not fade away as they approached. It was a single patch of colour that cleared to a flat white rock, just to the left of the track. "White stone," said Anson, and cut the motor and when they stopped leaned forward over the wheel as the clouds of steam billowed up in front of them. Stiff-legged, he got down from the driving seat and walked round to the back of the car. "Brew-up if you want to," he jerked over his shoulder as he went.

They left him for a time, but they were too exhausted to do more than make tea and hard-boil the eggs in the water; as all the cans were hot, it did not take long. When they had managed to swallow an egg each and chewed at the sweet stickiness of the dates, Zimmerman looked across at Tom Pugh and said, "He must eat something—otherwise——"

But Tom looked down at his feet. "I'd rather not do it—after this morning——"

Zimmerman had looked across at Diana. "Will you come?"

They put a mug of tea and some dates and an egg they had shelled and broken on the back of his map-board and took it into the back of the car. Anson was flat on a bunk, eyes open, bare chest jerking in convulsive pants.

The girl said, "Here's your grub, George."

"Grub," he said, "I don't want any."

"But you must——"

He turned his head slowly. "Is that an order, Sister? Yes, Sister, if you say so." Then his eyes slewed round to Zimmerman. "What's he—the matron? You would make a bloody good matron, Zimmerman." And he started to laugh—or tried to, but no sound came, only a quicker shaking of the throat and chest.

Zimmerman pushed past the girl. He shouted, "Eat

it," in a parade-ground voice and between them they managed to lift him up and hold him while he swallowed the pieces of egg. He whispered, "I feel bloody," and Zimmerman picked him up as if he were a baby, carrying him through the open door at the back to sit him on the step. He held him with one hand and said, "A can of water, Sister," and when she had passed it he tilted the whole of the two gallons over the head and the neck and the body, so that it ran down off the step and was sucked into the salt like a sponge. Then he scooped up the wet limp body in his arms again and carried him back inside; he saw that he was asleep before he had put him down. All the time the girl had been watching without a word.

He looked at her now, shame-faced almost, as he muttered, "A can of water—so little—for a brave man." Then he went round to the front of the car before she had time to answer.

The sergeant-major was there, head pillowed on his arms against the steering wheel as he slumped in the driving seat. He touched his shoulder and said, "Sergeant-major, the captain is asleep. But I think he would like you to go on. Would it be of any help if I went and sat out in front to help guide you?"

Tom's head had jerked up. "Not out there—in this heat. You would fry, sir. No. Come and sit here by me —and we'll manage somehow."

Perhaps because they had eaten, things seemed a little easier in the afternoon. By six they were forty miles farther on, ten halts for the boiling behind them, three more gallons of precious water gone. Anson was still asleep in the back, reported Diana, who had stayed with him. He had woken twice and asked for a drink, had not displayed the slightest interest in the fact that they were moving.

It was Tom who called a halt. There was no reason

200

for it from any consideration of geography. It was the eleventh boiling. He said, "We can't go on overheating her like this. Let's call it a day now—it will give us a better chance for tomorrow."

They just stopped. No turning off, no looking for shelter in that emptiness. The faint thread of the track went on and on in front, the firmer mark of their own tyres thinned to nothing behind them.

The sun was lower now, the mirage gone. No northern cliff was there to keep them company, only to the south the faint yellow, jagged line of Sand Sea, with the hazy plumes blowing sideways from the points like smoke from a row of factory chimneys.

"There must be a wind up there—to blow the sand off like that," said Tom.

Zimmerman grunted. "I wish the bloody thing was down here."

Slowly, drained of all energy, they fumbled over the making of the brew, and it was nearly finished when Anson came out of the back, followed by the girl. He did not remark on what had happened except to say, "Sorry to have been so long." He sat on the sand, sipping his tea, looking at the map-board. "Did you take the speedo reading?" he said.

"Yes. Forty-two from the white stone."

They all watched while he measured. "That's good. Only——" he turned to look down at the wheels of the ambulance "—only I wish we had got a bit farther. This part is the lowest of the whole issue. We're sitting on top of a bloody jelly here. We'll have to watch out she doesn't bog down in the night." He looked better, Zimmerman thought, the eyes were really taking in what they saw, the fallen-in look gone from the face in all he could see through the beard. But then he stared sideways at the smooth, flat mud, stretching unending on and on. It looked so firm, so safe. For the second time he thought, 'He doesn't know what he is talking about. . . .'

When they had finished, Anson said, "Tom—do the headlights work on this crate?"

"Should do, sir. But of course, we had them all disconnected."

"Well, in case of anything——" he looked at the wheels again, "wire them up. And have the sand-mats out ready."

The heavy air was cooling now. They sat on, smoking, basking in the blessed relief. They watched the sun go down, blood-red, behind them and the purple shadows flood out once more over the flats. Just before it was dark, Anson got up and went to the back of the car; he came out with two of the white water cans, walked ten yards back and put one down, then forward past the radiator to leave the other the same distance in front.

Then he came back to them. "Your territory behind, Diana, we'll take in front. You can sight on the gleam of the can going out, the bulk of the car coming back. But don't go a step sideways." He looked over his shoulder to where the sergeant-major was bending over the bonnet, fixing the wiring of the lights. "Did you hear that, Tom?"

"Yes, sir."

Zimmerman wanted to smile. Already there was a twinge of regret at his earlier feelings. They were not worth it. But . . . why this business about the lights . . . the detailing of the only path he could take . . . right in their range? Did Anson believe in these fantastic preparations . . . or was it a trap?

The other side of his thinking surged up stronger within him. Did they think him that much of a fool? . . . Then he would transmit tonight, even though no one might hear him. Just to show these clever English.

202

It would be amusing when they saw his footprints on the mud in the morning. . . .

He waited, smoking and listening to the snatches of dying talk until it was quite dark. Eight-thirty . . . just right. The girl had gone to bed and the sergeant-major had said he was soon following. He and Anson were taking first watch to see that the wheels did not sink. A waste of time.

He got to his feet, stretched, and moved towards the cab to unclip the spade. "I won't be long." No one answered. He slung it over his shoulder and with the pack bumping on his back, started to stroll away down the track ahead.

When the gleam of the water can came up to him, he turned sideways and took six quick steps to the right. His boots felt the gentle fall-away of the ground and then he was on the smooth mud, as firm and solid as he had expected.

Crouching, he fumbled with the straps and soon the flap was open in front of him. He was just feeling for the knob to extend the aerial, when the darkness was rent by the searing white light of the twin headlamps. The suddenness was a physical shock as they fanned out to miss him by a yard.

As he went flat, he swore. So that was it. Anger welled up in him at the charity he had wasted. Crouching again, bending double over the pack clutched to his chest, he started running farther sideways, away from the light.

The first steps were normal . . . but then something happened. The foot on which he had his weight would not come forward in the next stride, and for a moment he was left like that with the other one pawing the air. To regain balance, he dropped it quickly, hard.

There was a soft, shivering sigh . . . a crackling that

spread away from him in every direction over the mud. Now the back leg was up to the calf in tepid treacle that pulled . . . and pulled. He twisted, falling on his side, and the crust crumbled beneath him. The comfort of those headlamps seemed so far away now.

A horrible sour smell was coming up all around, and with it a noise . . . slow, heavy bubbling, like washing on the boil. But that steady downward tugging was the worst.

He started to scream.

X

DIANA was getting ready to slide under her blanket when she heard the first of the chain of events that led up to those screams.

After she had been out behind the car, she had come in through the back door and switched on the interior light—for Anson had said it didn't matter now they were so far out. Then she had got mirror and comb from her handbag and started to try and do something with her face and hair.

The door to the front had been ajar, and she could hear the soft murmur of the two men's voices. Then Anson had said, sharply, "NOW" and in the same moment the white reflection of the headlights had flooded back through the crack in the doorway. She dropped her bag and pushed through to see what was happening.

After so long, the twin beams, so white, so straight, seemed almost indecent. They slashed the track ahead, etching the faint marks of the old tracks, magnifying the height of the stones in the gravel, but there was no sign of anything else.

"What are you doing?"

Anson said softly, "Trying to catch our friend with his pants down," and Tom laughed.

She had started to say, "Well, you haven't," when the screams started; they came from ahead and to the right of them.

Tom shouted, "God! the bastard's gone in——" before Anson's voice cut in, tense and quiet.

"Start her up, Tom. Drive on slowly. Swing over a bit to the left of the track and come round to the right. But, for God's sake, don't go too far."

The headlights wavered a little to the left and then came round in a slow arc to the right. Anson was standing in the cab, ripping off his shirt, then boots and stockings, as his hand reached for the buckle of his shorts, he said, "Sorry, Diana—but that stuff stinks." Then, pale and slim in the headlight reflection, he was at the front wings, uncoiling the long, bamboo-stiffened strips of canvas that were the sand-mats.

At the edge of the light, something low and dark showed . . . another few degrees and it was in the centre of them. Tom stopped the car.

The mud looked grey and ten yards out on it there was a darker patch, jagged, with cracks running away from it like a hole in a frozen pond. In the middle, something that moved . . . a black slug that raised an arm at slow intervals to paw the air. The screaming was coming from it.

All was confused after that. There were vague memories of a naked Anson stepping out gingerly towards the hole as he unrolled a sand-mat in front of him; Tom wrenching off his clothes and following with the second one from a slightly different angle; shouting,

205

being told to stay where she was. Then they were both lying flat, reaching out to that black thing that had stopped moving, crawling backwards, dragging it after them, foot by foot, until they were safe at the edge of the track. The smell came back to her in great waves . . . the soft puffing of the bubbles. She was not looking at them now—only at that dark patch centred in the glare of the lights. On it, rocking, was a square pack. Slowly, it tilted to one side and disappeared.

Anson's voice was the first thing that came back to her, panting, as they dragged Zimmerman to the car. "A can of water—quick. Then look at the wheels and see if they're sinking. I wish to God we had a drink."

When she came back, she had the water and her flask. She said, "The wheels look all right." They were kneeling beside him, stripping off the stinking, sodden bush-shirt and she saw that it was split right down the back. Then Tom took the water from her and started to dash it over Zimmerman's face while Anson tried to clean out his mouth and nose and ears. She held the flask without speaking and he took it and opened it unblinking and poured the spirit back into the mouth so that it spilt down his chin and on to his chest. Zimmerman choked and spluttered and the breath came out of him in long uneven shudders.

"He'll be all right now——" Anson had got to his feet and was holding out the flask. "But we must move on a bit before we try to clean him up. Once that's happened, the whole strata's disturbed and the track might collapse."

They got Zimmerman on the step and Anson held him there while Tom backed the car to the centre of the track, very gently. When they were straight, Anson said, "Wait a minute."

While Tom held the sagging body, he got down and

went to the side of the track where the bush-shirt lay in a dark heap. He lifted it, holding it at arm's length, walking into the glare of the headlights to turn it round, looking carefully. Then, going to the edge of the mud, swung it to gain momentum and then threw it out so that it landed with a dull splash in the middle of the hole. He came back wiping his hands against his naked flanks. "He won't be needing that any more," he said.

When they had moved on fifty yards, they set about the task of cleaning both themselves and Zimmerman. Water was too precious and they used petrol. The smell of it was sweet beside that of the sour metallic mud. As she helped them soak and scrape and rub off with one of the blankets, it did not seem at all out of place. She thought, suddenly, of all the blanket baths she had done as a probationer—wondered if there had ever been another one like this.

They managed to get the silent, semi-conscious Zimmerman into the back and covered him up. When they had got outside again, she reached to the hip-pocket for the flask and held it out. "It's mine—but I think you've earned it."

Anson shook his head. "Not me—I'm concentrating on that Rheingold. You—Tom?" And when Tom had said "No" he went on, "I should keep it for Zimmerman, Diana. He's still pretty rough." Then he turned and switched off the headlights. "That's enough of them—though even if a plane did see them here, they just wouldn't believe it."

The darkness seemed intense after the headlights, she could only hear them groping for their clothes. Anson's voice came, "I'll see how he is—and get some blankets out. We'd all better kip down on the sand for tonight."

She said, "That pack——" and stopped.

"I know—I saw it. Closer than you did. Now it's gone—we need not discuss it."

They showed her how to make a hole for her hip and then they all curled up in a row on the sand and it was quite comfortable. Sleep came very fast and it seemed only the next second that the scratching noise wakened her. It was daylight, Anson was squatting a few feet away from her with a tin of petrol beside him, scrubbing away at Zimmerman's shorts with a stone. He stopped to smile at her.

"Good morning. We let you lie in. Tom's making breakfast and I'll bring it to you in bed." He held up the shorts. "That's the best I can get them. I've done the boots, but the stockings are impossible. I'll take them in to his lordship and tell him the rest of his stuff has gone down in the drink."

When he came back out of the car, she looked at him enquiringly. "He's O.K. Tried to make a speech, but I told him to forget it."

Both of them were beside her, eating eggs and dates, sipping tea, when Zimmerman came out of the back to join them. He had a blanket draped round his shoulders and she thought he looked so much older—as old as he had after the time he had held the ambulance on his back. A surge of pity went through her. 'When there are other things . . . that is what I must remember,' she thought.

Zimmerman came and squatted down beside them, he took the food offered him and ate it in silence. Then he put his tea down and cleared his throat.

"I wish to speak of last night—I——" She was looking at the streaks of blue-grey mud that still mottled his neck. But there was something else different . . . the voice seemed to have changed, deeper, more guttural, the accent not so clipped. . . .

No one said anything, Zimmerman took another date, chewed it, and spat out the stone. Then he looked at Anson. "It was madness—to disobey your orders, Captain."

"Well, it turned out all right, Zimmerman. Except that you've lost your pack and your shirt. But you'll have a tale to tell your pals—won't he, Tom?"

"He will indeed, sir."

Anson went on quickly before the big man could speak, "Now—today. It should be easier. Only sixty-five miles to the end of this rice pudding. With halts, I should say, five hours. We should be there at three, but it may take a time to find a good place to get up the cliff, even though they are much lower there. We can't be at the top much before dusk—and that last run to the coast, it's about sixty on one bearing, and I don't want to do that in the dark. I think the thing is to find the best place, lie up there, and then do the climb and the last leg in one crack tomorrow."

It was not as bad as the day before. The air seemed cooler and not so sticky, the view not quite so desolate as the ground rose and fell in slow waves that always gained a little in height. The track had edged close to the southern side of the Depression now and sometimes they had to cross thin tongues of hard ground that reached out into the mud flats. Beyond this, the dunes were still there, but they had not the massive structure of the Sand Sea, they were lower, in colour a paler yellow, and they could see the thin crests, ragged as a horse's mane, where the sand had blown sideways. "Ramak Dunes," said Anson, "—impassable."

On their other flank, the cliff was closing fast. It was lower too, more broken and in places there were what looked to be smooth, easy slopes. They still had to make their halts for the boiling radiator, but the gap between was creeping up . . . from six miles . . . to eight . . . to ten. At one halt while she stood by the bonnet, waiting for the engine to cool, a few puffs of wind came down from the north to ruffle her hair. It was hot and dry, but it was the first movement of air she had felt for days.

Soon the mud flats dwindled to isolated patches, there was a different sound to the movement of their tyres. Then the northern cliff curved round in front of them to block the way to the east.

They had made it. They were through the Depression. Tom, driving, gave a great shout, and Anson, sitting on the floor beside her, said, "Take her in at a gallop." She turned from the passenger seat and stepped over him to go into the back of the car. Zimmerman was lying there, quite still, naked but for his shorts.

She said, "We're at the end of the Depression, Captain Zimmerman. We've made it."

But he did not answer, did not even look at her. He lay there, hands clasped behind his head, staring up at the roof as he had done all day.

They turned towards the north end of the cliff, running close along it, looking for a likely place. She saw there were plenty of breaks in the rock wall now, all steep, covered with a smooth fall of sand that seemed to pour down between the spurs of rock from the level above. At last, Anson said, "That looks a good one," and they stopped and walked over to where the end of the sand-fall met the desert floor.

He started to walk up it, slowly, carefully. When they began to follow, he looked back over his shoulder and called, "No. Stay where you are. We don't want to disturb the pattern more than we need."

"Pattern——?" She turned to Tom.

"I forgot. On a slope, the grains always lie in a

certain way to each other. Once that's mucked up, they don't grip—start sliding. And our wheels wouldn't grip."

They stood watching Anson climb on. After the first few yards, she saw his feet were digging in, slipping back a little at each step, while the sand flowed down silent over the toes of his boots. When he came down to them he seemed preoccupied.

"It's pretty dodgy, Tom. I don't remember it being anything like as bad as that when we came last time."

Tom just looked at him and said, "You only had to come down it—then."

"Well, we had better look at one or two others."

They tried six in all, but the sand was the same and they came back to the first because it seemed the lowest. They camped a little way from it and had started the tea going when Zimmerman came out of the back of the car for the first time that day.

As they ate, between mouthfuls, Anson gave them details of the remaining supplies. "Thirty-two gallons of juice—that's ample, fourteen gallons of water, four sweet, and the rest from Qara. Seven days' vehicle rations untouched. And it's only a hundred miles to Alex." He looked over his shoulder to the sand slope behind them, glowing red-gold in the setting sun. "We'll go up that like a dose of salts in the morning— and you'll be drinking that Rheingold in Alex by six, Zimmerman."

Zimmerman did not answer.

Tom said, "Couldn't we spare a couple of gallons of the bad water now—to have a good clean up? I wouldn't like to be seen in a town like this."

Anson laughed. "A wash and brush up? We haven't got the razor—what about poor Zimmerman? He hasn't got a shirt."

Zimmerman spoke suddenly, "There's soap and a razor in that small pack of mine. Help yourselves."

"Well——" She could see Anson hesitating, "—it mightn't be a bad idea at that." He looked across at her. "I'm sure you could do with a swill, Diana. All right—a gallon for us, and a gallon for you. Would you like it heated?"

"Just tepid," she said, "straight out of the can."

They found her a tin and she went round to the back of the ambulance and stripped off all her clothes. It was heaven to feel the dry air flowing over her body and let the luke-warm water trickle down the back of her neck to spread out over her spine and fall down her thighs. With the dirty ball of her last handkerchief she scrubbed away all the stains and sand; there was only a pint of soupy, grey liquid left when she had finished, but she managed to wash out her socks in it and then hung them on the back step to dry. The clothes felt quite different when she put them on again, and barefoot she went round to the front of the car to join the others.

Tom was just finishing his shave. As he wiped his face on a towel she had not seen before—presumably from the Zimmerman haversack—and smiled at her, she hardly recognised him.

He said, "Captain Anson thought we might like to have the first shift. He's gone in the back with Zimmerman—he's still a bit worried about him."

"Shift——? What are we supposed to watch for? there's nothing to watch, now."

He looked at his feet. "I don't think that was quite his idea. He said, "Stooge around if you want to—but don't get lost.""

So it had come at last. She said, "All right—if you like. As it's the last night, let's go for a bit of a stroll."

He said, "What about your feet—won't they get sore like that?"

"No, I like it. It makes me feel clean."

They walked off along the hard flat bottom below the cliffs, towards the red ball of the sun that was dipping below the Depression, turning the rock walls into all the lovely shades of pink she had ever imagined. She thought of what had been said about it being the last night and where she would be that time tomorrow. She imagined for a moment the comfort, the table-cloths and the soft lights of the sisters' mess, the cutlery and china plates, and someone saying, "What was it like?" But she knew that she could never tell them. Tom was very quiet and she thought again. 'It was just one of those things—you must have imagined it all. So save your dignity, Diana. There isn't much else left.'

Soon the night came down and the stars pricked out one by one. She looked back and the ambulance was a vague blur over to the east. Without a word being spoken, they sat down at the foot of one of the sand slopes and Tom pulled out his cigarettes. As they smoked, the talk strangled in shorter sentences, died. Suddenly he got to his feet, throwing away his cigarette. "We'd best be going back."

"Why, Tom——?"

"Because it's better."

"But, why——?" She had got up to face him.

In the starlight she could see that he had turned his head away.

"Tomorrow," he said, "you'll be back in your hospital —a nursing sister—with two pips up. I'm a W.O. It— everything—would be too difficult . . ." His voice trailed away.

"But would it be——?"

"It might——" his voice was rough, "and it would

spoil even this. I want to keep this—don't you understand. . .?"

Time dripped out its slow seconds under the silent circling stars. She stood close, looking at him, eyes nearly level with his. "Am I that stiff, snobbish nursing sister now?"

"No."

"What am I, then?"

He did not answer, only turned his head away blindly, like something that is hurt. She said, very softly, "I think I know what I am—to you—now. I'm going to put my pride in my pocket and say that I'm hoping, so hoping, that I'm right. And I want to be like that to you, always. . . ."

There was only a dry sob and he was stumbling forward into her arms, and as she held him tight she knew that she was the last refuge for all the sorrow and loneliness of two barren years.

Afterwards, when they had finished the lovers' first bout of "Do you remember", they lay back against the soft warm sand, heads pillowed on arms, looking up at the wonder of the heaven.

She said, suddenly, "What was your wife's name?"

"Ann."

"Tom—do you think she would mind?"

He did not answer for so long that she turned to look. The dark eyes beside her were staring up, fixed on Orion. "Would she?" she said again.

He answered very softly, "I've never believed in much. But if she's somewhere—outside all that, then she'd say O.K. She was always so unselfish. I liked watching the cricket in the summer—and if she was tied up, with the teas, or the chickens, she would always make me go. It made her happy to see me happy—even if she couldn't join in."

214

"That makes me feel sort of cheap—a pick-up——"

"No."

There was silence again, then she said, "Are you, by any chance, working round to a proposal, Tom?"

"Sort of——"

"Then you needn't say any more. Because I accept, darling. But I'll always remind you that I——" The rest was lost as his big square hand was placed over her mouth.

"I've only been trying to think of all the complications —on your account."

"I can look after myself," she said.

When they got back the car was dark and silent and there was a neat pile of blankets stacked outside with the glimmer of a white piece of paper pinned to the top. Tom pulled it off and took it over to the dashboard light to read. She heard him chuckle and then he stuffed it in his pocket.

"What does it say?"

"Personal to me—from the captain—and it's rude."

She was aghast. "But he can't know——"

"Know? He's not a fool. And he's back in his old form again. That's what matters."

"He's nice, Tom. One of the nicest blokes I've ever met."

"They don't come any better than that," he said.

They made their beds together, side by side, and when they were down, she spread the blankets over both of them and came close, pulling his head down on her shoulder. "You sleep," she whispered, "I'll take the time from your watch—wake you before the others. You've got the worst of the driving tomorrow."

He lay still for a while and then turned his head restlessly.

She said, "What's the matter, darling?"

"I'm worried."

"About us——?"

"No. That sand up there. It's going to be dodgy."

"Leave it till tomorrow. You sleep now."

He said drowsily, "The captain said we'd go up like a dose of salts—I hope so." He did not speak again and soon she felt the steady rise and fall of his side against her breast. She held him close, thinking of everything, not back, only forward—the village, the garage . . . children. A tender smile played on her mouth and then she stared across the Depression floor to that sand-fall on the cliff, pale in the starlight, silent and challenging. "We'll go up you like a dose of salts, we will."

But they didn't.

XI

THE scheme was that the three of them should walk half-way up, leaving Tom to rush KATY up on her own, and run on behind, pushing if necessary.

The dawn was just coming when they made a start, she and Anson going up one side against the cliff wall, Zimmerman on the other. As she plodded up behind the captain, she looked across and back down the slope. It did not vary in angle from top to bottom, smooth, unbroken, the colour of clotted cream. She noticed that with every step her feet would sink in and slide back a little as the sand in front ran down, slithering over her ankle with a soft, persuasive sound. Like the others, she had gone barefoot.

About half-way up Anson stopped and said, "That's enough—he should be moving fairly well here. Just move across and get your shoulder to it and shove." He called across to Zimmerman, and he halted too.

The ambulance was clear in the new light below them, and it looked small and square, like one of those miniature toys. The noise of the engine starting came up to them and they saw it circle off to the far side of the hard ground below before turning to come straight at them, accelerating. The sound of the motor rose to a high-pitched snarl, KATY was flat out in third gear when she hit the bottom of the sand.

She seemed to rise up towards them as if she was in a lift, there was a feeling as though the car was stationary and the sand and the slope were running down it. The engine got louder and louder; under it Anson shouted, "I told you—like a bloody dose of salts." Twenty yards separated them . . . fifteen . . . and then Diana noticed something different.

The car had another movement now, beside the forward one. The bonnet seemed to buck from side to side as if it were a fresh horse trying to get its head; great plumes of sand were spurting from behind now, the sound of the engine no longer constant, but rising and falling in a sobbing. Then the whole thing slewed sideways as KATY seemed to sit down on her haunches. The motor cut to silence. When they had run over, she saw that the back wheels were buried up to the axles.

Tom looked at them from behind the wheel. "Too soft."

"Give me that spade," said Anson. "You, Zimmerman, get the sand-mats out. We'll dig her out and run her on to them. Then, Tom, you take her down backwards and have another go."

He tried twice more, and Anson three times, always making a fresh track, but they never got farther than the first mark. Always, just before that point, the wheels began to spin, the momentum went, and KATY would buck and bury her back wheels.

Minute by minute, the sun rose higher, hotter. Now that smooth slope was furrowed like a ploughed field. Then, at the sixth attempt, KATY started to boil.

Anson glowered at the steam billowing from the bottom of the rust-splashed radiator. "We'll have to take her up on the sand-mats—six feet at a time."

Two on each side, they took it in turns to clear a level trough in front of the back wheels and feed in the mats, holding them taut until the tyres had taken a grip. They made the whole length the first time and about half the second, before one wheel started spinning and sank in. The third time, nothing. Both mats ripped through to shoot out behind like two snakes while the tyres showered up sand as they bit their way down to axle level.

It was then that Anson seemed to go mad. He snatched the spade and threw himself down by the wheels, almost hacking at the sand in his fury.

"Get round the other side and dig," he shouted at them. "Don't just stand there——"

She said, "But you've got the spade."

"Well—use your bloody hands—but DIG. And when the mats are in, get round to the back—and push . . . PUSH."

After that he did everything except hit them. He seemed to be everywhere, never stopping, pushing and swearing at them . . . at KATY, tearing at the sand with his fingers. Once, when Zimmerman, bare to the waist, had stopped for a moment to wipe off the sweat, he turned on him, snarling, "Come on, man—you look like a Hyde Park whore—wondering how she's going to get through the winter." When she sniggered, he turned on her. "And if you'd stop grinning about your love-life, Diana, we might get this bitch nearer the top. Try

218

pushing—instead of leaning against the bloody thing."

It all became dream-like after that, a nightmare only pierced by the physical pain of her nails worn down to the quick from the scrabbling, the raw bruises on her shoulders from heaving at the back. But always beside her, pushing, cursing, there seemed to be Anson. Anson, with his yellow mask of a sweating sand-grimed face, the two holes in it that showed the insane eyes. . . . 'It mustn't happen . . . it mustn't,' she thought, '. . . he's going mad. . . .'

Twice she had slipped at the back and fallen on her face, while a sand-mat had smacked across her and the spurting sand had filled her nose and mouth and ears. Only afterwards, she remembered his sobbing voice beside her as he heaved and strained, "Get up—you bloody, sodding bitch——" and she did not know or care if he meant her or KATY. There was just one feeling now—that of a great resentment, they had all stripped off to the waist, they were cool. She felt the wet heavy weight of her shirt, the sweat trickling between her breasts. It wasn't fair . . . she'd show them . . . if he spoke to her like that again, she'd take it off.

Tom stopped it all. Suddenly, the engine cut, and as they sat down panting he came round to the back of the car. "It's no good, sir."

Anson, sitting on the sand with his head down between his knees, did not look up. "What do you mean—no good? You're a bloody fine one to talk—riding all the way."

The line of Tom's jaw hardened. "You told me to drive. I was meaning the engine. She's boiling—over heating all the time. And a seized motor won't get us to Alex."

"So what——? You want to walk, do you?" He looked wildly round at each face. "All right, b—— off,

the lot of you. Here's the compass——" there was a soft
sound as it fell at Tom's feet—"help yourselves to all the
water and food—keep on 30°—for two days. And I hope
it keeps fine for you. Only leave me alone."

He put his head between his knees and there was no
sound but the sawing of the breath in his throat. At last
he looked up again. "I'm going to get this bitch to Alex
—somehow. Do you understand——? I'm going to. It's
a personal thing."

Tom's voice was very gentle. "No one wants to walk.
I just thought we might try to wind her up."

Anson stared at him. "Wind her up—on the handle?
With the plugs out, you mean?"

"Yes. We've only done it over a few feet before. But
in reverse—the lowest gear—I don't see why it shouldn't
work."

"But how are you going to turn her round? She'll turn
over on a slope like this."

"I don't think so—not if everyone hangs on the inside
when she's across the angle."

Anson seemed to shrink. "You carry on." He got up
and walked over to the strip of shade by the far cliff wall.

Tom stood looking after him, then he said, "We'll dig
her out first. Then I'll let her go back and lock over
sideways. I shall do it right-hand down. So I want you
two to come and hang on the right side when I do it.
Lean out as far as you can—it may make just the
difference to stop her going over."

It took a long time to get her across the slope with Diana
and Zimmerman hanging out backwards as far as they
could. It seemed as if the angle was impossible, that any
moment the inside wheels would lift up under them, and
KATY would roll over down the hill. But Tom, from
the driving seat, said, "It's all right," and then he put
the steering hard over the other way and coaxed her

with the engine until they were facing downwards. In doing it they had lost all the ground they had made in the last hour.

She said, "What do we do now?"

"Wait—until the bloody plugs are cool enough for me to get out."

She left him and went over to the boulder by the cliff where Anson had stayed all the time, sitting with his head down. He was still breathing like a man who has run a losing race. She said, "He's turned her, George. He's waiting for the plugs to cool, he says. But I don't understand what he's trying to do."

He didn't answer for a moment, then to the ground, between his legs, he said, "Sorry—it's just that I counted so much—on getting there today."

"But we will—please tell me what he's up to."

He didn't seem particularly interested. "If you take the plugs out of the engine—there's no resistance from the compression. You put her in the lowest gear, that's reverse, and just wind the handle in front—the starting handle. Because the gear is so low, the wheels move so gradually that they don't disturb the pattern of the sand grains, and grip. That's the theory."

She looked up the yellow mound that went on ahead of them. It was only a hundred yards before it ended in the line of clear sky. For a moment she wondered why no one had bothered to trudge up and see if it was really the end of their troubles. Then she understood—no one had dared.

There was a noise from the ambulance and she saw that it was Tom shutting the bonnet and going round to the radiator with the starting handle. She held out both hands. "Come and watch him, George. Please. He's trying so hard."

By the time they had got over he had started turning

slowly, winding in rhythm like a man with a barrel-organ. It did not seem to take any effort. He looked up at them and smiled; without stopping the winding, he said, "I've just worked it out—thirty-two turns to every six feet up—that's if there's no slipping."

They went round to the back wheels, silent, watching them. They were turning, but so slowly that they hardly seemed to move at all, but as each bar in the tyre tread dipped down to bite at the sand, though it sagged, there was a fresh clean surface waiting to take the next one. . . .

"Look——!" It was Anson, crouching now behind one wheel. The firm pattern of the tread was beginning to show, moving away back from it. They were rolling up—not slipping.

"It's working, Tom!"

Tom, winding, not stopping, said, "I thought it would."

They took it in shifts after that, five hundred turns each. When it came to her, she was surprised at the little effort necessary to wind the great bulk of KATY backwards up the slope. It seemed that at any moment she must lunge forward, down at the one in the front, but they told her they had lashed the gear lever in position, so that it could not happen.

The sun was high now and Anson had ruled that the one winding should have Zimmerman's towel draped over their head and neck. But it was so slow. . . . Each in turn they wound, watching in achievement the straight, firm tracks stretching out behind them. But in between the two, there was something else . . . and she knew it was not so good. At inches distance, dark blobs on the sand where the drops fell from the radiator. When Tom came round as she was winding, he stared and then scuffled the trail out with the toe of his boot. "Don't let

Captain Anson see," he whispered, "he's got enough—already."

498 . . . 499 . . . 500. Each in turn reached the magical number and handed over to the next. Zimmerman was at it now, and there was only ten yards left to the unknown, beyond the barrier of sky. But no one made a move to find out if there was another ridge beyond.

Then Anson broke the tension. "Hold it, Zimmerman. We may as well look—and know the worst." They all scrambled up the last few feet to the top.

It was the end. There was nothing but a flat, stony plain that stretched on towards the horizon, with a faint ridge showing to the north-west. There was something else, a wind, hot, dry, bearing down on them from the north. As she stood there, feeling it search inside her clothes, pulling at the strands of her hair, she felt cleaner, happier, in the first moment.

Anson looked at his watch and then back down the slope to KATY just below, then the long, long way to the bottom. "Two and a half hours—for a quarter of a mile——" Then he gripped her arm and pointed. "But —look——"

The sky had that brassy tinge that she knew so well that she hardly noticed it. Now, to the north, almost on the horizon, it shaded to a deeper, clearer blue.

"The reflection of the sea," he said.

She sat between them, back to the door, feet straight out, listening to the singing.

Things had gone well since they had cranked KATY over the top. The radiator had been filled, she had heard the course—"Sixty miles on 68°, Tom. And if I can navigate at all, we'll finish slap in the middle of Burg el Arab railway station." It had been funny to hear of an ordinary everyday thing like that.

The singing was of no quality, even though it came from her too. Zimmerman had disappeared to the back, Anson was driving, Tom in the passenger seat, while she, between them, listened; not caring if they were out of tune, only happy because they were. As they went steadily over the plain, their spurs went jingle jangle jingle as they went riding merrily along, Casey waltzed with his strawberry blonde, and then came the detailed recital of the peculiar misfortunes of one Samuel Hall.

She did not try and join in; for one thing, she was not sure if she should know the words. It was nicer to let it all flow over her head, to think about more important things—how long it would take to learn the rudiments of keeping chickens, if she would ever understand enough to be able to work in the garage. . . . Without thinking, she put a hand sideways and took hold of Tom's.

"Oy, Oy." It was Anson from the other side. "Don't distract the navigator." Then, "I suppose I've got to do some congratulating."

She turned and smiled at him, not letting go.

"What do you think?"

"Another good man gone. But I think I'll wait—for active blessing on you—until we're at Burg el Arab. And I'm sure there aren't gentlemen in coal-scuttle helmets waiting to greet us."

She wondered if he meant that, looked away to the left, towards that faint ridge. But there was nothing in sight.

Tom's voice came, "We're counting on you—as best man, sir."

"No, Tom. I started the job—I'm going to finish it properly—give the girl away." Then he started singing, "Sand in my shoes" for no reason at all, and they all laughed because it didn't matter any more.

224

They went on steadily, there was no thought of stopping except to top up the radiator. The stages were getting shorter again, but at least KATY was not boiling the whole time. At one stop, Anson said, "Have a look at Zimmerman, will you?" and she went into the back of the car.

He was lying on his back, just as before, arms clasped behind his head. She said, "We're going well—half-way to the road already."

He did not seem to hear her the first time, so she said it again, and when he turned to look at her, there was something new, wary, in his eyes.

"What am I going to do about clothes," he said, "I can't go into the town with no shirt."

'Why not?' she thought—but she said, "We'll try and borrow one. Perhaps at the check post before Alex. We'll have to stop there and report."

"The check post——? Ah, yes."

They went on and twice they saw columns of vehicles to the north-west of them, but they were far off, running parallel, and impossible to identify. The ground was rolling now, with more sand in the bottom of the valleys and the first green things growing there—clumps of camel-thorn, once a stunted palm. The clear blue segment of the sky came farther and farther over their heads, the wind seemed cooler. At last, as they crested a rise, there was a row of thin wobbling rods in the mirage in front.

"Vehicles," said Tom.

Anson laughed. "No, you B.F. It's the telegraph line along the railway."

It cleared to that. Then they could see the tattered ant-heap that was the native village; beyond, the first proper building, the white walls and red roofs of Burg el Arab station. There was a train unloading, a swarm of khaki figures round it, but they were still too far away to be sure.

Anson leaned forward and peered at the speedometer. "I'm slipping. A mile short—and too far to the south." They changed course a point and went on slower, silent, searching for a sign. Then Tom said, "The flag, sir— just to the right of the station, on that dump. Red and blue—it's Ordnance." And then they knew they were right.

Across the railway track, bumping over the sleepers, with the troops working near-by turning to stare. Tom said, "Do you want to know the griff?"

"Hell, no. Let's press on. Four Rheingolds come before any bloody war."

They were on tarmac now—a real road at last—that led over the last ridge in a cutting. When they had reached the top the main road was below, crowded with traffic, all running west. Beyond, a thin line of palms and then the blue carpet of the sea. As they slowed down at the road junction to turn to the right, she saw the signpost.

It said, ALEXANDRIA 30 MILES.

XII

THE check post was at the junction with the Cairo road; much larger than Tom remembered it before—a small village of tents now.

Anson said, "Pull off in front of the office, Tom. I'll go in and grapple with officialdom."

They had been driving down the road for half an hour, doing a steady thirty with nothing to pass, nothing to overtake them; the stream of traffic was all going the other way. His eyes had lit as he saw the stuff that was destined for the front, wherever that might be: 25-pounders, tanks on their transporters—even under the camouflage, he could see there was a new type with the big gun mounted in the turret. 'Much more like it,' he thought. As the endless flow slid past them, men in the cabs would lean out and stare, sometimes a shout would be whipped into the emptiness behind. They did not wave or answer. They had been out of the world so long that unspoken consent held them in their own isolation. They did not want to know.

The palm-lined road was broken in places by fig groves. The only time that anyone spoke was when Diana said, "Oh, look——" and there, in a gap in the trees, was the sea again, so close, so cool, so inviting.

They were outside the tent with the flag now and Anson jumped down. "This is going to give them a shock. Give me your pay-book, Tom. Diana, have you got an identity card?" When they had handed them over, he looked towards the back of the car. "I'll fix him—but watch the back." He walked off into the office.

They stood waiting, leaning against the back of the car.

"Hadn't you better put that tin under, Tom?"

He looked at her. "That tin—not ever again. You don't understand quite how I feel about that tin. One top up before we start and that will see us through." Then he said, "Stay here. I'd better see how he is——" and climbed into the back.

Zimmerman was lying quite still, the blanket up to his chin; Tom could see the steady rise and fall of the barrel chest under it. But he also knew that he was not really asleep. He shut the door softly and went back to

227

Diana. He whispered, "Keep nearer those doors—he's pretending he's asleep."

They waited and no one in the camp came near them, only behind, the noise of the traffic on the road went on unabated. Then Anson came walking out of the tent with a tall captain of the Military Police and he watched her start to fuss with her hair, and said, "I shouldn't bother." Anson said, "Johnson—this is Sister Murdoch and M.S.M. Pugh," and they were shaking hands.

The captain looked at them as if they were beings from another world as he said, "Captain Anson's told me all about your trip. I think it's a bloody marvellous effort. I'll phone your hospital, Sister, and let them know you're coming." Then he looked at them again. "What about some grub—and a wash?"

He wasn't hungry—but a real wash, that would be something. Anson was shaking his head, though, saying, "I'd rather get on—unless you want to, Diana?"

"I'd love just five minutes, if I can."

The policeman said, "I'll show you my tent—and get that shirt for your South African pal at the same time." He looked towards the back of the car. "How is he—by the way?"

South African pal. . .? He opened his mouth to speak but Diana's fingers were biting into his arm. "Still asleep," she said.

The captain made to move off and then turned back. "Are you sure—you won't even have a drink?"

"No, thanks," said Anson. "We've got a date for that."

When they had gone, he stared at Tom. "Is he really asleep?"

"No—foxing. But, sir—aren't you going to turn him in?"

Anson gave him a strange look. "In good time, Tom.

All in good time. There's our date before that. But we'll have to watch him."

"But he'll rumble that—make a dash for it."

"I don't think so—not yet."

They had finished topping up the radiator when Diana and the captain came back. She looked a clean, very different person and Tom felt a surge of possessive pride in it. They climbed on board and the shirt was handed up. "The biggest I've got," said the captain, "I won't disturb him. Just see that he's handed over to his own people."

"I will—and see the shirt is sent back. Thanks for everything." Anson nodded at Tom and he let in the clutch and they were off on the last lap.

Anson was sitting on the floor now, Diana in the seat. He glanced down to where the captain was sitting cross-legged, with the shirt in his lap. He was undoing the shoulder tabs and pulling off the tubes of cloth that carried the three pips of a captain. "He won't be wanting those," he said.

The outskirts of Alex were appearing now, the clusters of houses perched on the side of the road, the Greek restaurants with their shady verandahs, the sea running close on their other side. Anson got to his feet. "I'll take him his present—and stay and make polite conversation for a bit. Those back doors open easily."

When he had gone, Tom listened to Diana's chatter, excited as she pointed out little ordinary things . . . half-listened to it, for there was something else more important to hear. The trained ear that always listened subconsciously to the beat of the engine had noticed something different . . . a fast regular clicking. Perhaps it had started on that last bitter slope—when she was overheating so badly. It didn't matter when, really. But the bearings were beginning to break up.

In instinct, he took his foot off the accelerator and let her coast, then picked up a little power, gingerly. Another quarter-mile and then from the back, on the other side, came that sudden sharp crack they had heard before. KATY sagged to the right and he swore and let her ride to a gentle halt. Anson's head came round the door. "What the hell, Tom?"

"It's that other —— spring," he said.

"Well, out of it—all of you." He looked back into the car. "And you—Zimmerman." They all got down in the road and walked round to where the clean, bright break of the main leaf stuck out behind them.

Tom scratched his head. "We could stop a truck—scrounge a lift, sir."

Anson stared at him. "A lift——? What the hell are you talking about? I just worked out with Zimmerman —we've done nearly six hundred miles, over every kind of stuff—and there's four left to do. No, we'll take her in on blankets. We've done it before, and I'm not leaving the old bitch now. Get the jack out." He smacked KATY's olive bonnet hard.

Tom, busy with showing the others how to roll the blankets from the back into tight sausages, wondered why Anson had got out the tool kit for a job when it would not be needed; understood, when he saw him take the largest wrench, holding it loose in one hand as he watched Zimmerman all the time.

On the other side of the road the traffic rushed by within feet of them, at their backs the sea hushed softly against the beach. But they did not notice either, nor the crowd of darting, chattering Arab children that had ringed round, waiting to steal anything that opportunity offered. They were back in their own special world.

The blankets were rolled in tight bundles and then wedged between the spring and the jacked-up chassis.

When the space was filled, the jack was lowered, squeezing the two together. KATY sagged, but not quite so much as before. Then Tom bound the whole with rope, down the sides and along, to prevent slipping. All the time, Anson stood to the side, swinging the spanner, watching Zimmerman. A silent Zimmerman, who looked strangely smart in the shirt that was two sizes too small for him.

Tom straightened. "There's another thing, sir. A big end. Come and listen." He opened the bonnet, started her up and worked the throttle. Anson frowned. "Big end as well—sounds like number four."

"Shall I take the plug out, sir?"

"God—yes. We'll go in on five cylinders and a pile of blankets. He looked round them all, swinging the spanner gently. "And we want the weight as far forward as we can get it—so you can all get in the cab. Take her in—in style."

He did not see the beginnings of the city. He was too intent, watching the road ahead, wary of the stray donkey—the children darting ahead, deliberately, just under their wheels. The rumble of the tyres told that they were on the cobbles now, and then the stench of tannery, reminding him of that night on the Depression, only two nights ago. There was something else to worry him, above the whistling pump of the open number four plug—the clatter was growing again. Other big ends were starting to go.

No one talked, there was no thought of singing now. Only an unbearable rising tension. He was not hungry, not thirsty—but once when the captain said, "I hope that beer's bloody cold," his mouth started watering uncontrollably.

The dim shapes of the warehouses drifted by, just out of his range of vision, then there was the narrow cleft of

231

Sister Street, with the dark buildings towering high to the narrow strip of blue. At the end of it, a patch of green.

Anson said, "Mahomet Ali Square." Diana said something else—something he could not quite catch. It sounded like "Zerzura".

People shouted at them, a tram gong clanged, but they took not the slightest notice, all their senses were strained in watching that patch of green that slid nearer and nearer towards them. . . . He wondered what Zimmerman was thinking.

The clatter was rising, a vibration coming up through the floorboards; for the first time a smell of hot oil, the well-known clouds of steam billowing out from under the bonnet. He shouted, "Shall I stop?" but Anson, sitting outside Zimmerman, still holding that spanner, said, "Christ, no! It's only the other side of the bloody square. Keep her going."

They limped out of the crack of Sister Street into the sunlight and there was the wide square with the gardens in the middle and the lines of tall palms streaming their crowns over in the sea breeze. They crept round the square, he had to coax her now to move at all, every instinct rebelling at the torture of machinery.

Then Anson said, "Pull in. That's it."

He cut the switch and coasted to the kerb and there was no sound for a moment but the rumble of boiling water in the radiator and the sounds of the traffic that seemed to come from another world.

Anson got down and threw the spanner on the floor with a clatter. "Come on, you lot." Then he ran his hand very slowly down the length of the hot, rust-spattered bonnet. "You bloody good old bitch," he said.

As they scrambled down to join him, each, even Zimmerman, touched KATY's flank, although they did not speak. With Anson leading, he and Diana falling in

232

behind Zimmerman, they walked across the pavement and into the narrow side street. At the corner, he turned for a last look at her, lonely now, battered, with that strip of bullet holes running down her side, propped up on blankets, sizzling, but triumphant.

It was just six o'clock, too early for the usual drinking crowd and the bar was quite empty. It was just as the captain had said it would be; the high, marble-topped counter, the tall stools against it, the clean light room, the few tables grouped round the walls. After they had pushed through the swing door, they trooped up to the bar in silence, pulled out four stools and perched on them in a row. The barman yawned and got up from his seat to come forward and look at them without enthusiasm.

"Yes——?" A pause, and then, "Sir."

"Set 'em up," said Anson.

"What up——?"

Anson turned to Tom. "He thinks we're tramps. He thinks we can't pay. He's forgotten the order we put in six days ago." He fumbled in his pocket and produced two crumpled pound notes that he put on the counter.

"Get cracking, Joe. FOUR VERY, VERY, COLD RHEINGOLDS."

When they came up, again they were as he said they would be, pale amber, in tall thin glasses, and so cold, the dew had frosted on the outside before he put them down. They stood in a row now, but Tom waited, as he knew the others were waiting, for Anson to make the first move. He stared at his for a moment, looking all round it as if it were a rare specimen, then ran his finger up and down the side of the glass, leaving a clear trail in the dew. He said, "That's that," and lifted the glass and tilted it right back. Tom watched the ripple of the swallow in the lean throat, and there was a tight feeling

233

inside him and his eyes were smarting and he knew that in a moment he would cry. So he lifted up his own glass and swallowed it fast.

When Anson put his glass down it was empty. "I quite forgot to drink your healths," he said. Then, to the barman, "Set 'em up again."

It was easier with the second one and they started talking on the 'do you remember' line, but not beyond that lonely grave in the wadi—and Zimmerman never said a word.

Tom said, "What about KATY?"

"I'll phone the V.R.D. and get them to pull her in. It's gharries for me from now on." Then he turned to Zimmerman. "You are our problem child. No clothes, no identity card, no money, no nothing. I'm afraid they'll take the hell of a long time to vet you. I'll have to come—and I don't feel like answering any of their bloody silly questions tonight."

Zimmerman spoke for the first time. "I hadn't thought of that. But must I bother you? Can't I just slip off to my own people."

Anson shook his head. "No. I've a better idea than that. Let's leave it all till tomorrow. Come with me tonight to where I usually stay. Mother Thompson's— she's got a boarding-house on the front. She's very good to me—she'll lend us cash—and clothes, even if they are only civvies. Then we can bath and eat and sleep. Face everything in the morning."

All through this conversation, Tom had been watching Zimmerman. His face had shaded through every expression from indecision to resolve, brightened visibly at the mention of civilian clothes. 'Captain Anson' he thought, 'he's gone plumb crazy. Give that crafty —— civvies, and he'll dodge out at the first chance—and they'll never find him."

But Zimmerman was saying, "Thanks, man. It seems the best idea. It's very kind of you."

"Well, I'd better ring her now—she likes good notice." He slipped off his stool and went over to the telephone-box that was in the corner. Tom went on watching. Something was flowing back into that big man. He looked younger, stronger every moment. Tom knew what hope looked like now.

Anson seemed a long time, and when he came back he did not climb on his stool. He stood behind them and said, "That's fixed," and there was a subtle change in his voice. Then, "Will you bring your drinks over to a table for a minute. I've something private to say."

They got down, wondering, and then Zimmerman said, "I think I'll—wash my hands." Anson, standing between him and the door, said, "That's an idea, so will I." Tom saw his eyes flick at him, so he said, "Will you excuse us, Diana?" and they marched out to the back of the room in procession.

All the time in the toilet, there was bright talk on how the war was going. Anson gave details of how the line had been steadied at Alamein, how lucky they had been to come out east of that. Tom wondered where he had got this information—he had spoken to no one except the M.P. at the check post, and surely, then, he would have mentioned it before. Perhaps Zimmerman spotted it too, for he tried to dry his hands rather quickly, and get out of the door in front of them, but, somehow, Anson was there first, and they walked back to the bar in their single file. He only had one glimpse of Zimmerman's face then—it was grey, and the broad shoulders seemed to be shrinking.

Diana was waiting, standing by the swing door out into the street, peering over the pane of frosted glass. She said, "There is a truck just drawn up outside—it's full of——" She swung round and she saw Zimmerman and her face changed; behind her, they could all see beyond the edge of the glass . . . the flat red hats of military policemen as they spilled out over the pavement.

Inside the bar it was so quiet, so still, he could hear the flies buzzing. He looked once at Zimmerman's face and then at the ground. He could only think of two things: that straining, cracking back that had held KATY until he had got the jack underneath—and the other thing to come, the grey cold of a dawn, the wall, and the nervous firing squad. It seemed such a bloody shame.

Anson's voice was tight. "They've surrounded the place, Zimmerman—but I've arranged they don't come in for another ten minutes. So we must talk quickly. I'm sorry—but what else could I do but ring Kom-el-Dick?" And he knew that last desperate question was addressed to him and Diana.

He looked across to the barman, shouted, "Another round—over here." Then he pulled out a chair for Diana and sat down beside her.

The Greek came over with the tray, put down the four tall glasses, and departed, scratching. Anson leaned forward across the table. "Zimmerman. What is your real name?"

There was no answer. The big man just looked at his glass, rubbing his finger up and down the outside, just as Anson had done.

"I'll tell you why," Anson went on, "I'll tell you just exactly what I told our security people. That we came out of Tobruk; that, later, we picked up a German officer, whose truck had broken down, who had started walking, who had got a touch of the sun. That he surrendered, gave his parole to me, and had behaved in a most exemplary manner. And that I would deliver the body after we had had a drink together."

Still Zimmerman did not answer. The barman lifted a hand to the radio on the wall behind him and fiddled with the knobs, a bright, metallic voice started singing, "Sand in my shoes. . . ."

Anson said, "You can get away with a hell of a lot when you're moving round—but just with us three, so close, I don't think you had a chance. And you had bad luck with your own people. To get through once was a miracle—but twice, no. I was just in time to see that fooling with the buttons in the wadi, but I don't know what it was—I didn't look when I threw the bush-shirt away after I got you out of that bog." He looked across the table, "You saw me, Diana—say that it's true."

Her voice came very low, "I saw—he didn't touch it. Just threw it away."

Anson's voice went on, "I didn't look—because I didn't want to know. You see, there was no harm done till then—even with that precious pack of yours. I know it was a transmitter."

Zimmerman looked at him and then down at his drink. He picked it up at last and took a long swallow. Still he did not speak. Anson's arm came out across the table, gripping him by the elbow.

"Christ, man—can't you see? There's no time. Tell me your name—stick to our story. I'll vouch for Tom and Diana, though we will be risking a court-martial. But there will be no more bother. Otherwise, I'll have to tell them a lot of funny things, give them the map reference where they can find a pack and a bush-shirt. They wouldn't take a lot of digging out. And then——?" He spread his hands. "But we don't want it—any of us —because we know very well that we wouldn't be here if it hadn't been for you."

The swing door at the front slammed open and a lieutenant of the Military Police came in. He was tall and thin and Tom saw that he had pale knees. He said, "Captain Anson?" to the room at large.

"That's me." Anson looked at his watch. "You're early."

The lieutenant slapped his cane against his leg. "That may be—but this fraternisation——"

Anson tilted his chair back and said one short and very rude word. The lieutenant flushed. "Must I remind you—there is a lady present?"

Anson looked at him. "I know—and if she had thought of it, she would have said it herself. But it doesn't alter the fact you are over-riding your C.O.'s orders. Do you want me to phone and tell him?" Then he looked down to knee-level. "Just off the boat," he said to no one in particular, "got to learn—thinks all that ironmongery is the answer."

The red-cap flushed again as he fingered his revolver holster. "Then I'll wait outside."

Anson said, "Do," and when the door had closed he leaned over the table again. "For God's sake—can't you see? It's the last chance."

Zimmerman looked down at his drink, picked it up and drained it in one gulp. He said, quite simply, in a very different voice, "Otto Lutz—Hauptmann Engineer —21st Panzer Group."

There was a silence and then Anson's voice came again, urgent. "Now listen. You lost your way—the truck broke down, Otto. You started to walk, then the sun got you. We picked you up after we'd buried Sister Norton—you only heard about that. From then on, just as it happened."

He stopped for a moment to look at the others, "Is that all right with you?" Hardly waiting for their quiet "Yes", he went on, "Quick—is there anything on you—or left in the ambulance—that might need explaining?"

238

Zimmerman . . . Lutz, it was easier to think of him like that, thought for a moment and said, "Perhaps—in my pack, but I don't think so."

"Well, I'll dump the lot—without looking—off the deep water quay, just in case."

The door opened again, and pale-knees came in. "Really——" he said.

Anson got up. "Will you fraternise with us, Lieutenant —and have one?"

"No, thank you."

Anson smiled at Lutz and said, "That's that." Then he stared at those knees again. "He'll learn—one day."

The Hauptmann was on his feet now. He looked at Anson and smiled and said, "So you release me from my parole, Herr Captain?"

"Certainly." Anson looked across at pale-knees. "I've told your commandant that this officer has behaved in an exemplary manner. There's no need for a ball and chain. You'd better run along with nursie, Lutz."

Lutz looked round the circle of them. "It's been a great experience. Will you shake hands?"

They all murmured something, and while the lieutenant looked down his nose, he took their hands in turn across the table. For Diana, there was a special click of the heels and a quiet—"Fraulein".

He walked to the door with the lieutenant, and then turned back to look at them once more. He said, "It has been something. All against one—against the greater enemy. I have learned a lot." Then he gave them that silly stiff bow again, the door flapped twice behind him and that was that.

They stayed quite still, looking at the blank door, until they heard the truck start up and the noise of the motor fade into the background of traffic. The radio was still playing softly on the wall, the barman appeared to have gone to sleep. Anson broke the silence, "I'd better go and dump that bloody pack off the end of the quay before I get inquisitive."

Diana said, "And I must get to the hospital."

Anson looked at both of them. "I made another phone call. I took the liberty of ringing them. I said that you would be escorted by a W.O. who would need accommodation. You can beat me up in the morning, Tom, and we'll find our precious unit." Then his voice went grave. "Tell your matron, Diana, I'd like to call on her —about Denise."

She said, "I would like that. And I want you to wade in on something else. You can smooth out the marriage bother easier than anyone. And we want it to be soon."

The door opened and three customers came in, so they went out of the bar, back into the noisy sunlight of the square, to KATY. She was there still, cool and silent now, somehow dejected. Anson went into the back and came out with Zimmerman's pack. "I don't think there was anything else of his," he said. "Sorry I didn't have time to ask you properly about this business—but you do agree, don't you? And you'll stick to it?"

They both nodded.

He sat down on the step and looked up at them, drawn, dirty, without a cap, but his eyes were back in the living again. "I wish I had a camera," he said, "—two people, about to enter into holy matrimony— entirely blinded by sand."

Tom was holding her hand now, was surprised when she let go with a whispered, "Don't be cross." He watched her walk over to the step of the car and put both hands on Anson's shoulders as she stooped to kiss him full on the mouth. He was near enough to hear her say, "Find your Zerzura, George—you're half-way there now," and wonder what the hell she was talking about.

Anson got up stiffly. He said, "I'll try, Diana. See you both tomorrow." Then he smiled at them. " 'Bye for now."

They stood, holding hands again, watching the slim figure grow smaller and smaller as it went down the square towards the sea. She said, "I do want it to be quick, darling. And then I want a baby as soon as we can—so that I can get out of this, and home, and start things up—for you to come back to."

The little figure had almost vanished now. The tall palms looked so green and stately as they bent their heads in rustling to the wind. There was a red-cap standing on the pavement opposite, trying, obviously, to make up his mind to come over and check them for being improperly dressed and holding hands.

He tried to slip his hand loose, but she held on fast.

"Don't let go, darling. Everything—is going to be all right—for all of us."